Praise for Annie Jones

"Jones beautifully conveys a range of emotions, from the depth of despair to the pinnacle of joy.... Readers will nod their heads with empathy toward characters who seem like real people. Throughout the novel, compassion and family bonds bring hope, and God's love is shown to shine through even the darkest of circumstances."
—*Romantic Times BOOKreviews* on *Sadie-in-Waiting*

"Annie Jones writes about characters we all know and—despite their quirks—love. Sadie Pickett is an endearing character whose foibles and charms will leave you smiling as you think, *Yes, life is just like that.* Carry on, Sadie, and thanks for inviting us along for the ride!"
—Angela Hunt, Christy Award-winning author of *A Time to Mend* on *Sadie-in-Waiting*

"Annie Jones has a proven ability to bring to life characters with whom we can identify, and whose trials and triumphs become our own."
—Hannah Alexander, Christy Award-winning author of *Grave Risk*

"Jones adds a touch of humor to realistically depict the emotions that most moms feel on a regular basis. Hannah's struggles are down-to-earth and will touch hearts."
—*Romantic Times BOOKreviews* on *Mom over Miami*

"Annie Jones is a true champion of stressed-out moms everywhere, and her understanding of what being a mother entails can only have come from someone who has lived it herself. Every mother who has ever felt like packing her bags and running far away from home has to read this book! *Mom over Miami* is realistically funny.... Annie Jones is quickly becoming one of my very favorite authors, and I cannot wait until her next book comes out."
—*Romancejunkies.com*

The Sisterhood
of the Queen Mamas

ANNIE JONES

Steeple
Hill
Café

Published by Steeple Hill Books™

STEEPLE HILL BOOKS

ISBN-13: 978-0-373-78557-5
ISBN-10:   0-373-78557-7

THE SISTERHOOD OF THE QUEEN MAMAS

This edition published by arrangement with Steeple Hill Books.

® and TM are trademarks of Steeple Hill Books, used under license. Trademarks indicated with ® are registered in the United States Patent and Trademark Office, the Canadian Trade Marks Office and in other countries.

www.SteepleHill.com

Printed in U.S.A.

To the Clear Creek Writers of Shelby County—
Norm, Gail, Chip, Rob, Gary, Mary Lou, Stephanie,
Tachelle, Joan, Bill, Thelma, Kate (and Alexandra)
and Clarence. Did I leave anyone out? Also, Betsy.
You are all such talented writers and wonderful
friends. Thank you for the inspiration.

Chapter One

"Sisters, girlfriends and troublemakers—you know who you are—you are fearfully and wonderfully made! In other words, God doesn't make junk. Thankfully, his children do, and that's why we have been blessed with flea markets just about everywhere."

"The queen has spoken!"

"My name is Odessa Pepperdine, and I am *not* just some silver-haired small-town queen bee, my dears. I am the *Queen Mama of all queen bees* in the sweet little hive of friends I have made among the shoppers and shopkeepers at the Castlerock, Texas, Five Acres of Fabulous Finds Flea Market. And it was on my say-so that we titled this little bit here Chapter One."

"Even though, you'll soon discover, the real Chapter One doesn't actually get started in earnest for a few more paragraphs."

"That's Maxine Cooke-Nash, my sister in Christ and formerly—"

"Stranger in the community. That's what Odessa always says

about us. 'Sisters in Christ, strangers in the community.' We grew up living parallel lives on opposite sides of the proverbial tracks."

"What tracks?"

"I said proverbial. *You know, just my delicate way of letting folks know that we stuck to opposite sides of town, you keeping company with people from your church, and me staying mostly inside the African-American community."*

"Only back then, when we were young, they didn't use that term, African-American."

"Oh, no, they didn't."

"They say you can never describe things in terms of black and white, but Maxine and I can tell you, if you were coming up in Castlerock in the nineteen-fifties and -sixties you could."

"Amen, Odessa, Amen."

"And coming up back then, Maxine and I were both active in the Campfire Girls, then went on to play high school basketball—probably against one another more than once. Later we each graduated top of our classes at Christian colleges, married ministers and settled down to raise our children, all within a few miles of one another. And we never met until we both tried to buy the same thing at the flea market."

"Are we telling this *part now?"*

"Oh. Oh, no. No, actually, we really *do* have something in mind in starting out things this way. As I said, I'm Odessa and this is Maxine. Say hello properly, Maxine."

"Hi, y'all. Don't mind me. I may not say much, especially when Odessa is holding forth—and let's be up front, when is she not holding forth or holding court or holding just about anything except back?"

"Ahem."

"Anyway, I may not say much, but when I do speak up, I try to make it about something worthy of the effort."

"And she does. She certainly does. Take what she had to say about the way I wanted to begin to tell the story about what happened when…well, there I'm getting ahead of myself."

"Which she does, and I have to rein her in."

"We're a good team like that, aren't we, Maxine?"

"Yes, we are. In fact, when it comes to reining in Odessa, I'm just about the only one who can anymore."

"Before…well, before all the things between the pages of this book happened, I never needed reining in. I was raised to be seen and not heard. Encouraged to be a good little minister's wife in the way of ninja-style church ladies everywhere, who appear when they are needed and disappear into the wood-paneled walls of the church basement when their service is not required."

"I cannot feature that, Odessa."

"Of course you can't, because now I am what people like to call 'irrepressible.'"

I've heard other words used to describe you, Miz Pepperdine."

"Oh, Maxine, you crack me up."

"Likewise, Odessa honey."

"See, we *get* each other. We speak the same language, you might say. Though we did not start out on the best of speaking terms at all. Oh, there now, that reminds me! I was explaining about the way we decided to start our story out."

"How?"

"You know, with Chapter One, the way you said. Uh, oh, let me tell this right. *Maxine* said that whenever she sees a big bold heading like *Foreword* or *A Word from the Author* or sometimes even *Prologue*, she tends to just skim right over it."

"I do. I'm sorry. But I think reading a book is a lot like eating a bacon, lettuce and tomato sandwich—"

"Which is her favorite."

"Which is my favorite."

"My favorite used to be a nice simple chicken salad, but I like my food with a bolder flavor these days."

"Odessa's chicken-salad days are behind her."

"Ever since I finally got fed up enough to throw good taste out the window!"

"Odessa, she likes to come up with a catch phrase for just about everything that happens to her."

"And, oh, what happened to me at the flea market when… No. No, that's not what we were talking about. What was it, Maxine? Your love of a good BLT?"

"My love of a good book, actually, by way of my favorite sandwich. See, often I think reading a book is a lot like a bacon and lettuce and tomato sandwich on toast served up on my favorite lunch platter with chips and a pickle on the side. Done right, it all looks so good, but I am anxious to sink my teeth in and get to the meat of it."

"But the meat of a book to one person might be nothing more than the olive stuck on a toothpick to hold the thing together to someone else, Maxine. So a book is not a sandwich."

"Well, a case could be made for that metaphor, Odessa. You know, with all the layers of story and setting and themes and—"

"No. I absolutely reject that analogy. If you have to compare a book to something edible and layered, you'd have to go with a hand-dipped chocolate truffle."

"Sandwich."

"Trrruffle, Maxine."

"One woman's chocolate is another woman's BLT. Now clink coffee cups with me, so we can be in agreement and move on."

Clink.

"Anyway, when Maxine and I began this—"

"Ages and pages ago."

"Mumbling is not very agreeable, Maxine."

"Point taken."

Clink.

"We, Maxine and I, began this as Chapter One because we are both ladies of a certain age who were brought up right."

"That dictates that we take a minute to introduce ourselves before we launch into our story."

"I mean, really, I wouldn't just walk up to a total stranger in the library and shout, 'Call me Ishmael' or 'Scarlett O'Hara was not beautiful.' Would you, Maxine?"

"No, I would not. At least not without offering them my hand, giving them my name and telling them why I wanted to say what I had to say."

"That's just good manners."

"Good manners."

"And if Maxine and I are about *anything,* it's good manners."

"And using them to get our way."

Clink.

"Which is why you'll understand and hopefully forgive us that we stuck Chapter One on this part that might normally have said, you know, *Foreword* or *Prologue.*"

"Which is the part I usually skim over."

"And Maxine and I? Let me tell you, we are *not* women to be skimmed over!"

"Not anymore!"

"No. Not anymore. Our days of being skimmed over are past us. We put in our time as mild-mannered ministers' wives, and now have come the days of speaking our minds and acting on the desires of our hearts!"

"We were mild mannered, not our husbands. Just so there's no confusion. Because at this point, you might find it hard to think of either Odessa or me as ever having been the kind most likely to inherit the Earth."

"She means meek, for those of you who might not have picked up the Bible reference."

"See? We really are minister's wives."

"Though not mild-mannered ministers, though they are both darling men in their own rights."

"Oh, yes. Precious men. Smart and funny and Godly, both of them, through and through."

"And manly."

"Manly, Maxine?"

"Yes, well, I called them darling and you called them precious, and non-Texan types might take that to mean unmanly, which they are not, not one bit."

"No, they are *men*, through and through."

"Which is why, once they retired, Odessa and I started going to the flea market, to escape from—"

"To find respite."

"To find respite for a few hours each week from our retired hubbies."

"Oh, and to try to collect for ourselves the one thing we each wanted with all our worldly beings."

"Ever since we were each young—and I do mean young— brides in the nineteen-sixties."

"The entire twenty-piece line of chip-proof kitchenware made by the Royal Service Company of Akron, Ohio, the black-and-gold-on-white Hostess Queen pattern."

Clink.

"Anyway, we just wanted to introduce ourselves up front and let you know a little something about ourselves and this BLT of a story…"

"Truffle."

"…that we have to share, and why we have to share it."

"You see, Maxine and me, we weren't always Queen Mamas."

"No, we were not."

"Or queen bees."

"Worker bees, more like it."

"Regular drones."

"Which isn't a bad thing, now, but…"

"But the time comes when even a drone has to stop and look around herself and say, 'It's time to create a buzz.'"

"And oh, what a buzz Odessa made!"

"I did. Though I didn't do it just for myself. I did it for all of us."

"The drones."

"The meek."

"The women who are strangers in their own communities."

"Who are all wonderfully and fearfully made."

Clink.

"There's the meat of the story, Maxine, right there."

"Shh. You're getting ahead again, when all we wanted to do with this introduction part— That's what we could have called it, the Introduction."

"And you're telling me you wouldn't have skimmed something called the Introduction?"

"Well, no…I am a skimmer, I do confess."

"Right. And if we got other skimmers in the crowd, and they went into the story, and suddenly you or I popped in with a comment…"

"Probably you."

"It might throw things off. Say, Maxine, have you ever heard that expression a month of Sundays?"

"What now, Odessa?"

"I was just thinking how the story of when we first all got thrown together until the *incident* was just about a month—of flea markets."

"You mean the span of four flea markets?"

"No, I mean… let me see, from July Fourth until Labor Day, weekly flea markets, lasting three days—except we never come out on Sundays, being as that's the Lord's Day— but you can count it because some things happened on Sundays. So that means…"

"Hold on, Odessa is trying to do the math in her head. This could take a minute. I'd tell you to go read a book, but I'm sort of hoping you already are!"

"Got it. Three days a week over about nine weeks, plus extra for Labor Day weekend, makes twenty-eight days, so that's right. About a month of flea markets from start to finish to tell the story of how our new friends Jan, Bernadette and Chloe—"

"Ahem."

"Oh, right, don't want to give too much away."

"Let's just say it involves some collectible kitsch and some baked goods."

"Oh, and don't forget to mention—"

"The tiaras. The story is just jam-packed with tiaras."

"Hey, a woman wears a lot of hats in her lifetime. Why shouldn't one of them be a crown?"

Clink.

"And also a hot-air balloon."

"I got nothing for that one. So I'll see y'all on the next page, as I intend to start off and probably wrap up every chapter from here on out. Just my way of keeping things on track, you know."

"Odessa means just her way of being the big queen boss of all things, even your reading pleasure."

"Please note that Maxine wore the sweetest, warmest smile ever as she said that."

"I did. You know, it's always enjoyable to watch people doing the things that they are best at doing, and our Odessa, she is the very best at being the boss. So that's the way it's going to be. Me and Odessa having our say as we—and by we I mean mostly Odessa—see fit. God bless, and enjoy!"

"And don't forget…"

"Stay Queenly!"

Chapter One

(Really, we mean it this time)

The Book of Proverbs tells us—more than once, so you know not to take it lightly—that it is better to live on the corner of a roof than to share a house with a quarrelsome wife.

Jan Bishop Belmont was not what I'd call particularly quarrelsome. No, if pressed to find a word for the forty-something blonde with the sprayed-on suntan—Castlerock is a small town, so if you don't want folks to know how you got that golden glow, go out of town to get it—I'd pick… hmm…*malcontent*.

Mal from the French for "ill" and *content* as in all the stuff contained inside something. Or someone. That's right, inside of all that prim and proper exterior, Jan carried around something that ailed her. For the longest time, I didn't know what, and so all I could do was try to get others to be more tender toward her—and try my best to stay out of her way.

★ ★ ★

"Hot-air balloon rides! Tethered for your complete safety." Every Friday afternoon and Saturday morning, a gangly young man stood outside the old drive-in movie theater parking lot that served as the grounds for the flea market. Hour after hour, he shouted to passersby and handed out flyers for a ruddy-faced fellow who spent his time taking anyone with the price of a ticket twenty feet up above the crowd in a basket attached to a colorful two-story silk balloon.

At least I think it was silk, but honestly I didn't get close enough to know for sure at that point. Maybe it was that parachute material—though that would hardly inspire confidence, would it? Making something you want to fly through the air out of the same stuff you use to help you *fall* from the sky? Hmm. Either way, I guess it all boiled down to a matter of trust, trusting silk or synthetic. Trusting a ruddy-faced man with a woven basket. And trusting the Lord, of course, to keep a body afloat. Or is that a*flight?*

Whatever the word was, I did not, at that time, possess the amount of trust in anything but the Lord to give it a try. Me? In a hot-air balloon? Outwardly, I may seem just the type, but below this, uh, *colorful* exterior beats the heart of a woman who has lived most of her life in someone else's shadow. And been just fine with that. Mostly fine with it.

Well, I lived with it, anyway.

However, my trust in the Lord has *always* been mighty, so from the very first time I saw that breathtakingly buoyant conveyance, I couldn't rule out the prospect entirely. Which is probably why it was *this* Friday morning, just moments before the man who ran the flea market was about to fling open the gate to let the treasure hunt for bargains commence, that that young fellow rushed up to me and Maxine.

"Hot-air balloon rides! Tethered for your complete safety." The paper rattled in his hand. The wind picked up his shaggy brown hair and pressed it against his pale and slightly blemished skin. He hunched his narrow shoulders and grinned right at me. "All major credit cards accepted."

"No, don't waste good paper on a bad prospect, young man." Maxine pushed back his hand, and the bright yellow flyer he had in it. "Choose your battles, the Reverend Nash would tell you. It would take an army to get me up in one of those contraptions."

I stopped, because I always stopped to fuss over young men who think they can charm me into doing the improbable. I'm a sucker for charm in all its forms, and I could tell that this young man, despite looking like he had gotten dressed from someone else's dirty-clothes hamper this morning, fairly brimmed over with the stuff. I shook my head at him, smiling. "In what wild flight of imagination can you actually picture us two granny-ladies, loaded down with all manner of vintage jewelry and sporting fanny packs over floral jersey sundresses, hoisting ourselves up into a big ol' basket? Let alone allowing you to launch us heavenward under a canopy of…whatever fabric that is up there sporting an advertisement for the King of Beers?"

"Aw, that logo isn't permanent. The boss switches it every few weeks," he said, as if that might just change our minds about the prospect.

It didn't.

"I don't care if you tack on a banner lauding the King

of Kings—and you wouldn't do so bad to think about that, because wherever the Lord goes, He draws a crowd." Maxine paused for a minute so he could let that sink in, then scowled. "But no matter what you advertise, it won't help draw me into that contraption."

"Me, either," I told the young man, sounding a little less decisive than my friend. "Not at this point in my life."

"Don't sell yourself short, Ms. Pepperdine." He looked right at me and said my name. I'm not sure how he knew my name, but then, loads of people that I had never actually been formally introduced to knew me through the church and my many local activities. Still, it always surprises me when somebody uses my name and I don't know them. I took a step back.

"Don't write off the balloon ride just because you're a grandma." He took a step toward me. Guess he had sized up Maxine as a lost cause already, but clearly he had high hopes for me. "There's still a lot of fire in you."

"Still?" From ripe to rotten, in a single word. *Still?* That's the kind of word folks tacked on at the flea market when they wanted to convince someone to pay too much for an object that had long since lost its usefulness. *Still* hinted that I might have some doubt myself as to the depths of the well of my vitality. *Still,* indeed. "Did you just say I *still* have a lot of fire in me, son?"

"Oh, you've done it now," Maxine said. And she laughed a bit as she said it, too.

"Yeah, still. Is there…something wrong with that?" He cocked his head, his expression bright with an innocence that could not conceal the glint of mischief in his smiling eyes.

"Well, just you listen to that same sentence without the word *still* and see what you think." I would have pushed up my sleeves, had I been wearing any, and maybe flicked my wrist and done a little flourish, the way a magician does right before he pulls that rabbit out of his hat. "'There's still a lot of fire in you, Ms. Pepperdine.'"

He nodded to show he'd tried it on for size and found it fitting.

"Or…" This time I did waggle my hands about a bit, and narrowed one eye, trying to look mysterious, sultry and clever, or at the very least impish. I wet my lips and affected a low, playful tone. "Ms. Pepperdine, you have a *lot of fire* in you."

His eyes got big for a moment, then his smile grew wide. He bobbed his head. "I get it."

"I thought you might."

He nodded again, only this time he shot me a look, all coy and crafty and just darling in its ill-disguised artlessness. He winked and added, without so much as a snicker, "When I say you have got a lot of fire in you, that means you've never stopped being a hot babe."

Charm. Gets me every time.

"You're my witness, Maxine. That adorable young man called me a hot babe." I licked the tip of my thumb, pressed it to my shoulder and hissed like bacon sizzling in a hot skillet.

"More like a hot-*flash* babe." She licked her own thumb, stuck it to my shoulder and made a *pffftt* sound—more fizzle than sizzle.

We both laughed.

My young salesman did not. Wise kid for his age. "I bet

if you ever tried going up in the balloon you'd love it, Ms. Pepperdine. You too, Ms. Nash."

"That's Cooke-Nash, son," I put in real quick. Wise and educated are not the same thing, but I knew he'd never make that mistake again. "Maxine is one of the original liberated women who kept her maiden name and hyphenated it with that of her darling husband, the good Reverend."

"Cool." He gave her an appreciative nod, even though both Maxine and I knew once-controversial issues like women keeping their names didn't even register in his realm of reality.

"Honey, you are wasting your breath talking to me, no matter what name you use to do it." Maxine waved her hand and her impressive collection of 1930s polka-dot Bakelite bracelets clattered down her forearm. "There's not enough hot air in all of Texas…"

"A state famous as one of the world's leading producers of hot air," I hurried to add.

"…to get me up in one of those things." She looked at the fellow over the top of her pink-opalescent reading glasses—you know, the kind you get at a nice lady's boutique, not the kind you pick up at some discount place with *mart* in the name. *Très* cute, I tell you.

I'm not the only still-hot babe in this duo, after all. And us hot babes, even when we have to have help to read the fine print or see the marks on the underside of ceramic poodle statues, we want to do it in style.

So after Maxine gave him that look, she put her hand on her, um, *ample* hip. She looked toward the rainbow-striped balloon billowing along the ground in front of the old towering concrete screen with the words Satellite Vista

Drive-In Theatre painted on it. She tsked and shook her head. "Not enough hot air in all of Texas."

He took it well. It's hard not to take things well from Maxine, even rejection. She has that kind of face, dimpled and motherly. Her skin is dark, of course, but not so dark that you can't see the smattering of freckles over the bridge of her nose.

Now I ask you, how can you get your feelings hurt by someone with freckles on her nose? And a sweet, soft voice that meanders out of an ever-present smile in a slow Texas drawl?

So he took *her* refusal in good spirits.

Now, me…? Well, at this point in my life, I guess I looked an easy mark. I certainly must have looked one to that hair-dresser who put a wild white streak in the front of my usu-ally dignified silver hair. Tarnished silver. Okay, silver plate, worn thin and discolored. Which is why I got myself to the chichi-est salon in all of Castlerock for a new color and do and how I ended up platinum-blond with what the staff there called "chunky highlights" of almost pure white. If my husband, David, hadn't liked it so much, I'd have headed for the drugstore posthaste for a bottle of hair rinse and a floppy sun hat.

Anyway, either my hair or my demeanor or something else about me screamed *easy mark* to the balloon-ballyhoo-ing charmer, or that young man knew something about me that even I didn't know.

"I can tell, Ms. Pepperdine, *you* want to cut loose."

"I do?"

"Now that's a scary thought." Maxine turned her over-the-glasses glare on me.

"*You're* just itchin' to have an adventure." He pushed the piece of paper in his hand toward me.

"Me?" The page crackled in my hand. "Itching?"

"It's all the peroxide they used in her hair. Gave her a rash," Maxine teased.

The kid ignored her, which was exactly the proper thing to do after a remark like that. Then he fixed his winning smile on me—also not a bad choice. "You, Ms. Pepperdine, want to break free from the things that tie you down here. You want to rise up."

"Up?"

"Yes, up."

My eyes followed the line of his hand high into the air over my head.

"Up above this crowd." He waved his fliers over my head.

"Me? Above *this* crowd?" I could almost feel my feet lifting. My heart beat a little faster. I gazed skyward and swallowed hard. I could just about…

"Get a life."

A woman's voice broke through my thoughts and brought me rocketing hard back down to earth.

"You'd think they were giving away gold in there, the way y'all flock around the gate here," she said, a little too loud to be mistaken for talking to herself and yet not aiming her criticism at anyone in particular. "It's nothing short of a fire hazard. I can't believe anyone would be in such an all-fired hurry to be the first one to have a chance to buy somebody else's tacky trash. Is that the best thing you can think to do with your time?"

I sighed and gave the young man a gentle pat on the back. "Son, I think you've read me all wrong. I'm a lady. And a minister's wife for more than half my life. It's just not in me to ever, ever, *ever* put myself above anybody."

"It's just a few feet." He pointed again.

I didn't look. The unseen complaining woman was right. I had better things to do with my time *and* my money than to waste it on such a personal indulgence. "No, but I do thank you for thinking I might actually try it."

"If it's the money you're worried about, we do take all major credit cards," he called, and it seemed to me his voice carried a bit too much urgency.

"Oh, I would never bring a credit card out here, sugar," I said as I hustled along after Maxine, giving him a wave over my shoulder. My collection of bracelets—charm, of course—jangled like dozens of tiny dented bells. "Maybe you should look for someone who wasn't raised right and doesn't mind looking down on his or her fellow man now and again."

But the young man had vanished. Just like that. Disappeared into the crowd without a backward glance. "After all that time invested in getting me to just think about that ride, he sure did write me off awfully fast when I said I didn't have a credit card."

"Maybe you look like you don't carry enough cash on you to pay for the thing outright so he gave up," Maxine suggested.

"Hmm." Something about it all didn't ring true—except the not-carrying-too-much-cash part. I keep to my budget. A lifetime of good stewardship, prodded along by the ever-watchful eyes of certain members of David's—that's my husband David Samuel Pepperdine—of David's congregation saw to that. Trust me, I learned early that if I indulged in some extravagance, even something as small as a hat that I shouldn't have worn to church service, David would hear about it.

Maxine and I hadn't walked on far enough to get gravel dust on our favorite flea market footwear—nurses' shoes, if you must know; think about it, it makes perfect sense, being on our feet all day out here and all—when that precious young man took my advice about moving on to someone who didn't mind looking down on others.

"Hot-air balloon rides! Tethered for your complete safety!"

"Are you crazy?" The harsh voice was only a few footfalls in back of us now. "After what happened to my husband?"

Maxine yanked on my elbow to keep me from stepping into a puddle.

"Jan Belmont," she whispered. Even before I could whip my head around to gape, she tacked on, "Don't look!"

But I *had* to look.

Jan was that kind of person. The kind you didn't *want* to screech to a halt and stand and stare at but couldn't help it. How do they describe that inclination? Like looking at a train wreck?

Few people would describe the perfectly pulled-together former cheerleader—and this being Texas, that's not the kind of laurel that fades with time—as a wreck of any kind. But more than one poor soul who had gotten in her way certainly knew what it was like to be run over by a fully stoked locomotive.

Jan stopped. Well, her feet stopped any forward motion. Then she sort of juggled everything in her arms, without actually tossing anything up in the air. Although that would have been worth more than the price of the hot-air-balloon ticket to see, given that she had a sheet cake and four plastic containers of assorted baked goods to drop off for our church charity booth.

Anyway, she stopped walking just long enough to nail this poor young fellow with a spine-shriveling glare. Then she said, in a way only a woman like Jan—bless her heart—can pull off, "I've seen what becomes of a body that falls from even that short of a distance, thank you. And because of that, I have neither the inclination—or, frankly, the financial freedom—to take that kind of risk."

The young man's Adam's apple bobbed. He stepped back. "No, ma'am. I mean, yes, ma'am. I understand."

"I thought you might." She smiled in such a way that it looked as if it actually pained her to lift the corners of her mouth. Then she stormed forward, people getting out of her way as she went. "Now, if you'll excuse me, I have things to do."

Maxine pulled on my elbow again, and I slipped out of Jan's path.

Seconds later her monster-expensive—meaning the price of those things was more frightening than sitting through a scary monster movie—athletic shoe went plunging square into the puddle I had narrowly avoided.

Water splashed up, onto her skirt and legs.

She shut her eyes.

Someone else might have let out with a string of curse words.

Jan just gritted her teeth and announced, "This place is a pigsty. And I hate every second of the few minutes a week I am forced to spend here doing God's work."

Jan Belmont was indeed a malcontent. But then, life had not handed her much to feel contented about these past eight months. There'd been talk of trouble in the marriage, and of her not taking it well when both her children went to swanky East Coast colleges and hardly ever returned to visit. Then her husband had had what folks in town solemnly called "the accident," in that tone that made you wonder if it actually wasn't. An accident, that is. Whatever it was, it required a lengthy recovery period, with no return to good health in sight to date. The financial strain alone had altered the course of her life in ways that no one could really grasp, especially with Jan trying so hard to pretend everything was fine. Right or wrong, the burden of that pretense would have crippled most other people.

"I can't help but feel sorry for her," I whispered to Maxine.

"I hate this dirty people-blocking-the-aisles-devouring-corn-dogs-and-tossing-the-gnawed-on-sticks-on-the-ground health hazard, eyesore-to-the-community pigsty. And I promise everyone within hearing distance that one day I am going to do something to see that this flea market is shut down and that monstrosity of a movie screen bulldozed to the ground!"

"I can," Maxine said as we both watched Jan limp along with one soggy shoe toward the vendors' entrance. "Help it, that is. In fact, I don't feel sorry for her one bit."

Yes, in Proverbs they warn us that it's better to live in the corner of the roof than to share a house with a quarrelsome woman. I can't help but wonder if that was what Marty Belmont had in mind—taking up residence on the roof—the day he crawled out of a second-story window of his home, fell off, broke half the bones in his body and crushed what little bit of goodwill there was left in his now ever-malcontent wife, Jan.

Chapter Two

(As they say in the old movies, later that same day)

Just as heaven has its orders of angels—Seraphim and Cherubim, Thrones, Archangels and the like—churches have a hierarchy all their own.

You have the leaders and the laymen, the servers and the silent types, the vivacious go-getters and the perpetual victims, the nitpickers and the naysayers, the ones who show up every time the door is open and those you only see on Christmas and Easter. And in every church—at least every one that I have had the privilege and/or frustration to be associated with—there is a Bernadette.

When Bernadette Alvarez named the bridal-and-formal-wear boutique she started in her one-bedroom house At Your Service, absolutely everyone—from her grandmother to the kid who delivered her first box of business cards—said the same thing about her choice.

"Perfect!"

I think she should have seen that as a warning.

People, sometimes even though they are total strangers, often see things about a person that that person cannot, or refuses to, see about themselves. And when these people go to the trouble to point it out again and again in one sweet, concise, enthusiastically spoken word? Well, that pointed-out-to person? She should see it for what it is— a big ol' red flag.

Trouble with Bernadette was…when it came to warning flags, that girl was color-blind.

Having listened to her talk over the months I've known her, I think that's because ever since she was a child growing up in a home overflowing with family and cultural conflict, Bernadette Alvarez has tried to make *everybody* happy. She tried to be Texan enough for her "My forefathers died at the Alamo" mother, Gloria Perry Alvarez. But also Mexican enough to suit her first-generation-immigrant grandmother, Gallina Roja.

"Let me—it's Maxine again— just pop in here to emphasize that everyone in town calls that spry, ornery old woman Gallina Roja, which means 'red hen.'"

"They say it's because she has red hair, even though she is no spring chicken."

"What Odessa is too nice to tell y'all is that we all know she got that title because she has practically pecked her daughter-in-law and granddaughter and even her precious son to death, trying to 'improve' their lives for them."

Bernadette tries. She does try. To please both Gloria and

Gallina Roja, and not to mention she works hard to show herself as savvy enough to make her ever-ambitious father proud. All the while staying sweet enough to get along with everyone at church, who in many ways represent the extended family she had never had. That should have been enough, right?

Not if you grow up in a family where everybody wants to be in charge. Of everything. Everywhere. All the time.

Gloria has dominated the real-estate market throughout the county for years, and has served so long on the town council they say she can't be pried out with a crowbar. Mr. Alvarez, a deacon in their church *and* a successful local businessman, used to be a state senator. And Gallina Roja? Her grandmother topped them all.

Her grandmother thought she could direct the action of the Lord Himself.

Bernadette says she couldn't count the number of times she has seen her grandmother clasp her hands together, raise her gaze heavenward and cry out, "Please, Father, please, send this girl a good man to marry her and take care of her."

Or "Please open her eyes so she can see there is more to life than work, work, work and letting people push her into every chore at her church that no one else wants to do."

And when all else fails, "Father, I beg You, *do* something with this girl!"

Do something? Where had that grandmamma been? That's Bernadette's whole life—doing things, usually for everybody but herself.

At Your Service. She'd intended it as a play on words about the goods she sold being used mostly in wedding services, not a description of how she remained ever at her family's beck and call. Or how, what with her being single and over thirty, the whole church had begun to assume that she had nothing better to do than be at everyone's disposal. Because she worked out of her home and lived alone, they assumed she should serve on every refreshment committee. Because she had a strong, pure voice and had sung in the choir for more than half her life, they figured she was more than qualified to serve on choir fund-raising and hymnal oversight committees. Because she knew what it was like to live alone and be starved for company, they expected her to serve lunches to shut-ins. And because she wasn't exactly a petite thing, they even counted on her to serve on the business end of a shovel every spring, when they remulched the flower beds around the church.

No wonder she finally decided to open a booth weekends here in the lot of the long-closed Satellite Vista Drive-In. For two-and-a-half days—she only worked a few hours on Sundays, after church and fellowship hour, and before she had to get back to teach the junior high youth group in the evening—she remained blessedly unavailable to everyone who thought they knew better than her how to run her life.

It was the kind of plan I wish I had thought of years ago, as a young minister's wife. But I didn't, and even if I had, I doubt I'd have had the gumption to try it. So, you see, I both envied and empathized with Bernadette. And I couldn't help wanting to, you know, *encourage* her in any way I could.

"So, Bernadette, when does the new minister arrive?" I called as I paid for some of Jan's donated brownies at the church booth across the aisle from Bernadette's.

Before she could answer, Maxine leaned in, whispered in my ear and reminded me of something she'd mentioned in more detail earlier. It made me gasp. Big and dramatic-like.

Of course, I tend to do a lot of things big and dramatic-like, but this bit of news actually warranted it. "I'm sorry, Bernadette, sugar. What I meant to ask was, when does the new *single* minister arrive?"

Bernadette rolled her eyes and shook her head. Her long black hair fell softly over her shoulders as they rose and fell when she gave a kind of low-key sigh. Inhale. Hold. Then exhale, slowly. You know, nothing spectacular or overdone, the way some people—okay, me—the way *I* would have played it. I suspect Bernadette does most things low-key and unspectacular, just to keep herself below the radar of people who might want to get all up in her business.

I mean like her grandmother, of course. Not me. I wouldn't dream of telling that sweet girl what to do with her life. Even though I have some really good ideas swirling around my head, starting with getting a look—and maybe something more—at that new single minister.

Single.

The good folks at the Castlerock Church of Christian Fellowship had called to shepherd their small but faithful flock that rarest and most sought-after of all creatures around here, the SIPYCM. The Still-in-Play, Young Christian Male.

At least young to a church that tended toward retirees and whatever children or grandchildren they could drag in on Sunday mornings. This thirty-something fellow would be arriving any day now. And by all accounts, he was seeking his very own SIPYCF for friendship, possibly marriage.

That's what the secretary at Maxine's church said, and she got it directly from the director of Little Lambs Christian Day Care, who heard it from the wife of the chairperson of the selection committee at Bernadette's church.

"All I can say—" Maxine peered around me to nail Bernadette with a stern look, as if to let on that this was an important thing to consider "—is some church ladies someplace have certainly fallen down on their jobs. But that *cannot* last long. A single minister? I didn't know they allowed such a creature to exist."

Bernadette smiled.

"Here, these are for you." I slid the box of baked goods across the tabletop toward Bernadette. "Yes, I know—I bought them, why shouldn't *I* enjoy them?"

"Well, I, uh, I…" Bernadette stammered.

I held up my hand. I had chosen to ask that question, not the one that was obviously playing across her mind, because I did not expect a real answer to the real one. At least not an answer from *her.* I had my own answer, thank you very much, and I wasn't one bit shy about sharing it. "Only kind of person who would ask why I don't help myself to a plate of brownies is the kind of person who hasn't seen me in my, uh, full glory…from the back…in the bathroom mirror after all the steam has dissipated. Steam from the shower, that is, not me."

She smiled.

"Me, I haven't run out of steam yet!" I laughed.

No, I still had plenty of steam in me. Full speed ahead and all. That's why I had to buy the brownies. I saw it as the right thing to do, and I determined to charge right ahead with it. The way I see it, the church needs my money. Churches always need money. And Jan—who reportedly stays up all night making things to donate to the booth to assuage her guilt over never volunteering in it—needed the self-esteem boost of having everyone tell her that her contributions sell out every time. And overworked, underappreciated Bernadette needs the comfort of chocolate and the kindness of someone who isn't trying to make a contest of wills out of every simple gesture.

So when I checked my watch, I knew Jan Bishop Belmont would be back any minute—because she always expects her goodies to by gone by noon—to collect her plastic containers. Well, I just *had* to stuff some money into the donation jar and nab the last batch of brownies languishing there. This way, everyone benefits.

Maxine got it, of course.

"And don't start with us with all that nonsense about losing weight, now," Maxine warned as she pushed the delicious-smelling dark chocolate squares toward Bernadette. "You have a darling figure,"

Darling might be a bit generous a word for Bernadette's figure.

"My mother says I'm chunky."

"Chunky?" Maxine shook her head, her expression sour. "That word doesn't describe you at all."

"Chunky?" I repeated, with my nose crinkled up. "Sounds weighed down. Cumbersome. Like a block broken off from the whole."

"Not a *thing* like our Bernadette."

"*Zaftig!*" I love that word, and it fits when you're talking about someone still young enough that none of her curves have gone completely 'round the bend. "Now, *there's* a word for our girl."

"Curvaceous." Maxine waved her hands in the air, as gracefully as she could with a plastic bag over one wrist and those bracelets clacking on the other.

"Zaftig and curvaceous," I said, as if it was a queenly decree. "*Chunky,* that's a word best saved for women like me and Maxine."

"You got that right. If we are what we eat, then Odessa and I are fast, cheap and—"

"Dangerous to the hearts of middle-aged men everywhere," I hastened to add. I may not be much to see in that bathroom mirror, but I *do* have my pride, after all.

"Shh. You shouldn't talk that way in front of our little health-food friend over there." Bernadette nodded toward the young girl dressed—on purpose—in things I'd have been ashamed to give to the church clothes closet for the needy. "If she hears you touting the goodness of food that's bad for you, she might try to force you to take a sample of that wheat grass smoothie she's peddling today."

"What's she promising the stuff does for you? Give you a thick, healthy mane?" Maxine sucked in her cheeks. "I sure wouldn't feed anything she gave me to a dog."

"Meow," Bernadette teased.

"She's just doing her job, y'all," I said, trying not to stare at the girl's hair, which was dyed a color I'd never seen on anything but a pair of ugly shoes. To make matters worse it was matted in the back as if she'd slept on it for weeks, and yet was meticulously gelled into place in front and clamped down with the sweetest sparkly barrettes in front.

I felt sorry for *her,* too. I mean, usually she was snarly and downright ugly to people, as if she wanted us all to think she hated everything and everyone. But those sparkly barrettes told a different story.

Or maybe I'm just such a sucker for anything that glitters that I *imagined* a different story.

"Where *is* that child's mother?" Maxine tsked.

"Something about her just breaks my heart, Maxine." I shook my head. "I think we should talk to her, give her the benefit of our years of experience."

Despite the fact that she couldn't tell a red flag from a purple haze for her own self, Bernadette was very good at detecting warning signs on behalf of others. When you live to please people, that's a given. So, obviously determined to save me and Maxine from our own good intentions, the poor misguided girl slapped her hands together and said, "So, what have you two found so far? Show me today's treasures of the Tiara Madres."

"Tiara Madres!" Maxine surrendered to the distraction in a heartbeat. A sure sign she hadn't wanted to follow my lead and get mixed up with Little Mary Deathray and her wheat-grass concoction of doom.

"Don't you love it when she calls us that?" I said, accepting Bernadette's distraction and Maxine's reluctance.

"I'd love it more if *somebody* was up to acting the part a little better." Maxine arched an eyebrow. My dear friend gave me a nudge and gazed down on the portable showcase in Bernadette's booth—the one with the four sample tiaras glimmering up at me from a deep blue velvet backdrop.

I sighed.

She sighed. "Face it, Odessa, we are a couple of Queen Mamas without the proper accoutrements."

"One day, mark my words, ladies, you are going to break down and think of a reason to buy yourselves your very own queenly headgear." Bernadette tapped the glass.

"Me? Don't be silly." Spoken like a true minister's wife. "What would we do with those, Maxine? Perch one on top of our heads while we ride around in a golf cart keeping the reverends company for eighteen holes on a Wednesday afternoon? Use it to catch the light and signal passing airplanes to try to divert them from the flight path over our retirement village? Wear it to the Piggly Wiggly?"

"Why not?" Bernadette asked, you know because she was making a sales pitch.

"Why not?" Maxine echoed because she so clearly wanted to be sold.

"Those tiaras are for weddings, proms and quinceañeras." I speak more than the basic awkward Spanish that everyone in Texas has mastered. So I knew exactly how to pronounce the word for the celebration that Hispanic families have for a fifteen-year-old daughter becoming a woman. "Those are three things that have no bearing whatsoever on your everyday life, Maxine. Or mine."

"Or *mine,*" Bernadette whispered, eyes averted.

That did it. Made me feel a perfect heel. And suddenly I had yet another person who by their very presence in this place had touched my tender heart. I wanted to grab Bernadette by the hand and tell her not to give up hope. She might be long past her own quinceañera and prom, but one day she could have a daughter…especially if things worked out with that new minister. And a wedding… The new minister was *single,* after all, and *looking.* Why not allow a bit of speculation and hope? One should always hope.

"Though, from what I'd heard, she shouldn't hope for too much in the looks department." This aside came from Maxine.

The new minister wouldn't break the camera in the wedding photos, but he wasn't movie-star handsome. Or even reality-show–TV attractive. But he had a good sense of humor and kind eyes. That's what Maxine's church secretary had heard, via the child-care director, via the wife of the chair of the selection committee. The man had kind eyes.

"Don't forget, we need you and your sewing machine at the church every evening this week to help make costumes for the play at the end of vacation Bible school, Bernadette, honey," shouted a woman in a red hat hauling a plaid bag in a rectangular wire-framed cart from one booth over. "Most of the volunteers can only work one night, maybe two, so we're counting on you to be there Monday through Thursday."

"Of course, Mrs. Davenport. I'll be there."

I looked at Bernadette, who had her head hung just low enough to give a glimpse of how much the demands of her life had worn away at her.

Bernadette deserved a man with kind eyes.

But I didn't take her hand or try to give her comfort. I may be pushy, a bit too proud and past my prime, but I am not a fool. I know that even the most encouraging of words from a plump old lady in the flea market would not hold any value for a woman that age.

In a lot of ways, the real reason people like me and Maxine fit right in here at the Five Acres of Fabulous Finds is that we're yesterday's goods ourselves. Discarded, to some degree, by people who once cherished us but now see us and quaint and perhaps cute but not really useful anymore. What could we possibly know about a modern single girl's problems? What could we possibly have to add to help her cope with a world that we fit into about as well as June Cleaver would fit with those Desperate Housewives?

I'm realistic enough to know that Bernadette would think that way.

She'd be wrong. But her way of thinking would stop her from listening to what we had to say anyway, so why push more problems on her?

"What did you find today?" she asked, quick and bright, as if maybe she suspected I was toying with the idea of foisting some advice on her and had to be stopped. "Any of those Royal Queen party plates you two love so much?"

"Royal Service, Hostess Queen pattern. And no." Maxine plunked the canvas bag that she used for carrying around her purchases on the counter. She had that look in her eye. The same look I'd seen the first time she and I had met. It spoke of a young bride's dreams of owning one nice thing, just for herself, bumping up against the harsh realities of a young minister's budget and expectations. That look was all longing and wistful, a bit sad but tinged with gracious acceptance. "We didn't find any Hostess Queen today."

"Yet," I added, emphatically. I know it's corny but I do believe that someday Maxine and I will each own a complete set of Royal Service Hostess Queen partyware of our own. "We still have another acre and a half to explore."

"I got a couple vintage aprons, very cute." Maxine pulled out a yellow piece of fabric with big red apples stitched on it.

"And I bought a mint-condition eggbeater." I didn't open

my bag, just pantomimed the motion of cranking the handle of a small appliance.

Bernadette made the motion right back at me. "An egg— Do you *need* an eggbeater?"

"You'd be surprised." I laughed. Actually, I'd bought it out of pure sentiment. I remembered my elderly neighbor having one just like it. I grew up in a house with a Sunbeam stationary mixer myself. Anyway, the vendor said a man had almost bought it to crush flat and use in a "found object" modern-art piece, and I just couldn't bear the thought of that happening to it, so I rescued the thing. But I didn't confess all that to Bernadette, or else she'd never take romantic advice from me, ever, because she'd forever suspect I was just trying to save some piece of human junk from hanging in life's gallery of bad art. I know God doesn't make junk, but at that age, a lot of women don't realize it yet. So I smiled and said, "Even us mild-mannered minister's wives run across our share of bad eggs that need whipping into shape."

As an afterthought, I shot a glance in the direction of the health-food salesclerk with the toxic attitude.

Bernadette shut her eyes. "I know your heart is in the right places, Mrs. Pepperdine, but you can't whip an egg into shape once it's already been hard-boiled."

"Hard-boiled? At her age? I don't believe that. Do you, Maxine?"

"No, I don't. She may want everyone to think that about her. To give the idea that she is already hardened through and through. But look at the way her eyes dart around all the time. *And* she bites her nails, the act of someone consumed by conflict, not crammed with confidence. And even though I do not at all get what she's going for at all with her style, she does make an effort with her hair. Those are signs that she's scared inside and wants to be liked."

"Maxine's right."

"That doesn't mean we should mix in," Maxine added.

I opened my mouth to protest, but Maxine didn't give me a chance.

"Not when we have Bernadette here, and the case of the perfectly marriageable new minister—"

"Sounds like you've got wind of our big news, ladies." Helen Davenport, who I know mostly from seeing her name on the interfaith committee membership rolls that she loves to *sign* up for but hates to actually *show* up for, stuck her head over Maxine's shoulder. "A single minister! Can you believe it?"

"God works in mysterious ways," Maxine muttered.

"But certain Tiara Madres operate right out in the open," I murmured right back at her, before turning to Mrs. D. "Which is why I'm not one bit shy about saying that when your new man arrives I hope you and all the good ladies of your church will make sure he crosses paths with our Bernadette as often as possible."

"Oh. I, uh…" Mrs. Davenport glanced from me to Maxine to Bernadette, who had her hand over her eyes. Then she sighed and swung her icy gaze back to me again. "I'm afraid you're a little behind the times on our big news, Mrs. Pepperdine."

I blinked.

Maxine scowled.

Even Bernadette peeked through her fingers at the woman tugging at the brim of her fancy hat as she chattered on merrily, as if everyone standing there would understand her point of view, without exception. "Our new minister arrived two days ago. But you shouldn't count on anyone... 'crossing paths' with him for a while now."

"What?" Bernadette's hand dropped to her side. The color drained from her face, leaving her looking like a child having the gate closed in her face and being told the roller coaster she's waited all day to ride is full. I mean, even if she isn't sure she'd wants to take that ride, she doesn't want to have someone else tell her she *can't*.

"Oh, yes." Mrs. Davenport gestured with tight, nervous waves of her hands. "Absolutely everyone in the church has already filled his calendar up. He's single, you know, and a whole lot of us have unmarried granddaughters we wouldn't mind seeing married to a man of God."

Not only had Bernadette been shut out of her chance to get on board, she'd been pushed aside by line jumpers. She sighed again, low and soft and under the radar.

"Excuse me. *Excuse* me." Not one bit concerned about staying off anyone's radar, Jan Bishop Belmont made her way up the aisle like Moses trying to part the Red Sea. Step, step, stop and press your palms together, then yank them apart, straight-armed and with no qualms about smacking a few people in the shoulders as you do. "What if there was a real emergency here? What if EMTs needed to get through here? Or the police?"

I looked at Maxine and sighed, knowing she'd pick up the "There's another case that needs our help" message in my expression.

She rolled her eyes and shook her head. "No. No way, Odessa."

I smiled.

"I promise everyone here I am going to do something about this place," Jan hollered, which you might think was incongruous for her, but if you think about it, being an ex-cheerleader, she had a good set of lungs and a way about her that made hollering sound downright inspiring. "Changes are coming, my friends. Just you wait and see."

My smile slipped into a smirk, I could feel it happening and didn't even try to stop it. Changes coming. I liked that. Not in the way Jan meant it. But looking around me, first at the snarling darling health-food diva, then at righteous rampaging malcontent Jan, then at sweet, downtrodden, zaftig Bernadette, I couldn't help thinking that a few changes were long overdue around here.

"Don't forget, Bernadette—" Mrs. D. hurried off without a backward glance "—Monday through Thursday, we expect to see you in the basement, at your sewing machine!"

Yes, when it comes to churches, there is a hierarchy.

The workers and the whiners, those behind-the-scenes and those who rush the stage when they see a chance to gain the spotlight. The line of people who want a new minister's attention can be seemingly endless. And sometimes the one who is first in line for everything else doesn't even get a spot when it comes to getting the good stuff.

That was Bernadette Alvarez. And because she wanted to keep everyone else happy, she accepted it.

Lucky for her, she had me and Maxine to make sure she didn't have to!

Chapter Three

(A Maxine moment)

"*That right there was the exact moment that Odessa set her feet—set our feet—on the path that forever changed the lives of those ladies, and I dare say her own, as well.*"

"*Forever,* Maxine? Well, slap a sparkly crown on your head and call you 'Your Highness,' because you've just become the Queen of Blowing Things Way Out of Proportion, and done it all in a single word. Forever, indeed!"

"*Oh, I am the Queen of Blowing Things Way Out of— Have you listened to yourself lately, dear?*"

"Yes, but I am always like this. That makes Out of Proportion my natural domain. Whereas you, Maxine…"

"*Whereas I stand by my original statement. What you started that day set us all off in whole new directions. Not a bad thing, I'll grant you that, but a done deal. That's how it is with you, Odessa. When you make up your mind that something has got to change,*" *well, those involved might as well get out of your way, because changes are coming and nothing is ever going to be the same again!"*

"I can't argue with that. I guess."

Clink.

"And I am jumping in here to say that what seems like an everyday ordinary circumstance might just be the thing that sets you off in a whole new direction. Just like Odessa did. Keep your eyes and ears and hearts open, sisters. Because God has wonderful plans for you—even in the midst of some harebrained plan of your own!"

Sometimes in life, a thing just comes to you. Some might call it an inspiration, a creative spark. Others might say it's completely logical, that instant when the jagged pieces of the puzzle we call life fit together into a vague but recognizable shape and our brains make that leap toward the larger picture. I think it's a God moment, when the Lord, from whom nothing is hidden, opens our own poor, weak human eyes and shows us the truth of a matter.

It all seemed so simple. So clear. So inescapable. Jan Bishop Belmont needed to stop thinking about something other than her own woes. Bernadette Alvarez needed to start thinking about her own needs now and then. All *we* needed was to get them together, working toward a common goal, and that just might solve both of their problems.

Christians are called to be the body of Christ. We are often reminded that that means we each have important but vastly different roles in the church. A hand is not a foot, and the tongue is not expected to provide the same information as the eye. All separate. All divergent. All necessary to keep the body functioning and productive.

It is a pertinent and profound illustration of how things

should be. Church. Body of Christ. Working in unison, each to the health, edification and glory of the whole. That's the model.

We are also told that sometimes we must not let the right hand know what the left hand is doing. A more complex model, to be sure, and to some it might seem a setup for chaos and conflict. It's that second model, I suspect—the right hand keeping secrets from the left—that the Lord had in mind when He looked ahead and considered the formation of that thing we call a committee.

"Instead of trying to close the place down, I wonder if maybe we shouldn't be trying to find a way to better police the goings-on there" was all I said that day. The next thing I knew, I was the head of an action committee looking into safety issues at the flea market.

"I am going to resign from this, I tell you that, Maxine. As soon as we see who all shows up and it's clear there are better choices than me to lead this mess, I am going to quietly bow out."

Maxine showed no sympathy at all. Not a lick. "Oh, Odessa, you never did anything *quietly* in your entire life."

"Quiet or kicking and screaming, I am getting myself dislodged from this mess as quickly as humanly possible."

Maxine scooped coffee grounds into a filter with so much I-told-you-so energy that I feared it would make the ensuing brew bitter. "You should have seen this coming."

"How? How could I have seen this coming? All those years as a minister's wife, and I never headed up a single committee." I laid small white napkins on the table at the center of the basement room in the Castlerock Church of

Christian Fellowship. "You know, because I never wanted to take up a position over David's flock like that."

"Well, your David doesn't have a flock anymore, Odessa. And *you* do!" Another scoop. Maxine was making some strong coffee there. Which shouldn't have surprised me, because she didn't have any problems making strong statements to go with it. "A flock of misfits and malcontents. If you don't establish your place over them from the get-go, they will eat you alive."

"I haven't had my breakfast yet, so I am pretty hungry but I don't think I'm *that* hungry," said an amicable male voice. And in *he* walked.

He, of course, being the SIPYCM. The Still-in-Play Young Christian Male, Reverend Jake Cordell.

The denim blue of his shirt struck just the right contrast with his khaki pants and the leather portfolio under his arm. The gold of his simple wire-rimmed glasses highlighted both the first touches of silver in the dark brown hair at his temples and the warm glow of his deeply tanned skin.

Outdoorsy, I decided on the spot. Yet intellectual. And understated. The term *handsome* did not pop into my head.

I glanced at him again. He had long fingers, no rings, and his shoes were both a bit too worn and a bit too casual for the rest of his outfit.

That last bit, about the shoes, let me know that not only was he not seriously attached to any female, but he probably didn't live close enough for his mama to know how he went out of the house every day, either. Shoes will tell, y'all. Young single ministers often don't have the ego or the fashion sense to care about the shape of their footwear. And they certainly don't have some female dragging them down to the mall to take care of that kind of thing on a regular basis. It's just not a priority.

Oh, and by young I mean he was young enough to be my son, probably, provided I had married right out of college and had a baby straight away, which I did. I'd peg this fellow somewhere between a mature-edged thirty-four years old and a baby-faced thirty-eight.

The whole deal, sizing Jake Cordell up from spectacles to scuff-marked shoes, probably took an entire three seconds. I was just getting an overall sense of the fellow, after all, keeping in mind that no matter what I thought, his congregants had already determined to keep him away from our Bernadette. So, yes, I will be brutally honest, I was looking for reasons that was a good thing. Why our girl was better off putting aside any notions of getting to know the man as anything other than a spiritual caregiver.

Acceptable, I decided, trying to picture Bernadette standing next to him. But not exceptional. Our Bernadette, with her most gracious and gentle spirit, her womanly curves, her dark eyes and even darker hair, deserved someone…

He flashed a big ol' smile at me and Maxine. I caved right there on the spot.

Bernadette deserved a man with a smile like that.

"What a cutie-pie," Maxine whispered. She's allowed, of course, going back to that being-old-enough-to-be-his-mama thing. She hurried toward the man, her hand extended. "I'm Maxine Cooke-Nash. My husband is—"

He did not merely take Maxine's hand, he enveloped it in both of his, holding it more than shaking it. And there was that smile again. "Actually, I met your husband the other day, Mrs. Nash. Fine man. I'm so glad to be able to serve on this committee with you."

It is a testament to the power of that smile that neither Maxine nor myself bothered to correct his use of only half of her legal surname.

"And I'm Odessa Pepperdine." I held out my own hand, and I have to say I may even have sighed a little when he took it and held it a moment. Not the sort of gushy, girly, getting-a-crush-on-the-new-minister kind of sigh I'd had to suffer through more than once when my David was young. But the sort of sage, have-I-got-a-girl-for-*you* kind of sigh that meddling Queen Mamas have sighed since they first got the idea that young people might need a little help in the matchmaking department.

"Nice to meet you, Mrs. Pepperdine." His smile broadened.

"Odessa. Please call me Odessa." I didn't mention my David or his retired status. Maxine had rightly pointed out that this committee was my flock—should I decide to stay with it—not my husband's. It was important for me to stand on my own merits here, and take the leadership role as an individual. Besides, I'm no fool. A fellow like this, if he realized he was serving on a committee with two former minister's wives and a darling single member of his congregation— He'd run for the hills. And he was wearing the shoes to do it in.

"Fine. Odessa. I want to thank you for thinking our church was the place to hold your first meeting. And for inviting me to be a part of your...what are we calling it? An exploratory committee? An action council?"

Action council. I liked that. Had a ring of importance

about it. "Action council. Yes, I very much think that's what we should call ourselves. The Five Acres of Fabulous Finds Community Action Council."

Maxine leaned in to mutter in my ear. "Five Acres of Fabulous Finds Community Action Council? Sounds like something out of the old Saturday-morning cartoon shows! We won't have to wear those stretchy bright-colored super-hero costumes, will we? Because I don't care how much Lycra you weave into a fabric, they all have their breaking point."

I would have chided Maxine, but of course she'd hardly said the words when the image popped into my head of the two of us in shiny black-and-gold outfits with the Royal Service Hostess Queen logo on the front, leaping around the flea market. Of course I laughed.

"We'll try to keep it more low-key than that," I promised her. "Maybe just some fancy capes and a couple of those tasteful tiaras you're always trying to talk me into buying."

Reverend Cordell chuckled, and it dawned on me he had heard every last word.

So I plastered on my most dazzling expression, then used one hand to fluff my puffy hairdo and the other to take his arm as I cooed, "We know this girl, the sweetest girl in the world, if you ask us. Who sells them—"

"The tiaras, not stretchy missus-size superhero costumes," Maxine explained.

"Yes, the tiaras. Among other things, down at the flea market, on weekends. Bernadette Alvarez?"

The name didn't seem to register with him.

"She's a member of your church."

"Oh. Uh, great. Is she…is she any relation to Roberto

and Gloria Alvarez? I've seen their names on dedication plaques all over the church."

"Their daughter," Maxine said, while I was busy thinking that the man had not rolled the *r* properly in pronouncing Bernadette's father's name. Most people wouldn't have cared one bit. Roberto Alvarez would, especially coming from a man who might someday supply him with grandbabies.

Of course, the whole issue of grandbabies was getting ahead of the game at this point. Still, in the cutthroat game of prodding up-till-now-commitment-phobic Christians of a certain age toward their own happily-ever-afters, you had to consider every possible outcome.

"She's going to be serving on this committee," I said, a bit distractedly. Thoughts of babies and matchmaking and suddenly realizing I might have gotten into something that I really had no business mixing into—church and family politics—had a way of doing that to me. "You'll meet her any minute now. Along with lots of other people. I hope."

He nodded. "It sounds like the perfect way for me to really get my feet wet in the community."

"You go to that flea market, you *will* get your feet wet." Jan plunked a coffee cake on the table, not sixteen inches from where we stood, then dropped her gaze to the minister's shoes.

If she wanted to make a snarky remark about the effect of flea market mud puddles on his footwear, she kept it to herself. As she would. The woman was nothing if not focused, and today she had come with her sights set on just one thing. "That place is a pigsty and a menace and I say let's set the wheels in motion to shut it down."

"Hello, Jan." I pulled out a chair, wearing what I suspect

Maxine might have called my "game face." "Thank you for coming today. If you'll have a seat, we'll begin our meeting in a few minutes."

"Fine." She sat on the edge of the seat, leaning forward just enough that it seemed she might, at any moment, leap up and rush off. To where or to do what, I couldn't imagine. "But I hope this doesn't take up too much time. I left my husband at the physical therapist, and I have to pick him up in one hour."

I glanced at the clock over the doorway. "Well, I'm sure we can—"

"One hour." She plucked up a napkin, draped it over her nervously jiggling knee and began looking about the room.

Maxine appeared at her shoulder with a small white cup. "Some coffee?"

"Yes. I can see that." Jan studied the dark liquid, but did not take it. Instead, she wet her lips, raised her head and spoke in the general direction of the door, saying, "Is this everyone you anticipate coming? Where are the rest? Ten people signed up to serve on this oversight committee."

"Action council." I skimmed off the wax paper covering the still-warm coffee cake Jan had brought and inhaled the damp aroma of buttery cinnamon and brown sugar. How a woman so transformed by unhappiness could produce such a confection, I just didn't know. Good cooking, I had always believed, was an extension of the cook. It came from the heart. I couldn't help but hope that this delicious offering meant there was still some sweetness left in the woman before me. I had to think that, or I suspect I'd have resigned my chairpersonship on the spot. "We've decided to call it an action council."

"At least ten names, Mrs. Pepperdine." Jan smacked the back of one hand into her open palm, making me feel as if she expected me to produce that list, and those people, on the spot.

I know that even as the accidental chair of this gathering I should have had some kind of response to that, but I didn't. My stomach grumbled. I reached for a knife to cut the cake, and blurted out the only thing that came to my cake-and-sudden-uncertainty-about-everything-addled brain. "Yum."

Jan looked at me like maybe, just maybe, I had just implied that I found the ten names on her list positively scrumptious. I bit my lower lip to keep myself from making a truly tasteless joke about cannibalism.

"Now, Mrs. Belmont, I suspect you're an old hand at this committee thing, just like I am." Lack of a stretchy outfit notwithstanding, Maxine was coming straight to my rescue. She set the coffee cup in front of the pinch-faced former cheerleader in the pink-on-pink outfit with hair sprayed stiff enough to withstand a category-three hurricane and announced, "Ten names is fine. Realistically, we should be happy if half that many people show up. And for the first meeting, folks do tend to straggle in."

"I don't—that is, *we* don't—have time for stragglers. This situation needs immediate attention. Tear it down, I say." She faltered, and for an instant I thought she might actually go all teary-eyed. There was something more at work here, I suspected, than just her frustration over the dirt, the health issues and the tacky knickknacks. Then her expression shifted. Grew cold. She crossed her arms, her back rigid. "Someone is going to get hurt out there, I tell you."

Someone already has. She didn't say it. Yet it resonated after the words she had spoken, like a faint echo. For an instant, I wanted to go to her, put my arm around her shoulders, to lend comfort and perhaps find out what she really had against the flea market. It would do her good to unburden herself about it, no doubt, and it wouldn't hurt for me to know what those of us who wanted to keep the place open were up against. I had almost begun to feel like a real dog for thinking that last bit, when Maxine growled out her own opinion.

"Someone is going to get hurt out there?" Maxine passed me on her way back to the kitchenette counter. "If that poor woman doesn't settle down, someone is going to get hurt in *here*."

I followed my friend, feeling a bit like a lost pup. But I did remember my manners enough to ask, as I caught a whiff of the wicked-strong brew in the clear glass carafe, "How about you, Reverend? Coffee?"

"Thank you." He nodded, then pulled out the chair next to Jan's, thrust out his hand and opened his mouth.

"I don't know whether to slap you on the back and sing your praises for coming up with this idea, or file a complaint with the city of Castlerock and get our attorney to start sending out cease-and-desist letters." With that, Bernadette's mother took the room.

Took it. Gloria Perry Alvarez does not simply walk into any given space. She occupies it. She commandeers it. She was just that kind of woman.

Reverend Cordell closed his mouth, but boy, did his eyes open up wide.

"If you truly want to ditch this committee, I have a feeling we won't have any problems finding any number of people to run it in your stead." Maxine pointed her gaze first at Jan, then at Gloria.

Did I dare do that to poor Reverend Cordell? And of course our...

"Bernadette! Stop lollygaggin'." Only a woman like Gloria Alvarez could use a word like *lollygaggin'* and make it sound so crisp, so elegant, and so utterly condescending. You could practically hear her eyes roll in the way she made the hard *g* sound low in her throat. "Bring that box in here pronto."

Jan's head whipped up, and you could feel the first crackle of competition for control of the committee.

Jan had come with a timetable and that list of members to hold over my head. Gloria had one-upped her by bringing this mysterious box. This box that, in fact, required another person to tote it in for her.

"What box?" Jan asked, uncrossing her legs so fast her foot slapped against the cold vinyl floor.

"Over the last six months that the flea market has been open, we've collected a number of letters and complaints about it. Up until now we've just stuffed them in one of those big portable cardboard file boxes." Gloria spread her arms out to indicate a container of considerable size and heft. "I have Bernadette lugging it in from the car."

Lugging?

The first time Jake Cordell would lay eyes on our girl, she would be submissively lugging something into the room at her mother's bidding. Not good.

I put my hand to my throat. "You know, Maxine, it's not that I have my heart set on seeing these two make it to happily-ever-after land. I just want..."

"You want Bernadette to have the same shot at making a good impression on the man as any other girl." Maxine placed her hand on my shoulder. "And if that good impression leads to something more?"

"Because Bernadette wants it to lead to something more, not because we think she must get married to be happy." I said it the way superstitious people knock on wood to keep a bad thing at bay. Not from superstition, though, but from a need to have it out in the open that I still understood and respected the ways of romance, the hearts and wishes of the couple involved and the will of God in these matters.

"You just want her to have a nice 'how I met your daddy' story to tell that doesn't involve her mama using her to haul city records into a damp church basement like some big-boned zaftig pack mule."

"That's all I'm saying." I turned to my friend. "Is that so much to ask?"

"Apparently." She looked past me, toward the doorway.

"You should be lifting your own babies and little children, Bernadette. You should have a big, strong husband to carry that for you." Gallina Roja backed into the room. Her hands flapped with every word, and her bony little wings— um, *arms*—swung back and forth, giving the impression that she thought her granddaughter might crumple under the weight of the dark brown cardboard file box at any moment and she would need to catch the contents, piece by piece, like a circus performer gathering juggling pins. "Get that thing in here and do something with yourself before the new minister sees you and decides he should become a priest."

At that suggestion, Jake Cordell stood up. Whether he intended to go over and offer to take the box from Bernadette, or had just gotten to his feet out of deference at the ladies' having entered the room, I don't know. I will never know, because he had hardly taken a step away from his folding metal chair when his whole face lit up and his hand went swinging outward in greeting.

"Well, hey, there. You must be this Bernadette I've heard so much about. I am definitely very pleased to meet—"

Crack.

Splat.

Ooph.

In short order, the seam of the box split.

The contents pitched forward and hit the floor. Bernadette lurched. Trying to save herself, she clomped down her shoe, hit a piece of paper and started to flail and skid—until she plunked down on her well-padded bottom and went sprawling right at the poorly shod feet of Jake Cordell and the scuffed-up army boots of the young girl who ran the health-food booth.

That girl hardly missed a beat as she faced the man who had so clearly been enamored of her quiet entrance by saying, "No, my name is Chloe Morgan. I believe *that's* Bernadette."

As I believe I've mentioned, there is much to be said for the right hand not knowing what the left hand is doing. At least as far as committees are concerned.

Maxine and I certainly had tried to keep our mouths shut about our matchmaking agenda. But somehow it always seems that a woman like Bernadette ends up looking like she has two left feet.

Chapter Four

They say you never get a second chance at a first impression. When you meet new people, they pretty much make up their minds about you in less than a minute. No wonder commercials no longer bother to tell clever stories or offer testimonials. They know you are not going to take the time to listen and observe, to compare and evaluate. So they shout, tout and get out.

That's the reality of things these days. We are living in a shout-tout-and-get-out world. The clock is ticking. Impress me, or don't waste my time. One minute. That's a lot of pressure for a person like Bernadette, who in all probability hasn't actually made up her own mind about herself, about who she really is and, most importantly, about who she is capable of being.

"So, what do you think about Jake?" I asked Bernadette the next day as we stood in the side lot of the old drive.

In my brilliance and, frankly, my desperation to save the day and grant Bernadette that most unlikely of gifts—a second chance—I had suggested that those who had showed up for our first council meeting should form into two subcommittees.

It made sense, really, because by the time we got all the spilled papers cleared away and the introductions over with, Jan had to leave to pick up her husband from physical therapy. And because Jake and Chloe seemed to hit it off, and Gloria continued to snap at her daughter, and that still-redheaded terror Gallina Roja kept scratching around trying to find out if Jake was the marrying type, we weren't getting any work done....

And by work, I mean matchmaking, of course. I took it upon myself, as the chairperson, to tip the scales a little bit in Bernadette's favor. And to divide the group up according to their interests and abilities. *Really.*

You see, Jan and Chloe were on the side of closing the place down. Gloria had all those complaints to share, and Gallina Roja? I have my own mother-in-law, thank you very much. I did not need to deal with somebody else's while trying to conduct my first-ever action council.

So Maxine, the Reverend Cordell, Bernadette and I took charge of the side of making the flea market more community-friendly. It's not my fault that that also fit in with my goal of making the Reverend more Bernadette-friendly.

We all agreed that our first step should be to go over and eyeball the premises on a non flea market day. Which led me to be standing by Bernadette the next day, asking, "So? What did you think of him?"

"Jake?" Bernadette fidgeted for a few seconds with the

humongous ring of keys she'd picked up from the man who owned the drive-in property. Then she gave me a sly look—half teasing, half warning that I should tread lightly. "What is there to think about him?"

Tread lightly? Had the girl not spent *any* time in my company? Besides, I'd seen the look in her eyes when Jake spoke to her over the mess she dumped at his feet Wednesday. Not love at first sight, but something even more powerful. She liked the guy. They *clicked.*

Something in her gaze said, "I know neither one of us is perfect, but I don't mind if you don't." Hope, and the acceptance of someone, flaws and all—if there was ever anything more powerful than lightning-bolt love, that was it.

But Bernadette had a bad first impression to overcome, and one did not do that by treading lightly.

"The Reverend Cordell." I waved, big and bold, at the man unfolding his long legs from a nondescript compact car under a big old pecan tree. I went so far as to reach up on tiptoe to extend myself and make sure he saw me—*us.* I don't know how he could have missed us, of course, Bernadette's cumbersome white service van and my big old truck being the only vehicles parked in the flat expanse along the side of the drive-in. "So what do you think?"

"About…?" she said, and I just knew she was playing coy.

I pointed, shielding the gesture from the man's view with my body.

"Oh, about *Jake.*" Bernadette said the man's name as if she'd said it before. *A lot.* Over and over. The way someone does when they practice for a chance meeting—a much-anticipated and intricately planned for chance meeting, that is. "I like him fine."

She turned toward him and raised her hand to wave, too. Then, seeing that he was preoccupied with trying to clean up those sad old shoes, she dropped her hand to her side. She let out a low breath and chewed her lower lip.

If I'd let her, she would have stood right there and talked herself out of any kind of a chance with the fellow. *Oh, no, not on my watch.* I gave her shoulder a nudge. "Go welcome him out here."

"Me?"

"Well, you are the tour guide du jour, aren't you?"

She looked at me, then at the old concrete Satellite Vista Drive-In sign, then at the keys in her hand, and a slow smile worked its way across her pretty face.

"Go."

It was a hot day, even for the first week of July, and I welcomed the shade of the trees around us, both for their cooling effect and for the way they hid any telltale show of nerves on my part.

She hurried off without a speck of further encouragement.

I shook my head and joined Maxine, who had been sitting in my truck pouting, because she really hadn't wanted to devote this kind of time to my made-up-on-the-spot concerned-citizens' action council. She'd argued that she just wasn't all *that* concerned, and didn't see why she should have to get her shoes muddy tromping around a place she was going to come to and spend the day at twenty-four hours from now anyway. So I had a hard time this morning getting her to budge from the comfort of my truck.

This truck, now, it's a hoot, if I do say so myself. Maxine calls it the "Mama-mobile," and thinks we should paint it pink and glue acrylic gems all over the hood. David and I bought it to haul shrubs and mulch and landscaping tools and all manner of concrete lawn ornaments that we thought for sure would become a part of our daily life in retirement. Two years now, and I haven't lifted a spade, planted a bush or found a home for a single red-capped garden gnome. But I do love to tool around town, windows down and attitude up, in my beat-up old truck. It's way more fun than a chubby pale-haired lady ought to have. Certainly more fun than Jake and Bernadette were having.

"Young people!" I folded my arms and pressed my hip to the front fender of the truck. "Left to their own devices, I wonder if any of them would ever find one another and start to work on producing the next generation."

"Folks been managing to do it for a whole lot of years without your help, Odessa. I have an inkling most of them just might get the job done, despite your misgivings."

"Some of them." I watched Bernadette, the hem of her bright print dress floating around her sturdy but still lovely legs as she flounced up to the minister.

He stepped back, his hands up, and said something. Probably some lame joke, telling her not to hurt him today.

She stopped short and looked at the ground.

"But those two?" The tableau they made just about broke my heart. "They are going to need all the help we can give them."

"*We?*" Maxine looked genuinely surprised.

I found it cute that, regardless of how much she likes to tell people she knows exactly what I have in mind and usually wants no part of it, I could still catch her off guard. "You know, Maxine, I have never been one of those women who meddled in other people's lives."

She said nothing.

"You're not going to argue with that?"

"I'm still trying to decide how I got dragged into this we-have-to-help-those-two notion of yours." She got out of the truck and shut the door soundly behind her. "As for you saying you don't meddle in other people's lives...? Well, a statement like that is the kind of thing I'd have to leave between you and the Lord, because..." She winced, looked skyward, then cocked her head and aimed her gaze square at me. "Odessa, there are times when being a sister in Christ and being a woman of good manners just plain clash. For me, that used to happen maybe once or twice in a decade. Now, every day I spend with you, it happens once or twice...an hour!"

"You have issues with me, Sister Cooke-Nash?" A quick glance showed the targets of my matchmaking walking our way, Jake in long confident strides and Bernadette... What was she thinking, wearing those espadrilles out here? I mean, they are too cute for words, but look at the height on those heels and the flimsy ribbons around her ankles! She is going to fall flat on her face. Or worse. I could see the two of them trying to explain how they both got mud-covered backsides! Texas in the summer wasn't usually a wet place, but somehow the whole flea market parking lot and the walkway into the place seemed to remain forever soggy. Bernadette knew that. And she should have taken it into account. "You know, I have my nurse's shoes behind the seat of the truck. Do you think I should get them out and insist she get herself into some sensible footwear before—"

Maxine laughed. "Odessa Pepperdine, you are the most meddlesome woman I have ever met. How can I stand here and listen to you say otherwise and not have issues with it?"

"Fair enough." I laughed, too.

Then I put my hand on her arm and swiveled her around to see what I saw. Bernadette clumping and wobbling along, clutching her skirt for dear life, all the while trying to make light conversation and maintain control over her windswept hair and the cumbersome keys in her hand.

Maxine sighed, and I knew she had begun to see my point.

We'd been told we could come out today if we parked along the side, out of sight of the road. That meant we had to walk around the chipped but still impressive screen of the drive-in screen to get to the gate where everyone entered on flea market day. I don't think Bernadette had considered that little hike when she had dressed this morning, and I could just imagine her stomach clenching as she thought about the kinds of things her mother and grandmother might say to her about the foolishness of her choices. I was wondering what I might call out or do to help her along when Jake finally paused and reached down to slip the keys from Bernadette's hand.

She tipped her head up to look into his eyes. There were not many men who stood over her that way, and I could tell she liked the new experience. She said something, glanced down, then lifted one foot and rotated her ankle.

Jake laughed and held his arms up, and I could just imagine him saying, *Here, jump in my arms and I'll carry you away.*

Then, without making a big deal out of it, he offered her his arm to steady her as they began to walk toward us again.

Big sigh. "I mean, I was never one of those who found it her place to meddle in people's love lives. To try to get everyone neatly paired up and married off."

"Mmm-hmm."

"But I just have this good feeling about Bernadette and Jake."

"A good feeling about…" She put her hands on her hips. "Were you not at the church yesterday? Because I honestly believe that was you I saw there setting up this subcommittee and arranging for us to come out here this warm Thursday morning to take a tour of the place without the distraction of the flea market traffic and vendors."

"What's your point?"

"Did you not see that travesty yesterday? The man thinks the girl is a klutz. And he is not wrong in that thinking."

"Klutziness is no obstacle to love, Maxine." Though it suddenly occurred to me that if she stumbled while hanging on to his arm, and he ended up twisting his ankle or tearing his shirt, it might be an obstacle to other things— like wanting to ever be around her again. Now *that* would be an obstacle to love. "But I think, once he sees her here in her natural setting—"

"Her natural setting? She's not an exotic bird released into the wild." Maxine flapped her arms a couple times to bring home her point. "She is a never-married bridal-and-formalwear retailer who has a small and a tiny bit tacky booth peddling classy things at a not-so-classy flea market to people like you and me who stop to ooh and aah over them but never buy a thing, Odessa. Seeing her *here* is only going to cement in the man's mind that she is always out of her element."

"No. You don't think that of her, do you?"

"I think… Odessa, honey, all your good intentions aside, I think that anybody who has that feeble self-esteem and that family of hers will always seem out of her element until she learns to stand up for herself. You want to help Bernadette? You help her do that. Don't try to get her married off to a minister. You of all people know how easy it is to lose yourself in that role."

It was good advice.

I've never been good at taking good advice.

The pair reached us and greeted us. I must have smiled a little too long or too sweetly at them, because after a second or two, Jake glanced down at the arm Bernadette was holding, then at me, and then stuck out his other arm. It had all the markings of saying to me that he wanted to make me feel included, but I knew that to Bernadette it said what everyone from her closest family to the delivery boy who praised her company's name really thought. *You are nothing special, girl.*

I refused the offer with a pat, then stood back to let them lead the way around to the front of the drive-in.

"Don't you see, Maxine?" I tugged on her to keep her from marching right up and joining the others. "By doing nothing more than getting the Reverend to notice her, and thereby giving herself a chance to decide if she wants to go out on a date with him—just one little date—then she will be standing up for herself. She will show her family she is more than they say she is. And did you hear Mrs. Davenport the other day? All the people she has worked so hard to serve for so long pushed her aside for their own gain. If she doesn't rally against that…"

"They will hold sway over her the rest of her life. And heaven help her if one of them should actually succeed in marrying off one of *their* candidates to that poor man."

"Salt in the wound," I whispered, my eyes shut tight against the very thought of it. When I opened my eyes again, I could see I'd gotten to Maxine. I'd made my sale, but I hadn't driven it home. "Think of it, Maxine. Bernadette is like Cinderella, and we're her…"

She held up her hand, her expression a clear warning about making that particular comparison. Then she offered a sly smile and her own version of our role in getting this girl her shot at the glass slipper. "Godly Mothers?"

"Tiara Madres." I raised my chin. I could practically feel the delightful weight of the silver band and a hundred crystals winking and twinkling on my head. If we had had coffee cups right then, we'd have clinked for sure and sealed the deal.

Maxine was on board.

Now all we needed to do was find a way to transform Bernadette and elevate her to a whole new status in the Reverend's eyes.

"Anyone up for a hot-air balloon ride?" The young man who stood outside the gate every weekend pushed a large wicker basket upright in a spot smack-dab between the four of us and the entryway.

I caught my breath.

"Sammy?" Bernadette cocked her head, but did not relinquish her gentle hold on the Reverend's arm. "What are you doing here?"

"I asked him." Chloe stepped out from behind the basket, her eyes bright and her hair practically glowing with a new, brilliant streak of orange color.

"Chloe? You weren't supposed to be on this subcommittee." I was torn. On the one hand, I liked seeing her, or anyone, take an active interest in our work but on the other hand, as chair I had set up who would work with who—with whom?—and she was messing about with my plans. I wasn't angry so much as flustered, and I suppose that carried through in my tone when I leaned in toward the girl in the black jeans with the black-and-red pleated skirt over them and a couple of layers of T-shirts. "I thought you understood you were to work with Mrs. Alvarez and Jan Belmont, looking into regulations and the paperwork side of things."

"I know." She shrugged. No, not shrugged. Squirmed, really. She twisted her upper body and ground the ball of her foot against the damp earth as she went on to say, "But you see, this is one of things that really..." She pressed her lips together. I am not sure what she almost said, and the fact that I didn't know made me think it wasn't the kind of language she ought to be using. She must have realized it, too, because she cleared her throat, fiddled with the ring in her eyebrow and began again. "I know Mrs. Belmont doesn't like the hot-air balloon rides."

"But she's wrong to want to try to shut us down." The young man reached up to turn on a valve. A sudden blast of fire illuminated the side of his face.

I stepped back, and Maxine with me. "Chloe, I thought you wanted to see this place shut—"

"A lot of people depend on this place for their livelihoods, Ms. Pepperdine." The girl did not outright deny that she had been on the side of those wanting to see the flea market closed, but she sure didn't seem to want me to *say* it outright, either. Her eyes darted from side to side, and when the young man dipped his head to tell her to keep talking, she obeyed. "It's not fair to take this place away because some lady thinks she's too good to share the same air with the rest of us."

Another burst of flame underscored her impassioned declaration.

Again Maxine and I stepped back.

Jake held his ground.

Bernadette alone moved forward. "I don't think your being here on a nonmarket day is a good idea, Sammy. There could be problems with insurance, and… Does your boss know you're here?"

"It's all perfectly safe." Sammy neither answered Bernadette's questions nor looked at her directly.

I studied him for a moment. In cutoffs and a T-shirt, without flyers in his hand or the crush of the crowd around him, he seemed younger, somehow. And older, too—or more experienced, to be precise. But just at what I couldn't have said. Leaner and harder than the mental picture I carried of him. I wouldn't go so far as to call him menacing. Yet, when he turned his cocky gaze on me this time, I had the urge to clutch my pocketbook a little tighter.

Don't be one of those people who makes up her mind about someone in less time that it takes a marketing-whiz kid to peddle you a tooth-whitening system. My mind spoke reason. But my skin crawled, just a little. There was something about his being here today, and the way he seemed to have a hold over

Chloe, how her story seemed to have changed. Nothing out here felt as it should have.

"So, Sammy agreed to come out here and give a demonstration for y'all." Chloe, too, spoke as if she had not heard what any of us had said and wasn't trying to talk to any one of us in particular. "Mrs. Belmont would run them off if she had her way. It's not fair. You can't make up your mind about something like this if you haven't even tried it."

Slowly the colorful balloon began to billow and grow.

"I have to admit, it is beautiful," I whispered to Maxine.

"So are a lot of things you have no business getting too close to," Maxine shot back.

"Anyone want to climb in? Ms. Pepperdine?" He, this Sammy with the hard eyes and the slippery charms, held out his hand.

And I confess, it *was* tempting. Which, right there, set off all kinds of alarm bells in my head. You see, I learned a long time ago not to worry myself overmuch as a Christian about the things that repel me. But the things that I am attracted to, that appeal to me, that even seem to call to me? Those I knew I should be wary of. Not all of them were wrong or sinful, but I should treat them that way until I knew better. Then again, what could be sinful about going up in a tethered hot-air balloon? "Aren't there permits to worry about? Are you allowed to just…"

"I'll go." The Reverend held up his hand and took a long stride forward, leaving Bernadette behind.

"I, uh…" Bernadette blinked and began to raise her hand, as well. "I guess I might like to try it, too, if that would be okay."

"Maybe Chloe should go, since it is her pet project." The

Reverend reached out to the girl in the Goth-ish getup, seemingly totally oblivious to the look of disappointment that flashed over Bernadette's face.

"Sure. Why not?" And just that fast, Chloe seized the door to the big upright basket and jerked it open.

"Do you really think you should do this?" I asked Reverend Cordell, meaning taking the balloon ride, because of my own concerns about safety. Okay, and also asking—in that way women have of asking one thing but meaning another and then expecting the men to pick up on the undercurrent, which they never *do* so it's really a waste of everyone's time—if he really should pick Chloe over Bernadette.

"You didn't see the grip that kid had on Chloe's arm." Jake leaned in close, a calming smile barely playing over his lips. "If someone doesn't go along with this, I think he might hurt her later."

My stomach turned. I felt ashamed. I'd focused so much energy on trying to set up Bernadette, I hadn't kept an open mind or an open spirit about young Chloe. The girl needed help.

Of course, that didn't mean I'd given up on Bernadette. And, to my surprise, Bernadette hadn't entirely given up on herself, either.

"Is there room…that is, could that thing still get off the ground with one more passenger?" She flipped back her black hair and marched right up to Sammy. Shoulders back and eyes on the balloon overhead, she wet her lips, then glanced at everyone gathered there, one by one. "I am the one giving the tour today, after all. Seems like up in the air is as good a place to start as any."

"What do you think?" Jake moved to put himself between Sammy and Chloe, who were waiting in the basket.

"I think our girl is actually standing up for herself a little," Maxine whispered in my ear, giving the young woman a solid thumbs-up.

Sammy nodded. "No problem. Chloe knows how to work it from in there. That's how safe it is. You'll see. You only go up high enough to see the ground and the rooftops of nearby houses."

"All right, then. Let's go," Bernadette got in, and when Jake joined her, I got the distinct feeling that she would have felt lighter than air even without the basket and the blast from the flame.

"You're a good man, Reverend," I said quietly, then stepped away and tipped my head back.

The flame flared. The balloon loomed above us. It took my breath away, but I still found enough to whisper a little prayer. "Please, Lord, keep these passengers safe. Help us all to know the right thing to do to be of help and service to our fellow man. And let us know that we do not always have the big picture but You do and that is where we will place our trust."

"Hey, I can see the whole lot," Bernadette shouted. "There, see, Reverend Cordell? The number one-ten spray painted on the asphalt? That's where I set up my booth."

"I'm sure it's lovely," he shouted back.

"Mine's next to it." Chloe reached out over the edge of the basket to point. The whole thing rocked, just slightly.

Maxine gulped.

"Do you see anything that might be considered a problem that we need to look into?" Now *I* was shouting.

"Yeah, like does Odessa have any cavities?" Maxine called up.

I frowned at her.

"Hey, I thought as long as they were up above us and you had your mouth open... Oh, who am I kidding? You always have your mouth open. Lots of time to check your teeth, girl."

"I see a bridge, but it's not the dental kind," Jake called, playing along. "And I see..."

He paused, shaded his eyes with one hand, then said something to the girls. Both of them turned in the direction he had been facing and shaded their eyes, too.

Talk about something piquing a person's curiosity!

"What?" I shouted up, wishing I had overcome my reticence and taken the ride so I could see for myself. "What is it? Is it something our action council should delve into?"

"I think maybe it is." Jake did not look down, but Bernadette did.

"What is it?" I jumped. More a hop, really, as if that teensy bit of extra height would, I don't know...either let me see what they saw or help them hear me better. "What do you see?"

"Not what," Bernadette answered. "Who."

"Who?" Even Maxine had to get in on *that* question, and we both hooted it together.

"Jan Belmont." Bernadette enunciated every syllable.

"Is she... What?" I wondered whether I would recognize the woman's car on sight, as they must have with their view of the grounds. "Is she headed this way?"

"I hope not," Jake said.

"Why?" I asked.

"Because it would be a long way for her to jump." His gaze remained fixed in the distance.

"Jump?" I did it again myself, just a small leap for my kind—the old-lady kind. I couldn't help it. This whole conversation made me want to do...*something.* "Where is she?"

"Sitting on a roof." Jake shook his head.

A roof. *The* roof. The place from which her husband had fallen and altered the course of both their lives. I didn't know why she would be up there, but I do know that just imagining her in that spot sent chills over my entire body.

"That cannot be good."

Bernadette looked down at me. I couldn't really *see* her face all that well, but I could see by the way she gripped the side of the basket and the way she no longer seemed intent on standing as close to Jake as possible that the sight had rattled her.

People looked right through Bernadette, and in return Bernadette looked right into people's very hearts. Something about what she saw in Jan just then must have made her put aside her competition with Chloe for Jake's attention and call out a command. "Chloe, get this basket back on the ground. We need to get going."

"On the tour?" Jake asked as the balloon descended.

"I'm afraid this concludes our tour for the day." Bernadette moved into position to get out of the basket first. She and Jan certainly had their differences. Jan wanted to close down the only place on earth where Bernadette found respite and relevance. But what she had seen had moved her to action. "I think Jan really needs our help right now."

"*Our* help?" Jake asked, holding the curved wicker door open for Bernadette to step out onto the ground.

"I'm going," she said, without any special effort to make herself look graceful as she climbed out and started walking away. "I'd welcome anyone else who wants to come along."

"Anyone?" Chloe called out after her.

Bernadette slowed, stopped, turned around and tipped her head to one side. "Looks to me like Jan needs all the friends she can get. If you think you can be a friend to her now, then you should come. *Any* of you."

She turned around, took a step, sank espadrille-deep in mud and almost took a nosedive into a puddle.

I gasped.

Maxine clucked her tongue.

Chloe said something to Sammy that I couldn't quite make out.

Jake took a couple long strides and caught Bernadette by the arm. He steadied her there while she slipped out of her shoes.

Chloe caught up with them.

"He's going to offer to carry Bernadette, I just know it," I whispered to Maxine.

"If he does, Odessa, *I* will carry *you*." Maxine slapped her hand on my back to get me moving toward the others. "Piggyback, no less."

"Maxine, someday you are going to make a promise like that and have to keep it," I warned.

"But not today, Odessa."

Because Jake did not sweep Bernadette off her feet. Nor did it seem that he had even offered to do as much. He did, however, carry her shoes. When they got to her van, he helped her put them back on, and I may be wrong about this, but I think, when he looked up at her then, it was with a new sense of admiration.

"My plan is working," I whispered.

"You don't have a plan, Odessa!"

"You don't know that, Maxine. I *might* have a plan. And even if I don't have a plan, God does, and by putting myself in a position for Him to use me in His plans, maybe I will come up with something. Wait and see, is all I've got to say."

Wait and see? In a tout-shout-and-get-out world? It doesn't happen often. People just don't think like that. But Christians should. Bernadette seems to, and the Reverend, too. They say you never get a second chance at a first impression. But for some people, second chances are their only hope. That's part and parcel of the message of salvation. Second chances happen. Because of that, the people who get those second chances are changed people. *He who is forgiven much, loveth much.*

Bernadette loves a lot. And it shows in her concerns for others. I don't know if the Reverend sees that, or if it matters to Bernadette whether he recognizes the trait in her. She certainly doesn't offer her love as a means to an end. She doesn't do it for what she will get out of it. And for that reason, I pray that the people she encounters will wait and see and not make up their minds about her in less than a minute.

Because the Bernadettes of the world—and there aren't nearly enough of them around, to my way of thinking—understand that the time to give up on another one of God's children is never.

Chapter Five

Appearances. It's said they can be deceiving. Obviously, I agree. Chloe, it now seemed, might be more intimidated than *intimidating*. Sammy might be more snake than charmer. Maxine, who is the one always pushing me to get us a pair of sparkly tiaras, wants all the trappings of being a *Queen Mama/Rescuer of Girls Who Just Need a Small Nudge to Find Happiness* but is less excited about taking on the responsibilities. And Bernadette just might have a little wildcat underneath that mousy exterior of hers.

Then there's Jan Belmont.

If ever there was a woman ruled by the deception of appearances, Jan was it. Cool, collected, in control. That's what she wanted everyone to see when they looked at her. And then she wanted them to make the next step in the old adage, "Seeing is believing." She wanted everyone to believe it. She did not just hope for this, she relied upon it, as sure as Maxine and I rely upon the goodness of the Lord.

It was her husband, she wanted everyone who looked upon her situation to construe, who was the needy one, the helpless one, the wounded one. And over the past year, he had worn the casts and contraptions and carried not one but two canes to show everyone the extent of his broken-ness. Her? She was fine.

No one bought that, of course. But then again, no one had reason or the means to challenge it. Until this morning.

This same morning, when I had made up my mind to no longer allow myself to think I know anything about a person based on outward appearances, Jan Belmont chose to put me to the test by sitting all by herself on a rooftop— a universal distress call, make no mistake about it.

"I'll drive." Bernadette had said it in a way that left no room for argument. And what would anyone have said to dissuade her anyway?

Me? *No, let me take my truck. Y'all don't mind riding in the open truck bed, do ya?*

Or Jake? *Hey, let's all pile into my junk heap and see how many it can hold without the doors actually falling off and sending half of us flying out into the street the first time we hit a bump.*

Why not Sammy? *Why don't I untether this hot-air balloon and show you what this baby can really do?*

That's how it happened that we pulled into the Bel-monts' driveway in a big white van with silver wedding bells and At Your Service painted on the side. And out we came, like clowns spilling into the center ring, me and Maxine, the gangly but gallant minister, the suddenly take-charge Bernadette and the little girl in the twirly skirt over a pair of jeans and orange-streaked hair. I don't know why Mr.

Belmont didn't rush right out to welcome us, maybe even invite us into his home and offer to make us cold lemonade and hot pigs in a blanket.

"What's he doing?" Jake asked, focusing on the man in a rumpled pajama top and baggy sweatpants staring blankly out the big picture window in the front of the white circa-1970s split-level house.

"He gives me the creeps," Chloe whispered, and considering the source, we all took that comment seriously.

"Jan must be around on the back side of the house. That's the direction of the drive-in." Bernadette pointed. Then she bobbed her head and shifted around in a way that made me think she was actually trying to see the flea market grounds from there. "We wouldn't have been able to see her from over there if she'd been sitting in the front—I mean, *on* the front of the house."

"But her neighbors would." That was Maxine's way of agreeing with Bernadette. Jan would be unhappy enough to know we had spotted her. She sure would never have exposed even this hint of odd behavior, of potential weakness, to the whole neighborhood.

Maxine clearly did not think I shared that trait—the unwillingness to act like a big nut in front of everyone—because she shoved me to the front of the group and said, "Go up there, Odessa, and ring the bell. See if he'll talk to you."

"Me? Why me?" Even though the Belmonts had been members of our church, or, to put it more humbly, David had been pastor of *their* church, for many years, I honestly could not see why I should be the one to confront Morty Belmont in his own home. And in his pajama top, no less.

Despite the size of my personality and sometimes my

hair—which can both be a bit too big, even by Texas stan-dards—in certain situations I become downright Charlie Brownish. You know, like I think I have the plainest, round-est face in the crowd and absolutely nobody will have any idea who I am.

This happens, for example, when I meet somebody who knows me from church, on their turf instead of mine. I'm just sure they won't know me. Even though if they were to see me in my proper place, standing next to David, flashing a humongous smile, shaking hands and ask-ing about their mama, their business or their vacation plans, my name would spring instantly to their lips. They'd even be able to dredge up a few small-talk comments about my two sons and what they are up to away at col-lege. But me turning up in a man's own driveway with this crowd in tow?

It's an entirely out-of-context experience.

"Go." Maxine prodded. I mean, *literally* prodded.

"I will thank you not to jab me in the ribs again with your bony old fingers," I snapped.

You should be thankful that I don't have an umbrella, Sis-ter Pepperdine, or you'd know what jabbing feels like," she warned, not the least bit serious about the threat to poke me into action with the business tip of an umbrella. "Now, poor Jan is sitting up on her roof and her husband is… Well, look at the man, girl. He's standing at the window, but the man is clearly 'not home.'" She made quotation marks in the air. "Someone has got to intervene here."

Someone, I thought, my stomach knotting up like silk fringe sent through the spin cycle. But why *me?*

"Maybe we should call David." That was my instincts

talking. I learned early on in my career as a minister's wife not to overstep my bounds, or I would hear about it.

Hearing about things. Now that was its own peculiar problem, too. What if I went up there and the man babbled out something I couldn't understand? Or, worse, something I didn't want to hear? What if he started to cry? He looked like a man who cried often and without much provocation.

Or what if he refused to come to the door at all and just kept standing there staring?

What if he came to the door, spoke clearly and innocently enough, didn't shed a tear…but he stank?

My nose twitched. I started mentally thumbing through Bible verses about dealing with lepers and the lame and even demons, but I couldn't find a single one about how to go about showing Christian love to stinky people. Should we hold our breath? Offer them soap? Always carry a spray can of air freshener?

Of course, I didn't *really* need a verse to guide me about how to love the person while hating his odor. This was just the kind of nonsense that was going through my mind as I tried to get up the courage to do what Jesus would have done…or find a plausible excuse to get out of it.

"Maybe we should just go around to the back of the house," Bernadette suggested.

"And do what?" Maxine laid her hand gently on Bernadette's shoulder. When she spoke, her question sounded as soft as her touch looked. "Shall we shout at Mrs. Belmont? Shall we make a scene and have everyone look from their windows to find her out there and us trying to coax her to come down like some wayward kitten?"

"I don't think anyone thinks of Mrs. Belmont as a kitten," Chloe muttered.

Maxine poked me in the back a second time and said, "Go up and ring that bell, Odessa. Ask the man to let us go upstairs and see if we can talk to Jan."

"I'll go," Jake said, taking a long stride forward.

I sighed in relief, but deep down, I felt anything but relieved. Was this what I really wanted? Was this the real Odessa Pepperdine, who talked a good game but then, when it came down to it, did not have the nerve to ride in a tethered balloon or even walk up to the door of a member of her own church family? Suddenly I wondered if my hairdresser, when throwing that white streak in my hair, hadn't been trying to make my outsides match my insides. Odessa Pepperdine, coward. Or skunk.

I didn't like the implication of either one. No, not one bit. How could I have not seen it before this instant? If I couldn't meet this small, everyday challenge, then I didn't deserve to chair a committee, much less claim that I was willing to make myself part of God's plan for someone else's life, as I had with Bernadette.

"No, I should go." And just like that, with my lips still rounded to speak the word *go,* I took off up the sidewalk that led to the steps that led to…me stopping cold in my tracks.

"What are you waiting for? One of us to whip out a little toy trumpet and go…" Maxine formed a circle with her thumb and forefinger, pressed it to her lips and sounded out a fanfare.

"Charge!" Chloe thrust her arm in the air. When she looked around and saw that no one else had joined her, she lowered it again, more than a bit sheepishly.

And in those few sweet gestures, the girl got to me, endeared herself to me entirely, and I smiled. She really did want to be a part of this, or at least a part of something larger than herself. Bigger than the flea market. Better than her relationship with Sammy the belligerent balloon ballyhooer. She didn't look the type at all, but this girl was something I was not—brave. She had not just come along on a mission to help a woman she knew would reject her out of hand, but had done it by joining a lot of old fuddy-duddies. (Do they still use that word? I don't care if they don't, it fits us right down to a T and I don't want to imagine what other words kids might use these days to describe a bunch of over-the-hill-ish do-gooders.) She had come knowing that we were all Christians and that we suspected she was anything but a member of our faith. Brave girl. And bravery like that had to be rewarded.

It was that feeling of goodwill and good humor that enabled me to take those steps and cheerfully knock on the Belmonts' door.

No answer.

Well, the man had suffered a terrible accident. You couldn't expect him to up and bound over to the door. I knocked again.

Still nothing.

I drew a deep breath and turned my head, not to peer into the window a few feet away, but to check the expressions of my companions, who were still standing by the van in the driveway. "Is he still just standing there?" I mouthed, and threw in a jerk of my thumb to indicate poor Morty.

Everyone nodded. All at once, you know, like those joke videos they make of cats watching Ping-Pong.

"'Ask, and it shall be given you,'" Maxine urged, using the familiar verse from Matthew 7:7.

"Hello? Mr. Belmont? Um, Morty? Can we talk?"

"'Seek, and you shall find.'" Jake picked up in the verse where Maxine had left off.

I leaned over, peeked into the window, then motioned toward the door. Mr. Belmont's seemingly unseeing gaze bore down on me.

"'Knock, and it shall be opened,'" Maxine finished up.

"I *did* knock," I protested.

"Is the door open?" she asked.

I held my breath. It couldn't be that easy. "I couldn't just try the knob and stick my head in, could I?"

Maxine cocked her hip. If she *had* had that umbrella, I think she might have waggled it around like a fencing sword to help make her point. "Honey, at this point you've already stuck your nose in. Might as well go for the whole head."

Jake laughed.

Bernadette gave me a look that dared me to challenge Maxine's statement.

So I did it.

Yes, me, who was raised far better than this. I seized the doorknob of somebody else's home, turned it, opened their door and walked right in.

In all the years we had shared Christian fellowship, I had never been in the Belmonts' home. And yet it looked exactly the way I would have expected it to look. Flawless. Nothing fussy or fluffy or fur-bearing in sight. Cool tones of pale aqua and white accented with gleaming unadorned silver. Silver candlesticks on the mantel. Sleek silver-encased photos that looked so perfect, it made me wonder if she had hidden her real family's pictures behind the ones of professional models that came with the frame. A silver tray crowded with medicine bottles, and an empty glass rested on the coffee table.

A place for everything, and everything in its place. Except the two occupants of the home, of course. I looked at Morty at last, and that's when I noticed the oversize brown recliner behind him. Definitely out of place. As was the man standing there, his hand curled around a TV remote, his face unshaven and his hair uncombed.

Poor man. He looked as out of place here as Jan must have sitting on the roof. I blinked, and tears bathed my eyes. My nose tingled. There was a reason I didn't do this kind of thing, I realized then. It wasn't because of my personality or my fear of foul odors. It was because…I'm just not any good at it. I'm too tenderhearted. Too empathetic. Too prone to dramatics and blowing things out of proportion and blubbering like a baby over situations that touch my heart and make me just want to—

"Get out!"

"Jan!" *Gulp.* Honestly, I think I actually made a big gulping sound. It's understandable, when you take a woman on the verge of busting out blubbering and scare her half out of her wits by storming into a room where she…where she, meaning me, has no business being in the first place. Which was why, as soon as I realized how it all must look to Jan, I started trying to explain myself as fast as my tongue could tattle. "I… Morty was standing there. They said somebody has to go up there and knock and the door shall be opened and the door *was* open, and everyone said, stick your head in…just like cats watching Ping-Pong. And we couldn't go around back and holler, even though you were on the roof and—"

"Stop!" She threw up her hands. She scowled, and not just her regular everyday scowl, either. This one looked like maybe I had given her a first-class headache with all my blathering. Finally, rubbing her temple with one hand, she made a "Go back" motion in the air with the other one and said, "How did you know that? About me being on the roof?"

"We saw you."

"How?" Every last bit of color drained from her face. Even her salon-bought tan seemed to wash away. "How could you see me?"

"Well, not *me.*" I shifted my weight, glanced back at the still-open door, then at Mr. Belmont, who had not moved an inch or changed his expression. "Bernadette and Chloe and Reverend Cordell saw you. From the hot-air balloon." I threw that last part in, as if it made perfect sense.

She blinked at me.

"They're outside."

"In a hot-air balloon?" She almost sounded hopeful, like maybe she thought we had come to whisk her up, up and away. Away from her worry. Away from spotless floors, where everyone trod so lightly it scarcely left a footprint, and fanned-out magazines that no one ever read or touched. Away from her husband and his easy chair and the constant blare of the television set.

"No, we came in Bernadette's van. We had been over at the drive-in, to take a tour of the place without any booths or people there. You know, to see what we were dealing with in terms of the layout of things and what kind of shape everything is really in." I was babbling again, but at least this time she seemed to follow me. She nodded. Her perfectly plucked eyebrows pinched together above the bridge of her nose. She even glanced in the general direction of the driveway without any perceptible hint of anger in her eyes.

This was good. This was all good. Jan Belmont was listening to me. I had no idea if I was making sense to her, but she was listening. Hadn't I started all this to help both Bernadette *and* Jan? And here God had given me what appeared to be the chance to reach out to Jan. I couldn't let it slip away.

"Why don't you come with us?" I said.

"But that's not my subcommittee."

"It's not Chloe's, either, but there she is!" I took a step back and gave the others a wave. As soon as Maxine started toward the door, that simple means of greeting turned into a panic-driven attempt to keep the lot of them at bay. I did everything but shout, *Shoo, y'all! I have this covered!*

I didn't have it covered, of course, but God did. And I saw no reason to tromp on His plans by bringing everyone into Jan's disquieted little world.

"I would love to, to do anything to get out of the house, but I hate to leave Morty."

"Is there any reason Morty can't come with us?" I don't know where that question came from. In truth, the last thing I wanted was to haul Morty out of his easy chair and into the world of the Five Acres of Fabulous Finds Action Council. But I had said it. I had promised to make myself an instrument of God's plans, and that was what had come out of my mouth. I couldn't take it back.

"I, uh…I suppose Morty could come along." For the first time since I'd gotten there, Jan looked at her husband. Her whole countenance shifted, softened…saddened. There was no mistaking the look on her face then. She loved the man.

He stared back at her with the same intensity he had shown the picture window.

"I want to get him out more. He has to have someone with him, in case he gets unsteady. And of course he can't drive, so unless the kids come home or somebody comes to get him…"

He looked her way then. His eyes narrowed, and he began to shuffle off again toward the dark blob of a chair.

She bowed her head. "He doesn't like having to depend on me and me alone so much."

I dared to touch her shoulder, just barely. "There isn't a one of us that couldn't use more than one person looking out for us, I suspect."

She smiled, briefly. So briefly I actually doubted it at all. Then she nodded, grabbed my wrist and took a deep breath.

Head up, she turned to face her husband, who had draped himself across that old recliner. In the time it took for her to go from facing me to speaking to her husband, Jan's whole face brightened. "Did you hear that, honey? Mrs. Pepperdine is inviting you to join us on our tour of the drive-in grounds. What do you say? Don't you want to get out?"

He just stared at the TV.

"Excuse me a minute." Jan went into the living room and said something to him.

He did not turn his head or acknowledge her in any way. She spoke again.

I wanted to look away, but I couldn't. I felt I had to stand there and witness this, to show Jan that I did not feel ashamed of her—or for her.

"Morty?" Her shoulders slumped. She hung her head. After a second, she gathered her composure, then took up the remote control and turned the sound down. "Mrs. Pepperdine wants us both to come with them out to the old drive-in. You know, for the committee I'm on, to…"

She didn't finish.

But then it didn't matter.

Morty wasn't listening. And if she had any question at all about that, he proved it to her by raising up the remote, pointing it firmly at the TV and cranking the volume up full.

"I'm sorry." Jan took my arm and headed toward the door. "I don't think we can make it today."

"But, Jan, you could still…"

She opened the door. "Give my regards to the others, please."

"But I never found out why you were on the roof," I whispered.

"Oh, didn't you?" She raised an eyebrow and then, pointedly, her face a mask of propriety and pain, she fixed her gaze on the man in the chair.

I wanted to burst into tears, but instead I simply nodded and started through the door.

"I'll see you Friday, when I drop off my baked goods," she said, her eyes as distant as her husband's had been earlier.

"Friday," I said softly. I took another step and then, knowing with all my heart that God had brought me here, and without one bit of concern for how it would look to my friends or the neighbors, did what I knew God would have me do. I pulled Jan Belmont into the biggest, warmest, most heartfelt hug I knew how to give.

She did not respond in kind.

I didn't care. And I didn't turn loose of her until I had said a quick prayer.

Morty Belmont was no longer weighed down with the cumbersome casts and braces meant to help his body heal. He wore his brokenness in other ways. And his wife did everything she could to hide hers.

Appearances can be deceiving, but God is steadfast. He had used a threat and a hot-air balloon to make me look beneath the surface and see how much my sister in Christ needed me.

Chapter Six

"They say when God closes a door, He opens a window."

Maxine replied, "That's pretty handy if there's someone you want to push *out* a window!"

I guess we shouldn't have been making fun like that, especially given Morty Belmont's fall, but the thing is, there are just times when you have to laugh or you think you'll do something drastic. And since a few hours after we left the Belmonts' house I'd convinced Bernadette to go and do something drastic…well, the least I could do was sprinkle a little humor into the mix and pray for the best.

So that's how it was that the predawn hours of Friday morning found Maxine and me sailing through the streets of Castlerock in my truck. Destination? The Five Acres of Fabulous Finds Flea Market, where we had taken on the assignment of running Bernadette's booth for the day while she trained a new employee to work out of the shop in her home a couple days a week. Yes, what you are thinking I did is *exactly* what I did. I talked Bernadette into hiring Jan part-time. Given Bernadette's nature and what we had seen at Jan's home yesterday, it hadn't taken much, just a reminder of how much Jan needed the money and the respite and a promise that Maxine and I would do whatever we could, *for free,* to pitch in and…

"Maxine Cooke-Nash and Odessa Pepperdine—businesswomen!"

"Would you stop saying that?" Maxine covered her ears, sort of. I mean, if she really hadn't wanted to hear me, she'd have stuck her fingers in her ears and started singing— probably a hymn. A real rafter-raiser like "Up from the Grave He Arose" or "Standing on the Promises," so she could really drown me out.

"En-tra-prah-new-wars." I sounded it out with a particularly bodacious Texas twang, if I do say so myself.

"Aren't-we-too-clue-less?" She parroted my accent, twang for twang. "That's more like it. Odessa, we have no idea what we are doing."

"Yes, we do! We're helping!" I didn't say who or what, because deep down I had the gut feeling we were helping the Lord more than we were helping any actual people. That is, helping the Lord help people. And I knew that if I put forth that idea, Maxine would suggest that if the Lord needed help with anything, He would have better resources than us. And she would be factual in that belief, though I can't say she could be right. "I can't hide my excitement here, Maxine. This is the first time I've ever worked at a real job, aside from motherhood and being an extension of David's ministry, since…ever."

"Are you kidding?" Maxine braced herself, straight-armed, against the dashboard. She used to hang on to the door handle, but one day, going around a particularly sharp curve, she yanked the thing clean open. This is not your sophisticated, modern all-electric and computer-regulated pickup truck here, y'all. Ever since then, she's clung to the dashboard instead, to make up for the bad springs in the seats, the bad shocks on the passenger side and the bad driver behind the wheel! So, braced for anything, she tipped her head to one side and eyeballed me good, her tone completely sweet but nonetheless incredulous as she asked, "You've never gotten out of the house and gone off to a job?"

"And you have?" I asked, also incredulous but distinctly less sweet. Whenever Maxine and I discussed our lives, they always seem to run side by side. In fact, they seemed so similar that I just assumed her life choices, especially about something as significant as being a working-outside-the-house mom or a stay-at-home mom, would be exactly the same.

"I sure have." She abandoned the dashboard death grip long enough to fold her arms across her bosom, all defiant-like. But that classic Maxine twinkle in her eye told me she wasn't setting herself up as my worldly superior when she proclaimed, "I was a carhop at the A&W."

"You were not!" I shot back, so fast I practically gave myself whiplash.

"You calling me a liar?" Maxine scooched over to the far side of the seat and gave me what older rural types around here would call the stank eye—meaning she scrunched one eye all up till it was nothing but wrinkles and opened the other eye so big it almost looked buggy.

I laughed, because I knew she didn't think I was actually calling her a liar and because how can you not laugh at a woman of so much grace and dignity who doesn't shy away from throwing the stank eye on her best friend when the occasion calls for it? "No, I was expressing my… When were you a carhop at the A&W?"

"When? Odessa Pepperdine! When I was in high school!" Now both eyes popped open wide and her smile broke through, even as she laughed lightly under her breath. "You don't think I made a career of carrying frosty root-beer mugs out to car windows, do you?"

"No. Not at all." Though I admit I did take a moment then and there to picture her as she looked today, with her carefully coiffed hair, meticulous makeup and senior citizen figure, in one of those orange-and-brown uniforms. And shame on me for it, but it made me giggle, just a little. Then I got right back to the conversations. "I just… Maxine, if you worked at the A&W, then there is an almost inescapable chance that you carried trays out to my car when I'd go there with all my friends after games and things. And I never even noticed you."

"Well, why would you?" She sighed and adjusted her shoulders, pressing them back against the cheap faux sheepskin seat cover. "It was 1961 in America, which made it roughly 1938 in Castlerock, civil-rights-wise."

Tension bristled in the cab of my bouncy old truck. This was a subject we had broached now and again, but we had, for the most part, decided that it was in the past and we had come too far and loved each other too much to let it mar our friendship now. But that did not erase the realities. We came from different worlds, Maxine and me, and in many fundamental ways it made us different women and that would always be so.

She pursed her lips and kept her gaze facing forward. "Why would a carful of middle-class blondes notice a dark-skinned girl in a carhop's uniform bringing them foot-long chili dogs and Teen Burgers?"

"Oh, Teen Burgers!" That did it. The memory broke the tension, and all but broke my ability to concentrate on my driving, as well. I could practically feel the foiled paper crinkling around the things and smell the aroma of the drive-in restaurant's long-ago specialty. It almost made me drive off the road. "With bacon!"

"Bacon!" Maxine's eyes lit up, and just that fast, we went from racially divergent oldsters to women of the same sisterhood. The sisterhood of women who know bacon is deadly to your arteries but cannot resist its crispy deliciousness.

"Let's go to the Wagon Wheel Diner and get a great big breakfast before we go out to the flea market and open up shop for Bernadette."

"We can't. As vendors, we have a responsibility to get her booth and goods there and ready for display before the gates open to buyers."

"Well, that's no fun," I grumbled, wetting my lips as if I could still taste the bacon and gravy that had slipped through our fingers...um, teeth?

"You should have thought of that before you volunteered us to do this."

"I had to do it, Maxine. You saw poor Jan and that husband of hers. She needs an outlet."

"Yeah, so she can plug a cattle prod into that outlet and make that man get out of his chair."

"Maxine!"

"I know. That wasn't very delicate or Christian-sounding, but sometimes I am not a very delicate Christian. I personally don't think Jesus was particularly politically correct. He spoke His mind and told that man on the pallet to take up his bed and walk."

"That *is* true."

"Well, someone needs to say the same to Morty Belmont."

"I have David going out there." It didn't feel like my place to call in the current minister. You know, that whole I-don't-meddle speech I'd made to Maxine, coming to bite me in the, uh…ankle. But to ask my husband to drop by and see what he could do to cheer up a former member of his flock—that's not meddling, is it? Well, if it is or if it isn't, I did it. "There's not much more we can do for Jan's husband."

"But getting Bernadette to hire Jan to work at the business a couple days a week?"

I followed the signs to the exhibitors' parking lot and flashed Bernadette's pass to the woman standing by an orange-and-white barricade there. She waved us on through and said we could only stay in the unloading zone for ten minutes, so to only use it if we had big things that we couldn't navigate through the parking lot. Except she didn't use the word *navigate*. She peppered her instructions with the kind of cursing that passes for ordinary language these days, and she didn't take the cigarette out of her mouth until she gestured toward Bernadette's spot.

After brushing ashes off my bare forearm, I guided the truck into the right row, all the while talking to Maxine like I was an old pro at all of this. "Bernadette having Jan help with shipments and orders on Mondays and Wednesdays gets Jan out of the house. It also frees up a few hours for Bernadette during the week."

"For what? So her family and church can boss her around even more?"

"No. So *we* can."

The wheels hit a pothole, and Maxine just missed hitting her head on the ceiling, but from her expression I had no doubt that my words had done more to jostle her than my driving. "So *we* can? So we can *what?*"

"Boss Bernadette around." I tried to drive more gently, but one thing we hadn't taken into account during our tour—probably because we'd been instructed to park on the side—was the pitiful shape of the big field they used for a parking lot. We had always parked far out, so as to make for an easy getaway when we reached our trashy-treasure saturation point, so I'd always assumed everyone else had had better conditions. "You know, how we're trying to give her a shot at dating the Reverend?"

"Are we still doing that?"

"Have they gone on a date yet?" *Thwump.* Another pothole.

"No," Maxine answered, her hand protecting her head.

"Then there is still work to be done. And we are on the job, Maxine."

"And you said you'd never worked. I guess you don't count meddling as a full-time job?"

"I don't meddle. I *encourage.* I'm like a…a…a…"

"Big fat meddler?"

I scowled at her. "Gardener. I am like a gardener. Encouraging tender seeds to take root and grow. To strive for their full potential."

"There is a joke in there, about what one uses to fertilize those tender seeds and about speeches like that making me think you have a lifetime supply." Maxine held her hand up. "But being a Godly woman, I won't go there."

"Good, because we're *here*." I pulled up to a roped-off section and cut the engine in front of a card with the number that corresponded to Bernadette's slot in the flea market. "Let's unload and get to setting up."

"Okay, but after we finish and the flea market opens…? I am going to run out and get a to-go order from the Wagon Wheel for a whole breakfast spread, with extra bacon."

"And you think I'd try to stop you?" Nothing stops Maxine. And from now on, nothing is going to stop me, either. I can do anything through Christ who strengthens me. It's not just a verse people print on a paperweight, it's a way of life. "And while you're gone, I'll be at Bernadette's booth, showing them what I can do if left to my own devices."

"Here, ladies, let me help you with that." The familiar voice of a young man, the tone far too friendly and familiar, told us that we were not going to be left to our own devices.

"Oh!" Maxine clutched at the clear plastic tub of tiaras she had naturally gravitated toward carrying in.

"Why…Sammy! It's…you." What was I supposed to do, lie and say it was nice to see him?

"Yeah. You know, it doesn't take no time for us to set up our operation, so after we're good to go I always come around back here and see if I can help anyone set up."

Bernadette had never mentioned this service. She'd explained how to sign in, how to put the tables and display cases together, how to hook up the electronic side of things in order to do credit-card purchases, where to stash checks, and how to reach her if we needed anything. Nowhere in the two hours of prep time we'd done over dinner last night had Sammy's name come up.

"Um, I think we have this under control, actually. I, uh…as I understand it, they have handcarts inside and we just unload onto them."

"Yeah. If we don't have enough to fill it up completely, I'm going to hop on and make Odessa push me on it!" Maxine snatched me by the arm and whisked me toward the back gate.

"Oh. Well, okay then. If either of you wants a real thrill ride, though, come around and try the balloon on your break. We give fellow vendors a really good…"

But by then we were inside the fenced area that was once the drive-in proper, the place that contains the main body of the flea market.

"Don't listen to him, ladies." Not two feet inside the vendor's entrance, a man wearing a straw fedora and what my sons would call a retro bowling shirt was rolling a flatbed handcart, the kind they use in those huge warehouse clubs to haul small furniture and enormous boxes of detergent, over to us.

Maxine put her tub down on the gray metal surface of the cart and gave the man a wary look. "Pardon me?"

"You want some advice?" He said it a bit shifty-like, even though he would have needed two-tone shoes, a pencil-thin mustache and a warehouse-club-size tub of gel in his hair to really pull off the act. Still, I had the feeling he knew what he was talking about when he warned us, "Stay clear of that Sammy Wilson."

"We would have loved to stay clear of him." Maxine grabbed hold of the waist-high bar that guided the cart and wheeled it around so that we could easily load Bernadette's goods onto it. "He just naturally seems to gravitate toward us."

"That's not good. Won't make you many friends around here."

"Why not?" I asked, before Maxine could decide to announce that we had not come here today seeking friendships.

But just that fast, the fellow disappeared.

The rest of the morning went by quickly, especially after we got set up and Maxine ran off to get us a big breakfast. I don't know if it was the extra bacon or the fact that I so wanted to do well for Bernadette, or maybe I just felt particularly compelled to taste a little bit of success on my first and only day as a bona fide working stiff, but along about noon, when the traffic hit its peak, I got an idea.

"I thought you were of an anti-tiara frame of mind, Odessa," Maxine said when I shared it with her.

"Buying them, yes. Wearing them to attract customers to Bernadette's booth? I am all for that." In went the key, the display case opened, and out slid the blue velvet stand where those four dazzling tiaras twinkled at us in the high July sun. "Which one do you want, Maxine?"

She put her hand on her hip, and all those polka-dot bracelets went clattering down to collect around her bent wrist. "Which one do you think?"

I plucked up the biggest of the four.

She accepted it most graciously, and put it on with such ease that it appeared she had done that kind of thing before. Maxine is a woman of many talents, but given her husband's occupation and her own early penchant for asserting herself as a strong woman of independence, situating a tiara on her head was not something I'd have expected her to have mastered.

"Come clean, girl," I said, even as I picked up a delicate glittering headpiece with pearl accents for myself. "You've won some beauty pageants in your time, haven't you?"

"A couple. In college. But Odessa Pepperdine, if you ever tell anyone…"

"Who would I tell?" I looked out over the vast array of humanity milling all around us and opened my mouth as if I was about to call out to everyone.

Maxine lunged at me to put her hand over my mouth.

"Who are you two supposed to be?" Chloe did not cross the narrow aisle, but she did inch over to the very edge of her own booth to get as close as she could when she spoke to us.

"We're the Tiara Madres!" I hollered back to her. "And we have the best treasure to be found in the entire flea market!"

"Guest books and unity candles?" She crinkled up her nose.

"No. Wisdom." I struggled to get my tiara on straight without deflating an hour's worth of work on my hair. "The voice of experience."

A woman walked by wearing stretch pants that showed two inches of bare skin above a pair of rolled-down white socks and a shirt that showed two rolls of bare stomach above the exhausted waistband. Maxine shook her head and added her two cents. "Fashion advice, too."

"Because we have it going on in *that* department!" I

yelled, pinching Maxine's voluminous yellow dress with the big orange poppies all over it.

At that, Chloe laughed.

Honest. The girl *laughed*. My heart swelled at the sight.

"Well, my work is done," I murmured, grinning what I supposed looked like an idiot's grin. "I can retire happy. We made Chloe laugh."

"Last time I looked, making Chloe or anyone else laugh was not on Bernadette's list of things we were to accomplish here today."

"It is never a wasted effort to lift a weary heart, Maxine."

She froze and looked at me. I could see the wheels turning behind those big brown eyes of hers, and knew she was trying to think of something smart or sassy or even a little bit stinging to say in response. Only she didn't. One beat. Two. Three beats passed before she couldn't hold it in any longer and she broke up.

"When you're right, you're right, Odessa. I say it would not be a waste of our day if were to spend the rest of our time here less worried about making a sale and more intent on making the day brighter for everyone who passes by here."

And so we did.

Or at least we tried.

And in the process, we made a few friends and more than a few sales. We put the checks where the checks belonged. We put the cash where the cash belonged. But when we put the credit card where the credit card belonged...?

"Nothing's happening."

"Where's our Bernadette?" Mrs. Davenport had strolled up late in the day, all porcelain-capped teeth and plastic shopping bags.

In the big family photo album in my mind, the one that showed my many sisters in Christ, Mrs. Davenport was always the one in the group shot who was throwing things off-kilter for everyone else. No, not the one sticking her tongue out or wriggling around so that she appeared more of a smudge than a smiling face. She wouldn't do anything that might actually detract from her own image. It was other people who had to watch out for her…input.

She was the one who, the second before the flash went off, liked to poke the person next to her in the ribs and say, "Your strap is twisted" or "Did you mean to have your hair that way?" or "I'm glad you're standing in the front row where everyone can see you. You know the camera adds ten pounds?" Then she would smile brightly and the person she had just "helped out" became the one who looked bad in the photo.

She wasn't a bad person. I don't believe that of her for one second. She just couldn't keep her thoughts to herself. She liked to poke. She was a natural-born poker.

And people like me and Bernadette, we were just ripe for the poking. I tried to swipe her credit card again.

"What's the matter? Didn't our Bernadette train you on this part?"

She's not your *Bernadette,* I wanted to proclaim. She belongs to herself, and maybe someday, if she should so choose and he should ask, to Jake Cordell, despite your efforts to steal that away from her.

Instead, Maxine chimed in, "She's taking the day off from the flea market. But we can take care of this for you."

I shot Maxine a panicked glance. To anyone else I might have explained that I wasn't sure what the problem was and the credit card thing had been working just fine all day and couldn't they pay cash or write a check, but Mrs. Davenport? One word from me, and I'd supply her with poking material for the rest of the year.

I said a quick prayer and slid the card through the reader again. Nothing.

"Maybe we should call Bernadette," Maxine whispered.

I whispered back, my face frozen in a smile and my lips hardly moving, "If we call Bernadette, she won't trust us to do this for her again."

Maxine rolled her eyes. "Then, by all means…*call* her."

"You get awful bossy when you put on a tiara, Maxine, you know that?"

She touched her fingertips to the fan-shaped silver frame set with all those sparkling crystals and her whole demeanor changed. Her shoulders went back, her eyes glinted. She set her jaw and took the card firmly from my hand. "We can do this now. And if we can't, then…well, then we can always ask—"

"Chloe." All day I'd been trying to think of a way to get close to the girl again, to try to open up the lines and maybe talk to her about her choices. In clothes, and in men.

"Oh, no." Maxine glanced from the face of the credit card to the face of determination—mine—and spoke softly, so no one else could hear. "You have that Lucy Riccardo look in your eye. You have hatched a scheme to meddle in another innocent life." She glanced at Chloe, then added, "In another *unsuspecting* life."

"Maxine, I am not going to dignify that with a reply."

"That's because you can't think of one."

"I am ignoring you."

"Odessa, just give me your cell phone so I can call—"

I held my hand up the way the kids do. Did. Yes, I am not too proud to acknowledge that by the time any trend trickles down to me, it is long past cool. Or phat. Or fly. Or whatever word they use now. Leaving Maxine with the card in her hand, I exited the At Your Service booth, talking all the way. "Look at me. I am the Queen of Ignoring All Naysayers. I am the Princess of Making This Card Thing Work and the Grand Duchess of Doing It Without Resorting to Calling Bernadette on Her Only Day Away from This Place in Forever."

"I'd shudder to see the sash they'd have to use to print that title on," Mrs. Davenport muttered.

"Luckily, I know just where Odessa could fit a sash that big."

"Is that a comment about my behind?" I spun around to ask as I reached the health-food booth. Up until then, it had been just fun between us, but whenever anybody makes a remark about a woman's behind, well, that's when the gloves have come off for sure.

"No! I would never, no, not ever, sugar. That was meant to be a swipe at the size of your big *mouth*." I know a lot of people won't get this, but that made it all better. Because it wasn't about my backside and because, well, I *do* have a big mouth, and it would probably take a big, big gag to shut me up.

Especially right then, when I was all worked up with the need to prove myself for Bernadette and *to* Mrs. Davenport and build a bridge to Chloe.

People were watching, and smiling. I guess that egged

me on, but I did notice it made Chloe cringe all the more when I stopped right in front of her at the health-food booth.

"Chloe, can you step over here and see if you can tell what we're doing wrong with this card over here?"

"I…uh…" She hunched up her shoulders and looked around her. I could tell she didn't like having all those eyes on her, which I found odd. A person who dresses the way she does, sticks rings and doodads in her eyebrows and earlobes and in her nose and then goes so far as to put paint in her hair, now that is a person one would think *wants* to draw attention to herself. But Chloe all but curled up into a ball and spoke so softly I had to practically read her lips to discern that she had said, "I guess I can give it a try."

"Good." I put my hand on her shoulder, you know, to try to bolster her confidence a little. Because hip young girls really do draw a lot of confidence from the approval of old ladies wearing prom tiaras, right? I sighed and tried to salvage it all by adding, "Maybe you can bring over that portable scanner you have, just to see if it's our mistake or a problem with the card."

"Portable?" She looked around, her shoulders drawn up even higher and her eyes dark and shifting. "I don't know what you—"

"Yes. I've seen you use it a couple times today. That little backup unit you use? It's really small and—"

"Never mind, Odessa!" Maxine's shout cut me off, and Chloe ducked away and hurried back to the safety of her booth. Maxine waved to me to return to our booth, as well. "I finally got it to go through."

At least we hadn't had to bother Bernadette. The day was almost over, and we had done well. I squeezed back behind the makeshift counter with Maxine and put my hands on either side of the tiara, ready to slip it off and go back to being just plain old Odessa Pepperdine, the kind of woman that everyone...

"Declined." Maxine squinted to read the glowing digital words on the small black screen.

"Declined? That can't be." Mrs. Davenport seized the small appliance in one hand and yanked it around to see for herself. "It's a new card. I only used it once before, and that was out here last weekend."

"It's probably us," I jumped in to say. David and I don't use credit cards, so I didn't really have any advice to offer. All I could do was try to take the blame myself. It was more than Mrs. Davenport would have done for me, I suspected, so I thought pretty highly of myself for doing it, too.

But the woman did not seem to appreciate my effort to ease her embarrassment one bit. "Something is not right here."

"Maybe we did it wrong. We're just filling in for Bernadette, you know."

"No. Not here." She pointed to the booth, then made a bigger gesture. "Here. At this flea market."

She fixed her gaze on Chloe.

I have to confess, that's right where my own eyes were drawn, as well.

The girl whipped around and suddenly began refilling the sample cups with gooey orange-brown liquid so fast you'd have thought she had a horde clamoring to taste the stuff. My heart pounded, and not just the way it does when I forget I'm not twenty anymore and try to dash up a flight of stairs. It pounded the way it did when I was a kid playing hide-and-seek and was about to be found out. Or about to find one of my friends and knew I had to run my heart out to tag the tree base and call them out.

Just as she would have been telling the truth when she warned her fellow photo subject that the camera added ten pounds, Mrs. Davenport had spoken the truth. Something was wrong here, and I had a feeling that if Chloe wasn't a party to it, she knew where the party was.

"I guess all I can do right now is go home and call the company that issued the card and find out what the problem is." Mrs. Davenport shoved the card back into her wallet. "But somebody really should look into this place."

"Somebody is looking into it," I snapped. I don't usually snap at people, I don't think, not even the Mrs. Davenports of the world, but this whole thing had me acting not quite myself. I mean, really, I was running a booth in a flea market wearing a tiara and keeping company with people like Sammy the snake and Chloe the…the…the wheat-grass peddler. That didn't sound like me at all!

"Well, whoever is looking into this place ought to get their eyes checked, is all I can say." Mrs. Davenport thrust her wallet into her bag, then took one long, sweeping look at everyone who had gathered to witness her predicament. "Because something fishy is going on right under their watchful gaze, and they are certainly falling down on the job."

★ ★ ★

Yes, when God closes one door, He opens a window. That's a lovely thing to contemplate. My question is, what do you do when God starts opening windows faster than you can get to them? I'm afraid it's going to create a backdraft, and before I know it, doors will be slamming all through this house of cards I've built trying *not* to meddle in everyone else's business.

Chapter Seven

Chloe Morgan had volunteered to be the first one to sign a petition to close down the Five Acres of Fabulous Finds Flea Market. She was the living illustration of the poor little lamb who had lost her way. Bah. Bah.

Bwhahahaha.

That's how Maxine liked to say it, doing that mad-scientist laugh, all big and sinister-sounding. Well, as sinister as a lovely sixty-something minister's wife with freckles and far too much Bakelite jewelry could sound.

And I understood her reservations. Really I did. The girl with the weird hair and sweet hair accessories, our Chloe, scared some people. Yes, she had now officially become *our* Chloe. Though Maxine didn't know it yet.

Our Chloe scared some people. Just as she drew pity from others. And if you paid close enough attention to the folks walking by her booth at the flea market, or even to the narrative of a certain sometimes scaredy-cat minister's wife—that's me, y'all, don't injure your brain trying to guess anyone else—some people clearly wished they were more like her. But pretty much everyone who saw her couldn't help but notice that Chloe Morgan was headed in the wrong direction.

When a sheep goes astray, the shepherd goes after it. It's a lesson that's clearly spelled out in the Bible, more than once. The shepherd calls and searches and climbs down into gullies and out onto the rocky cliffs to find the lost one and bring it back into the fold. We, with Christ as *our* shepherd, should follow that example. Even if it means we sometimes have to go out on a ledge.

"A tattoo parlor?"

"It's Chloe's other job, Maxine. When she's not working at the flea market on weekends," I told my friend, who had met me for brunch this Saturday morning and ended up dragged along on an unfolding adventure in search of someone—yet another someone—I thought probably needed our help.

Maxine balked outside the tall and narrow door, painted a sickly deep red probably to stand out in the dingy side alley. Body Art by Abner was painted in large black letters on the narrow panel of glass. Beneath a jagged break patched together with dirty white tape was a list of services and promises of hospitallike skill and cleanliness. "I thought the plan was to get Bernadette a date. We're not going in here to do that, are we?"

"The plan was to get Bernadette noticed. By Jake. And, by doing that, to give her the opportunity to perhaps, maybe, one day, if she wanted, go on a date, fall in love, marry and have lots of babies…with Jake."

Maxine shut her eyes, so tight it made her whole sweet, round face pleat with wrinkles. "You notice how nothing in that whole mess of an explanation contained the words *tattoo parlor* or the names Abner or Chloe?"

"Yes, but we've moved on from Bernadette for now, Maxine. We've gotten her sort of started on her way, and now it's time to turn out attention to Chloe."

"Why? How? When did I agree to this?"

"When you became my friend." I gave her a hug. "And when Chloe became more than just a surly-faced salesgirl across the aisle from Bernadette's booth."

"So you are saying it was inevitable? That my befriending you over our love of Royal Service Hostess Queen partyware put my feet on the path that would eventually lead to us chasing down a young girl in a tattoo parlor?"

"Why are you being so contrary about this, Maxine?"

"Because I don't remember signing on for any of it." She had raised her voice in frustration, then instantly, like the well-practiced minister's wife she was, whipped her head around to see if anyone had heard her losing her cool.

I laughed, because I knew that Maxine wasn't really all that cool to start with and because I totally understood why she felt she had to guard her every public response. "Don't bother checking. Nobody we know is going to be hanging around this alley."

"Except Chloe," she reminded me.

And I kind of went all gooey then, because I could see that in that instant of looking at our surroundings and thinking of the girl we had wondered about for so long,

Maxine had begun to soften. "I just wish you'd told me where we were headed before we got to the door."

"Tell you? Why didn't you ask?" I wriggled my way in between her and the sticky brass doorknob. "When we came away from brunch at the Blue Bonnet and headed directly away from either of our homes, you couldn't have said something then?"

"I was enjoying the scenery."

Which she might well have been. The Blue Bonnet Bed-and-Breakfast, where we had enjoyed a delicious brunch complete with linen napkins and bone-china teacups, is set on a really lovely piece of land outside town. It's not too far from where Gloria and Roberto Alvarez—and Roberto's mama—live, which is considered *the* direction for all future growth of Castlerock. In other words, it is prime real estate. Everyone who goes out that way looks and daydreams just a little about owning some property there.

"But that scenery didn't last right up until this very second, Maxine." The time for imagining was long past, and I had to deal with the present and *this* property, where I hoped we'd find some answers. "When we pulled off Magnolia into an alley past a row of Dumpsters by the back entrance to the soup kitchen a block back from here? Not a peep out of you."

"I've served meals at that kitchen dozens of times. It didn't seem so unusual for us to be near there."

Again, she had a point. Maxine almost always has a point. I both admire and am annoyed by that very fact at least twice a day. This time, I had to take her point and accept it. This *was* Castlerock, and save a few unsavory bars and questionable neighborhoods, there were few places anyone wouldn't feel safe.

"Okay, but I still think that if you had an issue with coming here you should have spoken up before I swung the door open and we walked in."

"But we haven't—"

"Now we have." I swung open the door and walked in.

Maxine did not follow immediately, so I had to crane my neck to slap a steely-eyed glare on her and jerk my head to tell her to get herself inside. Maxine and I are a team, after all, and she is my backup. And when she acts like this, all stubborn and sensible, well, it surely does—get my back up, that is.

Teeth set tight, I whispered hard and low, "Get in here. It's a legitimate business, and we have every right to come through that door."

"I know. I *know*. But I just...I just can't help thinking...a tattoo parlor?" She bent forward so that just her head and shoulders appeared through the entrance as she said, "What kind of person comes to a tattoo parlor?"

"Someone who wants a tattoo?" A man with his hair pulled back into a tight braid studied us from behind a freestanding counter. He was lean as a leather strap, with long, angular limbs and the saddest, scraggliest goatee I had ever seen. If one of my sons had come home sporting that pitiful sprout of facial hair, I'd have handed him a washcloth and told him it looked like he'd dribbled hot cocoa down his chin. So right off, I had kind of a warm feeling about this fellow.

Still, if I was going to describe his *demeanor*, and I was, I'd have chosen the term catlike. Deep-set eyes with heavy lids. He had this cool, detached air about him that did not hide a sense of tightly coiled keenness.

"Or maybe somebody who wants to learn about some-body who has a tattoo," he said in a quiet, cautious tone.

That was his way of asking us why we were here. I knew that. Maxine knew that.

Still, she looked at me and frowned, "I'm just not sure about this place."

I looked around us. Actually, it didn't look all that differ-ent from your average beauty-school-graduate shoestring-budget hair salon. Only instead of pale walls, hair products on glass shelves and posters of the latest ever-changing cuts and colors on the walls, this place had dark walls covered with examples of artwork that I assumed one might choose to have permanently applied to one's skin. Or should that be *under* one's skin?

The atmosphere had sure gotten under Maxine's skin, I could tell. She came on inside, though, and planted her feet in one spot. She still gave off the impression of someone about to cut and run when she shifted her weight from side to side and said, "I don't think this is the kind of place Chris-tians should be seen in."

"Really?" The man came around to the side of the waist-high counter, his long fingers trailing over the cor-ner. "Me, I'm of the opinion that Christians should be seen anywhere there are people who need to hear the message of Christ's love."

"The man has a point, Maxine." Yes, people other than the all-knowing, all-know-it-all-ing Maxine could have a point, and furthermore, sometimes that point could put my friend right in her place, as she so often did to me. I held out my hand to him, fully aware that I was skirting the sin of pride when I smiled gratefully at him for his words to

Maxine and said, "Odessa Pepperdine. And this is my *sister in Christ,* Maxine Cooke-Nash."

"I'm Abner." He grasped my hand and gave it a firm but gentlemanly shake. You know, as though he thought if he delivered the full strength of his grip he might bruise my delicate elderly hand.

Talk about having the pride deflated right out from under a person!

He released my hand, stood back and gave us a subdued once-over. "So, you ladies come for a tattoo today?"

"Us?" Maxine practically yelped in surprise.

"Does it hurt?" I asked, my pride definitely on the up-swing again.

"Odessa!"

"What? I just want to know." I'd always been curious about the kinds of things people get up to in the name of self-improvement and beauty. After all, I wasn't immune to their allure. Hadn't I endured my share of permanent waves? And this was back in the day when they stank worse than rotten eggs and burned your scalp like fire. And high heels! Teetering around town on tiny stilts with your five little pig-gies jammed into skinny little pointed toes? My feet still ache from the bunions I got back then. Oh, and don't even get me started on the things we wore as young women, the things the catalogs advertised as foundation garments. How those double-stitched and paneled creations pinched and squeezed and cut off circulation to your extremities. All in the name of slim thighs and a flat tummy. Which I never quite achieved, anyway.

I was no stranger to the agony of fashion. So I was under-standably curious about this new fad of using one's own skin as a canvas or a pincushion. "It just looks so painful. All that jabbing. All those needles. So I don't think it's so bad to ask, does it hurt?"

"Yes." Abner offered a faint, crooked smile, his head nodding slightly as he answered with bluntest honesty.

"I thought it would," I said, suddenly a wee bit happier with my fashion-battle-scar bunions.

"But if you want to give it a try, we could start with something very small, and I promise I'd be extra gentle. I think you could tolerate it if you really wanted—"

"Don't you even start down that way, girl," Maxine said to me, raising her finger like some scolding schoolmarm. "This isn't going bumpity-bump down a Dumpster-lined street or hitching a ride in a hot-air balloon."

That made Abner blink, and I think he looked at me with a newfound respect.

"Sorry," I said. "But I don't think we'll be taking you up on the tattoo offer just now."

"Then why are you here?"

"We're looking for Chloe Morgan."

"You cops?"

"Us?"

"That's not an answer. If you're cops and I ask, you have to give me a real answer. That's the law."

I didn't know whether to be concerned that the man knew that or curious because I didn't. Either way, we weren't cops, so I told him that, then brought him back to the reason for our visit. "Like I said, we're looking for Chloe Morgan."

He hesitated, then cast his eyes downward, like a man laying down a heavy burden. "She doesn't work here anymore."

"Why not?" I blurted the question out without thinking. Clearly, the man was not happy about Chloe leaving, and I had jumped on him as if he'd said he'd personally kicked her to the curb with a steel-toed army boot. I took a deep breath. "But she did work here? I mean recently, right?"

She hadn't lied about that, I hoped. Bernadette had come up with this place for us to find Chloe via her mother, who, unlike me, had asked the members of her subcommittee to write down all their contact information, home numbers, cell numbers, work numbers. And now, to learn that information was wrong? Had Chloe lied? Was any of this a sign that she was in deeper trouble than I suspected?

"Yeah, she worked here." Abner was still playing it quite protective of our girl.

On the one hand, I wanted to laud him for that. On the other hand, I wanted to nab him by the gold ring in his ear and twist until he told me everything he knew so that I could get right to saving Chloe from the kind of people who…who would grab someone by the body piercing and strong-arm them into cooperating. Another deep breath. "How long ago did she stop working for you?"

"I'm not sure I should tell you that."

"Hey, we told you we aren't cops," Maxine protested. "Don't you believe us?"

"Of course he believes us, Maxine. What do you think, he suspects we're actually undercover Texas Rangers?"

He chuckled softly.

"Maybe." Maxine gave a considered display of pride herself. Why shouldn't someone see her as potentially a female-senior-citizen version of Dirty Harry or James Bond? Not that she saw herself or us that way, but the truth is, I don't think Maxine likes being counted out of anything, even absurd stuff like that. "I don't think it's too far a stretch to see you and me as members of the thin blue line."

"There is nothing thin about us, Maxine. More like the plump blue-*haired* line."

Another chuckle. We were winning him over.

"Blue hair? I don't think so. Not us. The only things that belong on our heads are—"

"I know. Tiaras." I raised my hand to receive a high five, and Maxine delivered with a smart, crisp slap.

"You see, Mr....Abner—" Maxine smiled that sassy freckle-nosed smile of hers and raised her chin like a true woman of regal bearing "—we *are* members of a very special order."

He quirked one eyebrow higher than the other, which gave him less of a catlike quality and, coupled with his crooked smile, made him look like a lop-eared pup. "Oh?"

"The sisterhood of the Queen Mamas." I gave a flourish with one hand.

He shook his head, his crooked lips almost forming an actual smile at last. "You got ID?"

"Do we look like we need ID?" Maxine put her shoulders back and her chin down.

"Just think of us as members of the God squad. We're here trying to help Chloe."

"God squad, huh?" He looked out toward the front of the place. The sunlight from the front window lit his face. It was a good face. Well traveled, but brightened from within by kindness and a sort of wisdom I suppose folks like Maxine and me will never acquire. "Just so happens I'm a member of that team myself."

"Who'd a thunk it," Maxine muttered, and in her eyes I could see that she had, indeed, *thunk* it and she believed his words even before he spoke them

"Yeah." He moved his head slightly, and both Maxine and I followed his apparent line of vision to a section of the wall that displayed Celtic crosses and references to Bible verses.

Maxine and I looked at each other.

Finally, I stepped right up to Abner and spoke. I knew I had nothing to fear from him, and anyway, if I had really committed to allow God to use me I had to go places I would not normally go and trust people I might not normally have been open to trusting. "I think Chloe is in trouble, and we want to help."

"Trouble?" His narrowed his eyes. "Something to do with Sammy?"

"Yes, Sammy certainly seems at the heart of it, to my way of thinking," I said.

Abner squinted even more until I could not even see the color of his pupils anymore. "That Sammy, you want to like the guy. You want to give him the benefit of the doubt. But don't let yourself, ma'am. That Sammy is no good."

"Here now, if you're on our team, you know none of us are as good as we should be," Maxine reminded him. "That's why we need a shepherd to help bring us home."

Abner blinked, and that odd angle of his lips returned. "Did you say you were a lady minister?"

"Ministers' wives," she said.

"Both of us," I chimed in.

"Formidable." He nodded. "I think you can handle this, then. Sammy is the reason I fired Chloe. I didn't want to do it. Kept giving her another chance, and another, until finally…"

My shoulders slumped at the thought of what her relationship with Sammy had cost Chloe. "Poor kid."

"She got distracted." Abner glanced over at a workstation that had none of the kinds of photos and personal items of the other workstations. "Whatever is going on with Sammy distracted her. Got her mind off her work."

"As a tattoo artist?" I, too, looked at the seemingly abandoned workstation.

"She was apprenticing."

"Oh," I said, as if I had a clue what that entailed.

"Mostly she did body piercings." He fingered his earring. "She was really good with those."

"Takes one to pierce one, I guess." I laughed at my own lame joke.

He shrugged. "But recently, the more involved she got with Sammy, she started to get nervous. Jumpy."

I didn't know a thing about apprenticing at a tattoo parlor or doing body piercings, but it did seem to me that jumpiness and nerves were not the kind of thing you'd look for in this line of work.

"Do you have any idea what they are involved in?" I asked.

He shook his head.

"Do you think she's in danger?"

"You mean physical danger? Like he might do her harm?"

My stomach churned.

Maxine looked at me, and I knew she was thinking this was a job for someone with a little more experience. I also knew that, like me, she believed the Lord had brought us this far and would see us to the end, no matter what.

"Does he hit her?" I asked.

"If I knew he did that, if I ever had any evidence of that, I would have stepped in."

Maxine finally spoke, and I wondered if she meant the message as much for me as for Abner. "She wouldn't have listened to you."

"I know. But maybe *he* would have." He curled his hand into a fist.

"That's not the way we generally do things on our team." Maxine's tone was soothing but uncompromising.

He relaxed his hand and met my gaze. "What makes you think she's going to listen to you?"

"She probably won't," Maxine said.

I sighed. "But we have to try."

"Gotcha." He dipped his head to acknowledge our effort. "I hope you find her, then, and that you...you know...make a difference."

In other words, he didn't think two chubby old ladies could pull a lost little lamb like that from the brink of whatever danger she had chosen for herself.

"We're not alone," I said. "We have some other friends— and, of course, the Lord. We'll keep looking."

He nodded. "Guess there isn't much else to do, then."

"Pray for her," I suggested.

"I do," he said, and I had no doubt that he did.

Now the problem with looking for lost sheep is that they can get themselves into all kind of places where shepherds and middle-aged Christian ladies might not always have a strong foothold. But that doesn't mean we should just stay home and knit.

Chapter Eight

Some say beauty is only skin-deep. But then, so are most rashes. And so are those tattoos down at Body Art by Abner, some of which made my skin itch, just looking at them.

I often wonder about the people who get tattoos like that, if they give any thought to when those ornaments and the bodies sporting them are no longer a thing of beauty. I mean, in sixty or seventy years, will sweet young caregivers named Hazel and Ike, working in senior settings, use those faded barbed-wire armbands and withered hip-riding butterflies to tell all the Lindsays and Ashtons apart? Do these children not understand what happens to skin with age? A whole bouquet of red roses on a fellow's shoulder at twenty will more closely resemble a bowl of raisins, with hair sprouting out of some of them, at sixty.

And what about those piercings? Some young people have turned their entire heads into pincushions. Most of them don't even know what a pincushion is, either! Some of them have enough metal in their faces to attract magnets right off their grandma's fridge, which I think is a pretty clear way of saying, *Hey, look at me!* But when you do—look at them, you know—they get all surly and say, *What are you looking at?* and I want to grab a mirror and hold it up, saying, *Isn't it obvious?* Though some people might say that us oldsters aren't much better, with our dyed hair and bright-colored accessories, and that it's all vanity, I say…

"*Odessa?*"

"What, Maxine?"

"*Beauty may be skin deep, but babbling bores clean into the brain.*"

"Point taken."

Beauty is more than skin deep, and we all know it. That doesn't mean a person shouldn't try to clean up and look presentable whenever possible.

"*Good job.*"

"Thank you."

Clink.

"Where to now, Odessa?" Into the truck we hopped again, and out we went into the wide, wide world—by way of the narrow path prescribed in the Bible, of course.

To get from where we'd parked to go to the tattoo parlor to Main Street required a sharp turn and getting us over a big, jutting bump of concrete. That bumper-chunker, as anyone who ever went over it too fast and surveyed the damage later might call it, marked the end of the pothole-pitted back alley and the beginning of the main roads. Those very main roads were the ones that high-profile taxpayers used, and so they were kept in much better shape. I held on to the steering wheel with both hands, both fore-arms and one knee, to try to make the transition smooth going for my pal and me. That's what friends do, isn't it? Try to make life smooth going whenever they can?

That's all I wanted for our flea market foundlings, after all. To try to smooth the way and illuminate their feet and, well, yes, maybe give them a push in the right direction. But to do that, I had to find my foundlings, and right now one had gone astray.

I eased my truck onto Main and took a left on Mock-ingbird. Gloria's contact sheet had listed phone numbers, but the only addresses had been the e-mail kind. But I thought since Chloe worked around here, she might live around here, and if she lived around here, she might just be, as the kids say, hanging out around here. If the kids still say that. If not, you know what I mean. "Let's see. If you were a girl…"

"I *was*. Once." Maxine resumed her straight-armed po-sition in the passenger seat.

"If you were *Chloe*…" I began again.

Sincerity, not sarcasm or even the tiniest hint of con-tempt, filled Maxine's expression, and she shook her head, saying, "Oh, I was *never* her."

"Not even a little bit?" I caught Maxine's gaze, and though I have no proof whatsoever that I am capable of doing this, I felt sure that I had a twinkle in my eye. It sug-gested that I thought my upright and proper friend *had* had a bit of an, uh…flamboyant streak in her youth.

She pressed her lips tight, and for a second I thought I wasn't going to hear a peep out of her. Not even the slightest concession, much less a full and complete confession. But suddenly a schoolbus filled with kids trundled by, and she sighed. "As soon as I walked far enough down the street that I knew my mama, nor any of her friends, nor any of my friend's mamas, nor anyone from church, would see me, I rolled up my skirt at the waistband to hike it up to my knees and put on pink frosted lipstick."

"Why, Maxine! You wild thing! I am shocked!" I wasn't. I could totally see Maxine looking achingly adorable with her skinny legs poking out of a box-pleated plaid skirt and her smile framed by sugared bubble-gum-colored lips. But what I'd said wasn't a lie. It was hyperbole. In other words, I was making something big out of something ordinary, just for the joy of reveling in said bigness and the foolishness that often accompanies it. It's a Southern thing. And speaking of making something big out of nothing, you know I just had to ask, "Did you also tease up your hair?"

"Oh, no!" It was Maxine's turn to look shocked. But her response was clearly the real deal, not a sky-high case of Texas hyperbole. "I didn't dare mess with my hair!"

She touched the cropped-short-and-too-cute-for-words cut that she now wore.

I checked my own coiffure-du-jour in the rearview mirror. It didn't have the flair of my circa-1960 upswept beehive, but it still had style. Big style. And so I smiled and waited for Maxine to finish her story.

"No, ma'am. I did not try anything fancy with my hair. Not after all the things my aunts and older sister did to get it ironed and flattened out and softened and straight so that they could slick it down and curl it up and give me that immovable stiff flip." She made a motion along the side of her head and shoulder to show the line her hair would have followed in those days.

"Kicky," I said, using the vernacular of the day—after *keen* and before *groovy*. "Me? I used to tease mine, but I really could never get enough height to suit me."

"I can see that about you." Her eyes lifted to the top curls of my pumped-up and pale-streaked hairdo.

"You should have seen me on my wedding day!"

"Oh, my! I bet they had to put a red flashing beacon in your do to ward off low-flying aircraft."

"Rhinestones."

"Rhinestones?"

"I had twinkling rhinestones sewn into my three-tiered quarter-length veil, complete with blusher. You know, the…" I motioned with one hand to show something covering my face, then being lifted away.

"Yes. Yes, the…uh, I know what you mean." Maxine made the same motion. "I refused to have one of those, even though I think Mama and Daddy thought I should, tradition and all. But I said no, I am going into this with my eyes wide open, thank you very much!"

A woman who kept her own name and hyphenated it with her minister husband's name, she would think of a thing like that.

"But then, for me, after that one last gasp…"

"Gasp?"

"The rhinestone veil. Everybody said it was time to put aside childish things—"

"Childish? How is showing some personal flair childish? How is being yourself childish?"

I stared straight ahead. The town where I had grown up,

where almost everyone I knew had grown up, the place where I had formed all of my attachments and most of my ideas, stretched out before me. And Maxine's question expanded inside me. *How is being yourself childish?* "I don't know. It's just what everyone said."

"Everyone?"

"My mother, for one." I loved my mama, but she believed that things should be done a certain way, and woe to anyone who got them out of order or colored outside the lines.

I didn't have to say all that to Maxine for her to comprehend it, either. Mothers of Castlerock of a certain era, no matter what their races, tended to come from the same mold. "Uh-huh."

I came to a stop sign and stopped. And stayed stopped while I added softly, "And David."

"David?" That caused Maxine to turn loose of the dashboard and twist her whole upper body around to face me. "Your own husband called you childish?"

He *had,* and I remembered exactly when and what over. I did not turn to Maxine, however, when I said, in a sheepish voice, "When I got upset about losing the few pieces I had of my Hostess Queen partyware."

"Few pieces? I assumed you had the whole set at one time!"

"Something that showy?" Now I did look at her. I mean, Maxine was talking crazy talk for even suggesting such a thing. I *had* to look at her when I explained. "For a bride and groom right out of seminary? No. No, ma'am. I got four pieces as wedding gifts, and that was it. Mama didn't even think I should ask for those. They were too sophisticated-suburban for Castlerock, she told me. Something straight out of TV."

Maxine chuckled at that. "But you had a few pieces. All I ever had was the luncheon set—you know, eight kidney-shaped plates with a place on one side for the matching cups?"

I nodded. "What happened to them?'

"Oh, I still have them. Still in the box."

"Really?"

"Oh, yeah, because you know, being a minister's wife, I never had luncheons that didn't involve more than eight people, and even if I did, nobody I knew ate the dainty kind of lunches that would fit on those plates."

"Castlerock, *not* the home of the sophisticated suburba-nite," I joked.

"But you had four whole pieces? And you lost them *all?* Now that's a pity. They get broken over the years, or what?"

"Worse. They got…appropriated." It still stuck in my craw a bit, all these years later. Stuck in my craw, and stung a little bit, too.

"Apropri—what?" Maxine folded her arms.

"You know." I gave the truck some gas at last and went rolling slowly onto the deserted downtown street. "One morning the women's Bible study needed something to serve refreshments, and David handed over my hot and cold beverage carafe."

"You had that?" Maxine's face went all dreamy. I know it's corny, but this Hostess Queen service? It really was the stuff of dreams, back in the day.

"And my six-compartment relish tray," I added, so she'd know exactly what had been at stake.

"He lent them *both* to the women's Bible study?"

"I thought he lent them, but next thing I knew, somebody wrote 'Property of' and the church's name and address on the bottom with a permanent marker, and that was that."

"David didn't get it back for you?"

"He told me not to be childish."

"Oh, Odessa." She put her hand on my shoulder. She didn't need to do or say another thing. I knew she understood completely how that had made me feel.

"Same with the other pieces I had, when they got carted off for use for some church event, never to be seen again." I sighed, turning to take us around the block one more time. "That was when I knew."

"That you were going to dedicate the rest of your life to finding and replacing all those pieces and completing the entire set of Hostess Queen partyware? No matter how long it took? No matter how much junk you had to look through or how many vendors who had to bargain with?"

"Oh, Maxine, you say that like it's some kind of military mission." I sat up a little straighter, and smiled at last. "I am so proud of you!"

She beamed.

"But no."

That, as we say around here, took the shine off her penny. She scowled my way, just a little, and with her silence asked me to explain myself.

"No, that's not when I decided to try to replace my pieces. *That* is when I knew I was never going to come first."

"With David?" Disbelief softened the edges of what might otherwise have sounded like a harsh accusation.

"With *anybody*." Again, I did not look at her, but kept my

eyes on the road, and occasionally the sidewalk—because we were still looking for Chloe, after all—and drove. "I knew I was never going to be important enough to have my own full set of partyware, for one thing. And by extension I realized that anything I did manage to have or accomplish or even create was never going to be mine to keep. Not my household goods, not my children, not even my husband. I had to share with everyone, and put myself at the end of the line. Bottom of the heap."

"Bottom of the...?" Maxine's mouth gaped wide open. She huffed. She rolled her eyes. "Odessa Pepperdine, that is the... Oh, I just don't know.... Odessa, if ever there was a person destined to hit the heights, you are that person."

I shook my head. "I don't think so."

"Well, I do. Top of the world, Odessa, that's where you belong. And I am so sad that you didn't have friends and family who made you feel that way."

I gave a faint smile.

"Well, never you mind. You have a friend like that now. One who never thought of you as the bottom of the barrel."

"Heap. I said bottom of the heap." There was a difference. Slight, but a difference.

"Whatever. The point is that we are in the same sisterhood, girlfriend, and from now on it's up, up, up." She pointed skyward.

I wanted to believe her, but... "I don't know, Maxine. It doesn't seem that simple. I mean, despite our present flabby, age-ravaged carcasses..."

"Excuse me?"

I cleared my throat. "Uh, despite our fabulous and ravishing…"

She sat back in her seat. "Much better."

"…carcasses."

Maxine held her hand up between us. "Girl, when I am around you, I never fear of suffering the sin of pride, is all I got to say."

I smiled. "Despite all *that,* can we agree that inside each of us, we still have a sliver of that scared, insecure young girl wanting to be loved, to feel special?"

"The only sliver of anything I have in me is pie, honey. That scared little girl in me is gone for good."

"Gone? Really?"

"Yes."

I have to say I admire that about Maxine more than probably anything she ever told me. Because my scared young woman, my inner Chloe, Bernadette and even Jan, is still alive and kicking. And not in that hip, happening, kicky kicking way, either.

"I am so glad you are my friend, Maxine, you know that?"

"Right back at ya, Odessa. I love you more than Hostess Queen partyware and a sparkly tiara combined."

We drove for a few seconds before I asked, "Do you love me more than bacon?"

"Don't push it."

I laughed and exhaled hard, breathing out a lot of the self-doubt and sadness that the discussion had churned up inside me. We had a task at hand. "Okay. Back to finding Chloe. Where would you go if you lost your job, had a scary relationship and even scarier hair?"

"Jan went out onto the roof."

"That's entirely different." I scanned the few open shops on the town square, knowing they were not the types of places Chloe would frequent.

It got real quiet then. And as you can imagine, real quiet is not the natural state between Maxine and me.

Finally, softly, with an almost reverent tone, Maxine whispered, "What was she doing up there? What did she go up there to see?"

"Or to avoid seeing?"

"You mean her husband?"

I raised my eyebrows and shrugged. "I used to think maybe he went up there the day he fell to get away from her."

"No."

"Well…yes. I wondered… You know what it says in Proverbs about living on a roof being better than living with a cantankerous woman."

"In what translation do they use the term *cantankerous?*" She chuckled softly. "But I get your point."

I nodded. "It's not the kind of thing I would ever ask Jan about, but it did occur to me. Why *else* would a man go on the roof?"

"Doing repairs?"

"Let me rephrase that. Why would a *husband* go out onto the roof?"

Maxine laughed at the subtle difference. A man might have all manner of reasons to tackle big, unappealing chores, but a husband…?

"Speaking of husbands, I think it's time I spoke to mine." With that, I pulled over to the side of the street and parked in front of what used to be a dress shop but now sold used paperback novels.

"Speaking of husbands? That's not why you want to call David. You want to call him because we were speaking of Morty Belmont and chores and you want to make sure your own man followed through on the assignment you set out for him." She cranked the window down to let some air blow through while the engine was off. Maybe it was the prospect of the Texas heat that put a little bit of attitude into Maxine's voice when she mumbled, "And here you haven't even completed the task you set out to accomplish this morning."

"You want to keep working on our task? Then scoot over here and take the wheel, big talker." I popped out of the truck, walked around the front and opened the passenger-side door. "*I* am going to make this call."

Never in my wildest dreams did I think Maxine would actually start up the truck, much less drive off without me in it!

Luckily, she noticed her error in leaving me standing in the streets of downtown Castlerock. She said she thought I had jumped in the seat, when in fact I had only just tossed my purse in and then stepped back to try to see the numbers on my cell phone. Tiny things. And on a gray-on-gray screen in brilliant daylight!

Anyway, Maxine backed up and allowed me to climb into my own truck and started driving while I made contact with my own husband, to whom I promptly told the whole story, including our stopover at the tattoo parlor.

"No, for the last time, we did not get tattoos, David!" I wasn't cross with him, so much as curt. "Yes, I know. Go get your lunch and we'll talk this evening. I love you, too."

I squinted to find the minuscule red symbol on the button that would end the call. Would that I could have cut the connection between Maxine and the steering wheel and gas pedal with so little effort.

Turns out Maxine was not a devotee of that smooth-driving school that I adhered to, or maybe she had never driven a beat-up old truck with bad shocks and mushy brakes and a steering wheel that tended to resist all attempts at using it for steering. So we'd gone bumping along for the whole five-minute cell-phone conversation. And not a sign of Chloe, to boot.

"Tattoos?" Maxine took a turn so fast my whole side flattened against the door. "David did *not* think that of us, did he?"

"I sort of think maybe he did." I pushed myself away from the cold, unyielding door. "He says I am not myself lately, so he didn't know what to expect."

"Not yourself?"

"That I'm running around more, going places without him, driving a truck, chairing action committees, making friends with people it would seem I'd have nothing in common with…"

"Oh, that." She waved her hand, and the truck veered slightly. "That's not like you?"

"Well, I think it is." My own hand shot out, as if it had a mind of its own, and grabbed the wheel to get us going straight again. "But I can see where he might think it's a new development."

"Because it *is* a new development, or because David hasn't been paying attention to the real Odessa?" Her driving might be all over the road, but her thinking was right on track.

"A little of both. You know…ministers." More than

once, I'd thought that if I were a total stranger who'd come in off the street, sat down in David's office and told him the story of my life, I'd have gotten more empathy and understanding from him than I had sharing his home and life for more than forty years.

"Men." Maxine sighed.

"Husbands!" We both said it at the same time, and instantly shared a laugh, as well.

"I don't care what he says. I haven't known you in person for all that long, Odessa, but I know you in my heart. I *am* you in many ways, and I have to say this—you are more like yourself than anyone I have ever met."

"And that's a good thing?" I asked.

"That's a terrific thing!" She hit a speed bump without so much as tapping the brakes.

I covered my head, the way we had been taught to protect ourselves from tornadoes and nuclear blasts in grade school, and uttered a most sincere "Thank you, Maxine."

"T'weren't nothing. What did I do?"

"You liked me."

"Oh, Odessa honey. I told you, I love you."

"I love you, too, Maxine. But I also *like* you."

"I get it," she said softly.

"In fact, I like you *so* much, my friend, I am not even going to demand you pull this truck over and let someone who knows how to drive it take over."

"Meaning?"

"I am going to let you drive us all the way to where we are going."

"We're going somewhere?"

"Yup. To find Chloe."

"Where to?"

"Jan Belmont's house."

"You're kidding."

"Nope. David said he didn't get anywhere trying to talk to Morty, and had to leave when Jan threw him out because she was expecting her subcommittee any minute. They plan to go over all the letters of complaint about the flea market."

Maxine sighed and pointed the truck toward the Belmont house. "Do you ever get the idea that the two halves of our action council are canceling each other out?"

"I do, and I am going to put a stop to it."

"How?"

"I have a *plan*."

A plan. Beauty might be skin-deep, but there was something more going on under this pretty hairdo of mine.

A distraction was what was called for, I figured. But not a distraction merely for the sake of distraction. This distraction had to serve a greater purpose. I didn't discuss it with Maxine, or let myself dwell on what David might have to say about my solution and how unlike me it was. It was unlike me, I suppose, if you only looked at the skin-deep Odessa who always did what was expected. That hesitant young woman who wore rhinestones on her veil and let her husband give away her favorite wedding gifts and only wanted to be liked.

But to anyone who thought of me as the woman most like herself, a woman destined to rise above her fears and shortcomings, it would have made perfect sense when I hit Jan Belmont's door, stepped inside and announced, "Hey, y'all! Maxine and I think that since we have the collective knowledge of so many mamas here all at once, and we only want what's best for our girl, we should perform an emergency makeover on Chloe!"

Chapter Nine

I hope you're not looking here for some opening remarks by Odessa, because she is indisposed right now. You see, she has totally lost her mind.

Not gone-around-the-bend lost her mind, but more gone-hog-wild-with-this-whole-making-over-Chloe-deal lost her mind. Lost track of time, and certainly lost control over her action council, which had gathered here to discuss complaints against the flea market and what actions we would recommend to address them. Unless we can slap some moisturizer on those complaints… (Odessa says, "This is Texas. We have big winds, bright sun and bad habits. If you want to have a dewy complexion here, you either got to sleep facedown in the grass or start moisturizer young!") Now where was I? Oh, yes, unless you can slap some moisturizer or costume jewelry on those complaints and call them intriguing alternative impressions, they will stay pushed to the side for today. Just like some sad wallflower that never had the benefit of what henceforth I shall call Odessaizing.

I have to admit, last time I peeked in, our scary-haired Chloe had cleaned up pretty good. Not that she was dirty. Around here, "cleaned up" refers to what you do when you get out of your every-day work or play clothes and put on what we used to call your "Sunday best," though people don't even dress all that well for church anymore, have you noticed that? When I was a young woman, even social invites came with "Sunday dress acceptable" printed on them, right where they might otherwise have put "Black tie," "Formal" or "Casual."

Not that that has anything to do with what's going on in the back bedroom of Jan Belmont's home. Guess now you know why I don't do these introduction bits. I tell y'all, if this story were a sandwich, this right here would be the cheesy part!

Now, I know Odessa tries to impart some wisdom or offer some-thing to think about before just jumping into the next part of the story, but for the life of me I can't imagine what we can learn from all that primping and pretty-making. Unless you need grooming and hair tips. I am in awe of what Odessa can do with a rattail comb and a can of Aqua Net. Guess it just took the challenge of taking a young girl's look from havoc to, as Chloe puts it, hot.

Oh, there you go. That's it. Hot.

Sometimes you just don't know what another person is capable of doing until you see them under fire.

"No open flames, Maxine!"

"You said you didn't have time to do this, Odessa."

"I don't."

"Then stay out of it, or get out here on this page and do it proper."

"I can't leave right now. It's a crucial moment in com-pleting the structure of the hairdo."

"Why do I suddenly feel like that child is going to walk out here with her hair sculpted into a replica of the Alamo?"

"It won't be the Alamo, but it will be worth remembering, I tell you what, Maxine. And in the meantime, no open flames. There's so much combustible vapor saturating this room that one flicker or wayward flash and Jan's house is liable to go up in a blaze like…well, like a house afire."

Picture me rolling my eyes at that.

Okay, how about this for the introductory life lesson or thing you might not otherwise have considered?

Most folks are like a big ol' can of hair spray. You never can tell what they'll pull together until you put them under serious pressure!

"Ta-da!"

"Odessa?" Maxine sat dead center on Jan's couch, looking for all the world like someone terrified of so much as denting a throw pillow.

"What?" I asked.

My dear friend tipped her head only slightly. "You're ta-daing an empty doorway."

I spun around.

No Chloe. No ta-da!

To play up the big revelation of the brand-new Chloe, I had sent everyone out of the master bathroom while I put the finishing touches on the girl.

Before taking her place in a straight-backed chair by the white brick fireplace, Jan had tucked Morty and his ever-blaring TV in a back bedroom—heard but not seen, as it were. That left his recliner open for Gallina Roja, and she snuggled down into her roost until she was all skinny legs and arms, with two beady, watchful eyes peering over her crooked nose.

Gloria Alvarez, who I thought would have put up the

most fuss about me throwing her meeting out of whack, had instead gotten right into the spirit of things. Maybe she had wished she could do the same kind of thing for her daughter, I don't know. But I do know she had taken it upon herself to remove the full-length mirror from inside Jan's closet, carry it into the front room and hold it up so that Chloe could enjoy the full effect of my—of *our*—efforts.

"If there's one thing I hate, it's having a ta-da moment go to pot," I said. I leaned toward the door, careful in case the child should come hurrying down the hall and run head-on into me. I knew how stiff we'd made the hair on that particular head, and figured one wayward curl could probably put an eye out. "Chloe?

No answer.

Maxine shifted gingerly on the couch. "Maybe that hairdo is working like earmuffs and she can't hear you."

Jan blinked like a bored housecat.

Gallina Roja slapped the sides of her elevated feet together on the footrest and chirped something in Spanish about the girl not keeping us waiting. Or about time being fleeting, or maybe about time being a big girl. I'm not sure. The words are close, the woman was speaking fast.

Either way, Gloria glanced in the mirror as soon as she said it and prodded the soft pad of flesh under her chin and frowned.

From the looks of things around me, I could see if Chloe didn't get out here soon, the moment could go downhill fast.

"Chloe?" I stretched my neck out, as if those few extra centimeters might make all the difference in her hearing me through the long hallway, two sets of doors and those carefully coiled curls. "You coming out, honey?"

"Not until you promise" came the terse reply.

I jerked up straight and pressed my lips tight.

"Promise what?" Maxine called out, when I failed to respond.

I glared at my friend, shaking my head and hoping she would get my message: *Do not negotiate with rogue makeover models. You know where this girl has worked and seen the tattoo ink and metal studs she has applied to lesser folks than us. Pipe down. She will eventually come out if we don't say a word.*

Even in my silent moments, I tend to say too much.

"Ms. Pepperdine?" Chloe called again.

"Come out, Chloe." I said it all sugarcoated, too, and like I had never heard her request. "Everyone is so excited to see you. Don't make them wait any longer. Why aren't you coming out?"

"My hair is too poofy!"

I sighed real big, so everyone could see what all this was taking out of me—you know, like a regular tortured artist. Then I put the back of my hand to my forehead, extra-dra-matic-like, and closed my eyes. "The poof, my dear, is the pièce de résistance."

"It's resisting my pushing down on it, if that's what you mean" came the answer from the dark end of the long hallway.

"Oh, my dear! Don't do that! Don't push down on it." I raised my hands and tried not to dwell on the image form-ing in my mind. All that time and work with the curling iron, reduced to a lopsided flop under the pressure of a sweaty, determined palm. "Smooth over it. Shake it out. Even compress gently, if you have to, but don't *ever* push."

Maxine broke out in a hearty laugh. "Don't push?"

"What?" I said, snippy but dignified.

Still laughing, Maxine shook her head. "It's just those words coming from you, Odessa. 'Smooth over.' 'Shake it out.' 'Compress gently.' *That* might be advice we could politely overlook without a snicker, but 'Don't *push*'?"

I got her point. As I may have said before, Maxine is nothing if not a woman with a point. That kind of thing can really get on the nerves of those of us who, while not entirely point*less*, might embrace a less direct line of reasoning in forming our opinions and world views.

"'Don't push' is not a term I associate with the woman who just marched into Jan's home and strong-arm commandeered Gloria's subcommittee."

I glanced from Jan to Gloria. Both of them smiled to let on that they did not hold my actions against me.

Maxine was just being testy because she had signed on, and reluctantly so, only to help me give romance a little push where Bernadette was concerned. Now she suddenly found herself taking on Chloe, too, and Chloe was not cooperating.

"You came in here and ambushed that young girl." Maxine silently tacked on "and me" with a stern glance. "Now you tell her that the last thing she should ever do is push?"

I tightened my lips against my teeth. It was not quite a pout, but it was certainly not a sign of concession, either. On the one hand, Maxine was dead right. No argument. No justification offered to try to sway things even the slightest bit in my favor. On the other hand…Maxine was right.

Yes, no matter how you looked at it, my friend was right.

That made me wrong. Or wrong-*ish*. A state made all the more irritating by the fact that the longer she looked at me, the closer Maxine got to busting out laughing about my getting all petulant and…well, downright pushy, even as I warned against it.

But what could I say? Maxine just wanted to remind me that this was a case of reaping what I had sown. And while I wouldn't strictly compare Chloe to the whirlwind in the Bible passage she was causing something of a dustup where my plans were concerned.

"Well, thank you very much for your input, Maxine. I will certainly take that into account in my dealings with my action council and our little friend. Now, if you will excuse me…" I swiveled my head and hollered down the hall in a voice pulled from the depths of my gut, "Chloe, get out here!"

"Only if you promise," she called again, matching my indomitable tone with every syllable.

I held my breath. On the one hand, God had given me this marvelous opportunity to witness to and show His love incarnate in the kindness of others to this hurting, seeking, fragile soul. On the other hand, the girl had worked in a tattoo parlor sticking metal rods in people for a living, when she wasn't shoving compost-quality swill at them as a means of improving their health.

I *had* to ask. "Promise you what?"

"Promise if I come out there and pirouette and curtsy around for y'all that at some point you, Ms. Pepperdine, will let me take you shopping to get you a new outfit of *my* choice."

Maxine pointed a finger at me and giggled silently.

"Can Maxine come, too?" I asked.

"Does Maxine want to come?" Chloe shot back, without missing a beat.

Maxine shook her head so violently I thought it would send her lipstick sliding off onto her earlobe.

"She'd love to," I said, smiling in self-satisfied triumph.

"Okay." The voice from down the hallway got louder, and I could only assume that Chloe had left the bathroom at last and was moving into the master bedroom.

The TV droned through the door across from the bottom of the stairs.

"As long as I don't have to pay for anything, you can all come." Chloe's voice was moving closer to the hall.

Jan glowered, just daring me to try to include her in that expedition.

Gloria held her hand up in the universal sign for "Stop in the name of love," only I don't think love was her main motivator.

Gallina Roja alone clapped her hands together in delight and asked, "When do we leave?"

"All right, then." I spoke with my eyes cast upward, just imagining what David would think about this new twist in my evolving personality. No, not evolving, growing. Growing was better. I was not turning into something altogether new and strange, something adverse to my customary nature. I was only becoming more like the me I truly always was, or wanted to be. I was growing to take up more space in the world, in my relationships and inside myself. Blossoming. "Yes. Yes, I promise, Chloe. Now come on out and show everyone how lovely you look."

And she did look lovely. A bit retro, I suppose, given that

the last time I had done a young woman's hair up like this, that young woman had been…*me*. Well, as we say at the flea market, everything old is new again, and Chloe looked fresh and new and just darling.

Everyone oohed and aahed, just as they should have. And just as she had assured me she would, Chloe spun around for all to see.

I played fashion commentator, of course. "We borrowed the top from Jan's things. I can't believe it. Even though she's over forty, she still has the figure of a twenty-year-old."

"Twenty-one," Chloe corrected, stating her age proudly.

Maxine mouthed the number, rolled her eyes just a little, and rounded her lips to mimic an astonished whistle. "I don't know which one of them to be more jealous of. Chloe for being so young, or Jan for being so trim. And after…how many children, Jan?"

"Three," she held up her left hand and wriggled her fingers, making her heavy gold wedding band glow and her impressive diamond engagement ring wink in the afternoon sunlight. Then she turned her head toward the mantel and the photographs there, and the smile she had been wearing faded. She dropped her hand to her lap, curling her right hand around the three fingers she had raised before. "One right after the other. And that's how they left when they moved off to college, one and then the next and then the next. It all happened so fast. So fast."

"You look trim enough to be in college yourself," Gloria said, and we all nodded as if we actually thought shallow compliments might actually cheer Jan up a little.

"When I was young, they told us you should count on

gaining a dress size with every child you had." Gallina Roja patted her flat tummy and cackled. "What did they know?"

"You are not a fair example, Grandmother Alvarez." Gloria shifted her expression and spoke with terse deference to her mother-in-law. "You only had the one baby."

"Yes, but I've had him for fifty-five years now. If that doesn't put the pounds on you, what will?" Again she cackled, and the rest of us joined her.

Except Gloria, who moved to prop the full-length mirror against the wall. "*I've* had him for thirty-six of those fifty-five years. If either of us was going to gain weight from babying that man, it should have been me."

"You got married when you were..." Chloe started to scratch her head, then froze when her pink-painted fingernails brushed a stiff curl. "Um, when you were that young?"

"We were both nineteen," Gloria said, shaking her head.

"Wow," Chloe whispered.

"Twenty-one," Maxine said, raising her hand.

My hand went up too. "Twenty-two."

"The day after my eighteenth birthday."

"Really?" Being young herself, Chloe did not hide the surprise we all felt at Jan's disclosure.

I guess the others had probably felt, like me, that Jan Bishop Belmont had always done everything in perfect order for Texas girls of that day. High school cheerleader, pledge the right sorority, graduate with honors and marry your college sweetheart.

"My parents didn't like Morty." She sighed and gazed toward the doorway and the room near the unseen bottom of the stairs. The TV roared. She chewed her lower lip, and for a moment I thought she might add some other observation about what she or others thought of the man now. Then she shook her head, blinked and fiddled with her bangs. "He's almost a decade older than me, you know. He was a football coach, and we met the summer after I graduated high school. They wouldn't let us get married, so as soon as I reached legal age…"

"So you just…ran off together?"

"Actually, yes. We eloped."

"Was it romantic?" Only Chloe would ask that. The rest of us—and I know this isn't the best of Christian behavior—were trying to wrap our minds around the idea of a football coach and a cheerleader running off together. What bitter feelings it must have engendered. What scandal. What…are the odds they really didn't date one another until *after* she graduated?

"I thought it was romantic." Jan looked to the mantel again, leading the rest of us to do the same. I don't know what she had expected to see there, but I had thought we'd find a wedding photo or some evidence of the connection between Jan and Morty. There was none. She exhaled in one hard rush, her shoulders slumping. "But then, I was young and in love."

"And you're still in love, all these years later." Chloe didn't ask it, she declared it, in that hopeful way young people have of speaking their fondest wishes, then looking to others for confirmation.

Jan smiled weakly.

Chloe turned away from our hostess then, her face ever bright, and addressed the rest of us. Her eyes pleaded for someone to salvage the conversation. "How did you all know so young that your marriages would last?"

"I listened to my heart," I blurted out, without really giving it much thought.

"I listened to the Lord," Maxine added, and it could have sounded all snooty and like a bad case of one-upmanship, but it didn't.

"Gloria listened to me!" Gallina Roja said, shaking her carrot-topped head.

We all looked from the older woman to Gloria, either for confirmation or to see if there was going to be an argument. Which—I confess it did cross my mind—would have been a really good way to get us off of feeling sorry for Jan and trying to tiptoe around the situation with Morty. Nothing detracts from one person's obvious unhappiness like another person's petty squabbles.

"Tell them, Gloria. You knew you that if you married my son you would have to work to make it last forever, because you listened to me." The old woman made repeated staccato motions with her index finger. "Tell them."

"I listened to my mother-in-law," Gloria conceded, spreading her hands open. "How could I not? She talks to the Lord."

That broke the tension just enough for all of us to catch our breath.

Maxine sat back on the sofa.

I went to Chloe and peered at her image over her shoulder in the mirror.

The young girl tipped her head. "Well, I hope you won't be mad at me for saying this, but I don't see how any of that could make you sure you were doing the right thing. That your relationships would last."

Gloria gestured with one hand open and out, flipping

from palm up to palm down and back again. Her thin, dark eyebrows crimped down, and she pursed her lips.

Though she didn't say a word, I knew exactly what she meant. "There aren't any guarantees in romantic love, Chloe, no matter how old you are."

"You can say that again." Jan stared blankly at the doorway again. We couldn't see into the hallway to the stairway or the door with Morty and the TV behind it.

"But it helps if you have faith, if you share the same beliefs and if, when you take your vows, you really mean them." I brushed some lint from Chloe's shoulder, then rested my hand there as I leaned in to add, "You really have to understand their importance, and do everything within your power to honor them."

The elder Mrs. Alvarez nodded her head slowly. "It takes a lot of hard work."

"And it doesn't hurt if you laugh together," Maxine said to the room in general, not just aiming her remark at Chloe.

"And pray together," I whispered.

"And even then…" Jan sighed.

"A man must love his wife the way Christ loves the church. That's what we believe. No compromise there. If the fellow you are with hurts you or manipulates you or…" Maxine struggled to find the right word. I couldn't help thinking she wanted to find something that could do double duty and apply both to Chloe and her smarmy charmer and to Jan and whatever had gone awry with Morty. "If a man disrespects you…"

"Then you shouldn't marry him." I gave Chloe's shoulders a squeeze. While I understood Maxine's desire to reach out to Jan, a part of me wanted to remind her that we had already taken on two women's love lives and helped get Jan a job and some money and respite. Were we really ready to tackle Morty, as well? "I hope you aren't really considering anything that serious with Sammy, Chloe."

The young woman met my gaze over her shoulder, then turned to study her image in the mirror still leaning against the wall.

"Sammy's the one you're not sure of, isn't he?" Maxine asked, scooting to the edge of the sofa now.

"Has he hurt you, Chloe?" I looked directly into the mirror and met her eyes. "The Reverend Cordell said he thought he saw Sammy squeeze your arm, that he was trying to force you to do or say something…"

"I didn't ask for your advice." Chloe twisted away from my touch and stuck her fingers in her hair to work them through and free some of the stiffness of her curls. "And if Jake has something to say to me, then he knows how to get ahold of me. He can tell me to my face."

Okay, a little part of me wanted to ask when she had started calling the Reverend by his first name and whether he had suggested it and under what circumstances. And also how would he know how to get ahold of her and when would he have occasion to tell things to her face? But the fact that the window of opportunity to get Chloe to listen me was closing made me focus on what I had to say to her. "I don't think you need our advice. I think, deep down, you know that a man who doesn't cherish you is only going to hurt you more and more as the years go on. Deep down, you know the truth."

At that exact moment, Jan Belmont burst into tears.

"Jan, honey!" When I focus, I focus, and so I hadn't even

thought of how anyone else in the room might take my words. And even now that they were out there and I had seen Jan's reaction, I couldn't quite believe it. So I had to ask, "Are you okay?"

"Of course she's not okay, Odessa, she's bawling like a baby." Maxine slid across the couch as best she could, stretching her arms out toward the woman who looked absolutely flawless except for her big red nose and the streaks of mascara under her eyes.

Jan bolted up from her chair. "No. No, I'm fine."

I suppose I should have felt vindicated by her claim, but I didn't. I stepped up to put my arm around the woman.

Jan squirmed out of reach. "Uh…oh… I'm just… I get emotional ever since the…my husband's…" She glanced around, most pointedly at the hallway where she had disappeared with Morty an hour earlier. "In fact, I should go check on him. I don't usually leave him to his own devices for this long."

And she rushed off, leaving all of us standing—or sitting—there staring at one an other.

We might have stayed in awkward, awful silence until Jan returned—which, given her ashen color and the absolute anguish in her eyes, might have been hours—but Chloe came to the rescue.

"I hope I didn't sound ungrateful, Ms. Pepperdine and y'all." She gave a twirl to draw our attention. She stared into the mirror and tipped her head to the right, then to the left. "I *do* like my new look, and I thank you for being so nice, doing this for me and all. But…"

"But?" I asked, trying not to seem so obvious about keeping one eye on the doorway where Jan had disappeared.

Chloe smiled. "I have to say, I *do* miss my barrettes."

"They were sparkly," I said softly, wiggling a few fingers to indicate to Gloria and her mother-in-law how the light played off the faux stones.

"Not as sparkly as what you two had on the other day," Chloe used all ten fingers and waggled them like crazy on top of her head.

Gloria frowned.

"Tiaras," Maxine explained. "From Bernadette's booth. We wore them to bring in customers the other day."

"I thought you wore them because you call yourselves the Tiara Madres." Chloe dropped her hands to her sides.

"Tiara Madres? Very nice!" Gallina Roja clapped her hands and fixed her eyes on Gloria. "Can I have a tiara, too?"

Gloria shot Maxine and me a "you have really done it now" look.

"Bernadette could really use the business," I blurted out. "Not that her business isn't doing just fine. I mean, the advertising. She could really use the publicity. You know, to attract—"

"A husband?" Gallina Roja asked hopefully.

"Morty, no! Not today." Jan's voice came not from the room, but from the hallway, followed by footsteps pounding up the stairs. Upstairs there was nothing but two bedrooms used by the kids and, of course, the windows that led outside, to the roof. "Please tell me you have not done this again to me with all these people here!"

"Maybe she's better off without one." Chloe mastered a mix of anxious kid overhearing grown-up arguments and sarcastic young woman with multiple holes in her head making a contemptuous observation. "A husband, that is.

Having one doesn't seem to be working out all that great for Mrs. Belmont."

Maxine again, trying to finish what I began. But then, when I began all this, it was like another lifetime ago. Things were fun and light and hopeful. And now…

I don't know what to say. What is the big attraction for the Belmonts in going out on that roof? I almost want to try it myself, just to see. I suspect it has something to do with the theme I came up with at the start of all this. Some people, when pushed, will rise to the occasion. Unfortunately, other people, put under pressure, will break.

I guess in this case that if enough loving people pitch in, we can make like hair spray and hold everything together.

Chapter Ten

Everyone looks at the man on the ledge. Every eye is trained on his slightest move. Every ear strains to hear the whys and the hows and listen for some sign of what will happen next. Every pulse beats fast, then faster, knowing that should the most unimaginable occur, every heart will leap, then stop, then…break.

Everyone wants to help the man on the ledge. Some want to help him come inside and get his feet on the ground. Others, I suppose, want to help him take that last awful step, and thrill to the idea of seeing his body hit the ground. But what about the people behind the man on the ledge?

Who sees their pain? Their struggle? Their own lives, teetering between the heavens and the earth?

What do you say to them? How do you reach out to the ones not obviously in immediate danger and let them know that they are not alone? It was a question I grappled with even as we all rushed upstairs behind Jan to see if we could help her help her husband and realized even before the last one of us hit the steps that Morty wasn't the only one in peril there.

"You go out there and tell that man to come inside right now." Gallina Roja shook her bony finger in Jan's direction.

Life sure seemed easy for a woman who talked to God and held on to her only baby for over fifty years.

"I can't," Jan said.

Her meekness, the soft anguish of her reply, created a small ache in my chest. I wanted to reach out to her, to grab her arm and pull her in from wherever she had gone in that moment of quiet despair.

"You *can.*" The determined grandmother brought her fist downward, against nothing and yet with all the impact of Khrushchev pounding the podium with his shoe.

And if you're too young to know what that means, then you may be too young to fully understand the raw emotion in that perfectly appointed bedroom that afternoon. Not because it has anything to do with the Cold War, unless of course you mean the cold war that has raged between men and women ever since Adam and Eve. But you have to have lived awhile to have known what was at stake for Jan and her husband on that summer afternoon in that seeming perfectly ordinary split-level.

I am not apologizing for that. Young people have a lot going for them. There are certainly a lot of wonderful perks in being young, so let us old gals have this thing, this way of knowing just how precarious the whole world seems when a man crawls out on a roof and his wife no longer has the words to draw him back inside. And why she has to try anyway.

"You can do it, Jan." Maxine put her arm around Chloe, who looked about ready to charge the window and give the man a piece of her mind her own self.

"I can't." Jan's focus swung from the group to the window. She bit her lip. "I'm the reason he crawled out there to begin with."

"I knew it," I murmured. Honestly. I did not shout it or sound all gloaty, like she'd just proved every piece of malicious gossip I'd ever heard concerning the Belmonts. But still, I said it. Out loud. And I could tell it stung poor Jan's pride something fierce. "I just meant, well, it came to my mind more than once that…"

I glanced around what must have once been a boy's bedroom but now looked like something from a decorating magazine. Not a fancy decorating magazine, nothing fussy or filled with finery, but perfect all the same. Too perfect. Too perfect was just the right backdrop, I supposed, for this moment. This time when all the pretenses that Jan had clung to for so long could not protect her from the reality of what people really thought and felt.

I took a deep breath and folded my arms. In for a penny, in for a pound, and I was in for a whole lot more than a penny already. "It says in the Bible that it's better for a man to live on the corner of a roof than to share a house with a…"

"With a what?" Jan asked when I hesitated.

I didn't want to finish. I racked my brain for a translation that might fall more easily on the ear. But I couldn't come up with anything, and so I completed the verse as I knew it from the Book of Proverbs. "With a contentious woman."

"There you have it, ladies." Jan motioned toward me. I had more to say, but she did not allow me to follow up on my thought. "It's my fault. I accept that. It's my problem. You should probably all go now."

Probably. That single word kept us from turning then and walking out one by one. *Probably.* It meant "No one would blame you if you did this" and "any reasonable person would take the out I'm offering and run." It also implored, "Please. Please, please, don't desert me now."

I don't know if you have to be old enough to grasp the scariness and subtleties of Cold War diplomacy to know the real weight of the word *probably.* But it doesn't hurt.

"Let's go make some coffee and talk." I waved my hands gently, the way you do when you're herding a class of Sunday school kids, or maybe shooing birds into flight.

"You can't just leave the poor guy out there." Chloe bent at the knees to peer out the window.

I had been avoiding doing just that, much as I wanted to take a peek and see exactly what was going on. It felt like such an invasion of privacy, both Jan's and Morty's, for us to even be there, much less staring and gaping.

Yes, you think I'd have the poise and good manners not to gape, but I have to say, seeing a grown man in his pajamas with his hair all mashed to the side of his head clutching a TV remote in one hand and sitting on a roof staring at an old drive-in, well, I think it would be almost impossible *not* to gape. But Chloe started it.

Yeah, I know. I would never have accepted that kind of excuse from my sons, but this was just going to be one of those do-as-I-say-and-not-as-I-do moments. I have to say,

I am not a perfect person. I am one of those folks who is ever in need of the forgiveness of the Lord and grateful for it and that is why—even though I tried to tell myself not to do it—I bent down in front of the bedroom window and looked.

"Odessa," Maxine whispered in admonishment.

I winced. Instantly I wished I hadn't given in to the temptation to gawk, even if it was only a little bit. Not just because it was rude and intrusive, but because I knew that from that moment on I would never look at Jan again and not see this image. Before, when I saw Morty looking like a zombie from a bad B-movie circa the nineteen-fifties, it hadn't bothered me, because I could put that vision in context. The man had suffered a trauma. He wasn't himself. He would get better with time.

Well, time had passed.

So this? This climbing out onto the roof to sit and stare into the distance, ignoring all pleas from his wife to come back inside? This deliberate deed, one that pre-dated his injuries and had also caused them, was a choice. Electing to act on that choice when Jan had a houseful of people to witness it was his way of striking out at her. I don't know if, after hearing both sides of the story, I'd blame him for his decisions, but right now I knew one thing. Jan needed her husband to cherish her in the way we had told Chloe all men should. And she wasn't going to get that.

As her friends, we could not abandon her.

Yes, that's right. With that glimpse out of a spare bed-room window and into Jan Belmont's life, I made up my mind. We had to do more than just try to distract and placate Jan—we had to love her like the sisters in Christ we went around claiming to be.

We, of course, being me and Maxine. I couldn't speak for the others here. Okay, I can't speak for Maxine, either. That had never stopped me from doing it before, though, or for hoping and believing that my friend would feel as I felt, or at least not feel that I was so far-fetched that she would turn her back on me entirely.

I straightened up and backed off from the window and nudged Chloe to shepherd her away with me.

She blinked at me, then at the other women, then at Jan. Finally, she fixed her eyes out the window, on Morty, who had his back to us and his knees drawn up, hugging them to his body. And then she stepped back, too.

I put my hand on her shoulder in a tender show of gratitude, she followed my earlier edict and did not push. She might seem too young to appreciate the precariousness of poking your nose into another woman's marriage, but she had grace enough to trust that the rest of us would do the right thing.

Just as I trusted that Maxine would do the same. And I told her as much with a look and jerk of my head toward the door.

"Coffee it is then." Maxine clapped her hands together, then opened them wide and motioned for everyone to move along. "In the kitchen. All of us. Now."

No one said another word. Everyone just moved into the hallway, one by one, until only Jan remained in the sparse and spotless bedroom with the summer breeze flowing through the open window.

"We'll keep the coffee warm for you, Jan," I said as I reached to close the door. "Take your time."

"Don't bother." Jan pushed up from the bed where she had been sitting, strode the length of the room, brushed my hand from the knob and replaced it with her own firm grip.

"Is she just going to leave him there?" Chloe asked again. This time she whispered it, first to Maxine, then to Gloria. "She's just going to walk away and close the door? She isn't going to—"

"To what?" A soft metallic click underscored the cool, crisp quality of Jan's voice. "Try to talk to him? Do you imagine I haven't tried? That I haven't opened up my heart to that man? That I haven't asked for his forgiveness for whatever I have done wrong? That I haven't humbled myself in a thousand ways in hopes that something I said, something I offered, would finally reach him?"

She bowed her head, swallowed hard, then retreated from the door, letting her fingers trail over the doorknob for a moment before completely letting go. When she lifted her head, she had masked her pain in serenity and purpose. "Now, did someone say they wanted coffee?"

She headed for the stairs without looking back.

"But what if…" Chloe hung back, even as we all followed Jan's lead. "What if he falls?"

Jan froze.

I held my breath. It's that youth thing, I suppose. But I can't fault Chloe for it. In fact, hearing the concern in her voice totally renewed my confidence in the effect Maxine and me and all of us—and I suppose, as much as I hate to think of him aiming his attentions at anyone but Bernadette just yet, all of us does include Jake Cordell—could eventually have on the girl.

Jan did not seem to share my buoyed-up sense of optimism about the young girl, though. Chloe's question had hardly faded in the air when Jan's spine went rigid. Not just straight, but rigid, like someone had yanked a rope taut. She pressed her shoulders back in a way that reminded me of a cat laying its ears flat just before it hisses, spits and draws its claws.

All of us tensed right along with her, the way you do when you know something awful just might happen and you don't have the slightest clue how you should react. Of all the things we should get better at with age that—knowing how not to let people fluster the stuffing out of you— should be one of them.

And apparently, for some people, it *is.*

"If the man falls, he falls." Galina Roja waved one gnarled hand in the air and marched right on down the stairs. When she reached the last step, she turned and rolled her shoulders in a utterly nonchalant shrug. "We should be able to see him when he hits the ground outside the kitchen."

Chloe gasped.

Gloria groaned.

I opened my mouth to say something, though I cannot tell you what because my mind had gone completely blank.

And then Maxine saved the day by doing the only thing a person really could do in a situation like that. She laughed. Then she put her arm around Jan's shoulders. "Come on, sweetie. We'll make coffee and we'll talk."

"Not about this, we won't." Jan moved out from under Maxine's warm embrace. I know it was a warm embrace because I know Maxine and I know that in that moment she had done her best to envelop Jan in the special bond of friendship that forms between women and in Christian love.

And Jan had rejected it.

Not out of anger at Maxine or any of us, but because she wasn't ready. Maybe because there was so much more going on than she felt she could trust us with, or maybe because she thought if she ignored the truth of what had happened here, it would all go back to the way it was before. And even though the way it was before was just awful, it was familiar. Safe, in some sad and desperate way.

"Then we'll talk about the complaints about the flea market." I hadn't lost my mind or my sense of purpose about Jan. This was just a tactic. We couldn't very well show the woman how much we cared for and supported her if we all found reasons to hightail it out of her presence whenever things got ugly. This was Jan Belmont, after all. You couldn't avoid things getting ugly around that woman. Which is kind of ironic, given her gorgeous face, good figure, excellent taste in clothes and beautifully-appointed home.

Anyway, all that leads me to believe that loveliness is a natural state for her, and that given the chance and exposure to the gentle ministrations of me and Maxine, Jan would set aside her tendency toward ugliness altogether.

"Perfect." Jan's heels clacked over the glazed ceramic tiles in her large, updated kitchen. "Going over those complaints suits me just fine. The faster we deal with them the faster we can shut that horrid rat's nest of a place down forever."

Okay, so maybe Jan was a little more attached to ugly than I'd suspected.

"Not everyone wants to close the flea market down, though, Jan." Gloria helped her mother-in-law into a chair at the table. "Some people would, in fact, like to see it improved and helped to play a larger role in our community."

"Well, if any of those people are here right now...?" Jan whizzed by without making eye contact with any of us. She flung open the cabinet above the coffeemaker and pulled out a blue canister. She plunked it on the table, yanked open a drawer, then started rummaging through the silverware. "They can just get out of my house. I became a part of this committee to close that eyesore down."

Gloria sank into a chair.

Chloe did the same.

Maxine and I stood. Ephesians 6:13-14 tells us to put on the full armor of God and stand. So we stood. We did not run, even though flouncing out just then would have proved both righteously rewarding and big-time dramatic—two things I cannot usually resist. Not to mention something of a relief to be off the case once and for all, and not because of my own fear or frustration, but because of Jan's own ultimatum.

But I had promised to give my all to this plan, and I couldn't turn away from it. "Jan, honey. Maybe we should—"

"Compromise? Oh, no! I have had all the compromise I can stomach, thank you." Jan turned around with a spoon gripped in her hand, her expression positively grim. "I won't settle for anything less than what I want, than what is best and right. And the sooner we do that, the sooner life around here will return to the way it should be."

★ ★ ★

Maybe there's a reason you don't think too much about the person *not* on the ledge, and keep your eyes fixed on the one who's likely to jump. Because you realize that sometimes the only thing you can do in a case like this is get yourself down on the ground, hold out a net and pray. Some problems can only be dealt with like that—through faith and preparedness and damage control.

And if you don't know exactly what put that ledge stander there in the first place, your trying to reach out to them or to tamper with the ones they have gone out to leave behind just might be the thing that pushes them over the edge once and for all.

Chapter Eleven

Matchmaker. Hopeless romantic. Fix-up artist. Yenta. Cupid wannabe. Mom.

Every culture and historical time period has had those people—okay, women, mostly—who feel it is their duty to do whatever they can to smooth out that rocky road to love for the tenderfoots and gentle hearts and the, to my way of thinking, sometimes softheaded—or should that be *hard*-headed?—people who don't seem to be able to do it for themselves. "It" being to find someone to share a few hours or a few evenings or a few rest-of-their-lives with. (So I believe in love and taking vows and oh, let's call it laying the foundation of the family unit as the means to happiness and stability. I'm a minister's wife. Did you really expect otherwise?)

Anywho…we had just seen very real and painful evidence that the road to romance, to love and marriage— which are supposed to go together like a horse and carriage—may start out smooth, but doesn't always stay that way. That sometimes the horse kicks up or gets stuck in a rut, and all too often the shock absorbers on that carriage take a beating. I have to say my own trip on love's long and winding highway has taken an unexpected curve or two and hit some bumps along the way. But never once has it occurred to me, or to David, if I can be so bold as to speak for him, to jump out of the carriage and proclaim, "It's just not worth it."

It *is* worth it to me. The good stuff, love and warmth and companionship and laughter and having someone to depend on, that's all worth the risk. And the bad stuff? I wouldn't wish it upon anyone, but then again, I wouldn't trade what I got from it, what David and I both got from going through it, for a million miles of smooth road stretched out before me to travel on alone.

In the days following that afternoon at the Belmonts', Gallina Roja and Gloria Alvarez no longer seemed as convinced about the whole married verses single life issue for Bernadette as they once were. Or maybe they were spending extra time pampering their baby/hubby, out of appreciation that he had loved them well and provided for them financially and emotionally and not strayed from that path and left their family unit stranded in a broken buggy. Either way, the pair of them backed off from reminding Bernadette that she needed a man and gave the poor girl some breathing space.

To which I could only say, "Hooray!"

Because it gave me more room to do *my* work.

"I suppose you know the burning question on our minds, Reverend Cordell."

"*Our* minds, Odessa?"

"My mind, then." I gave Maxine a look—the kind I had perfected on my kids when they were young and got squirmy in church—then went on unfolding folding chairs in the fellowship hall of Bernadette and Jake's church.

I liked the sound of that. Didn't you? *Bernadette and Jake's church?*

Anyway, two days had passed since our last…whatever that mess was when we had all gotten together. I had called yet another meeting of my action council—the whole deal, not just my subcommittee—to address the flea market concerns. Honest! This time I had actually sorted through the complaint letters and written up an agenda, and I intended for us to now come up with a plan of action for Gloria Alvarez to present to the town council.

It just seemed the right thing to do, both because I was this new Odessa who did new things and had her own funny little wayward-ish flock and because…well, because things had not gone so well in the other areas of my plan…my plan to submit to God's plan. I needed to see some progress somewhere, with someone, to convince myself I hadn't just cooked up a crazy scheme out of boredom and good intentions. I needed to taste a little success. I needed…lunch.

All right, I had an agenda beyond the one I had typed up at home the night before. I had plotted and schemed, just a little, to find a way for Bernadette to show off her cooking skills by providing lunch for us all. Does it detract from my good intentions at all that I had done so knowing that Mrs. Alvarez had to leave the meeting early, and take her mother-in-law with her, as Gloria was the keynote speaker at a Realtors' luncheon? Or that our new artist friend Abner had promised to give Chloe another shot at her job?

"Shot? At her job? You say that about the girl who does body piercing and tattooing? Odessa, I just have to interject here and say you have got to stop with the bad puns before someone takes a shot at you."

"I am attempting to lighten things up, Maxine. After all that upsetting stuff with Chloe and Sammy and Jan and Morty, I thought we should focus on…on…"

"On a couple of people too nice to tell you to mind your own business?"

"I don't have a business, Maxine."

"That's why you have so much time to get into everybody else's."

"Noted." And I didn't say that just to get her to shut up, either. It was something worth thinking about.

Clink.

But as I was saying before Maxine dropped her two cents in, was it wrong that I pulled together this lunch meeting, when I knew Chloe wouldn't be able to attend at all? Or that Jan had respectfully…

"And by respectfully Odessa means that she didn't use any actual profanity when she pitched a hissy fit over the phone and told us that until we showed some real interest in closing that nasty eyesore down for good, she wouldn't be attending any more meetings."

…declined my invitation? Or that I had every confidence that at just the suggestion that we leave the young people to their own devices and head to my house to kick off our shoes and whip up some BLTs, Maxine would race out of the church and into my truck faster than a hog squeezing through a greased fence?

Not to compare Maxine to a hog, you know, it's just my way of saying that I know that if going barefoot and eating sandwiches were part of the deal, my friend would drop any pretense of a protest real quick and go along with me.

And with us out of the way, that would leave the Reverend and Bernadette all alone to enjoy a nice meal and even nicer company.

That's not a deception, is it? I don't think of myself as having a deceptive bone in my body. My hair, well, there is a wee bit of deception in that, if you take into account the dye and the back combing. But in the part of me that matters? I am one hundred percent against deception. And one hundred percent in favor of love, and giving it a little boost whenever I can.

So here the three of us were, waiting for our quorum of members to arrive, getting the place ready and, well…there was this question, this *burning* question that I was just aching to ask.

"Oh, Maxine, let's not play games." I said as I clunked the last metal chair down on the floor and shoved it under the long, rectangular table. "It's hanging in the air between the three of us like that proverbial elephant."

"There's an elephant hanging in the air in here?" Maxine, who had been busying herself getting out flatware, held a slotted spoon up for inspection. She spoke to me with one eye peering through the opening, as if it was Sherlock Holmes's magnifying glass itself. "Where?"

I took up the white tablecloth I'd found in the cabinet and unfurled it with a crisp snap. "*Proverbial,* Maxine. I said *proverbial.*"

"I don't see an elephant in here, and I certainly don't recall one in Proverbs, do you, Reverend?"

To his credit, Jake Cordell laughed at our antics. I had put him in an awkward situation to say the least, and he had rolled with it. Good for him. The more time I spent around the man, the more I liked him. And the more I wanted to know…

"So tell me, Reverend, why aren't you married?"

He did not wince. He did not blush. He did not stutter or stumble or mumble or do a comical spit take with the coffee in the paper cup with the trendy café's label that he'd brought in a few minutes earlier.

Maxine didn't, either, but then I suspect she had known exactly what was coming. She just went on about her work, humming as if she didn't care how the conversation went, keeping one ear cocked to hear every last word.

Jake did clear his throat. Then he turned to me, smiled warmly and said, "Congratulations, Mrs. Pepperdine."

"Congratulations?" I asked.

Maxine huffed or…something I don't know the exact word for the sound she made but it let us know that the man had gotten her attention and she was impressed with his tact.

As for myself, I wasn't exactly on board with it. "Congratulations for what?"

"For being the first, and perhaps the *only,* minister's wife, retired or otherwise—in fact, probably the only good Christian woman I have met since my ordination—who did not ask me that question within forty-eight hours of having made my acquaintance."

I didn't know whether to beam with pride or hang my

head in shame at that distinction. So I chose something altogether different—I became skeptical. "What about Maxine?"

My friend waved the question off, using her spoon with
all the regal dignity of a Queenly scepter. "Oh, I asked him
the first day I met him."

And you didn't tell me? I didn't say that so much as show
it, by dropping my jaw and plunking my fist on my hip. After
giving the pose a moment to sink in, and maybe hit Maxine's guilt center, I gave my head a waggle and asked, "And
what did he say?"

"Ask *him.*" Again she waved the spoon in the air. "He
can speak for himself."

He met my gaze with his arms folded and his feet—
still in those shabby shoes—anchored shoulder-width
apart. "I said…"

"You can't teach an old dog to change its spots. It's all I'm
saying." Gallina Roja's craggy voice carried into the fellowship hall a full ten seconds before her small body came scur-
rying into view.

"Are you calling my daughter an old dog?" Gloria Alvarez had ignored the mixed metaphor coming from her
mother-in-law's mouth and gone straight to the heart of
matters. "Your own granddaughter? An old dog?"

"She is not clever like a fox. You got to give me that,
Gloria."

I pressed my finger to my lips, intending to hush their
less-than-flattering bickering over Bernadette with my less-
than-attractive bug-eyed not-in-front-of-the-potential-life-
mate expression.

Which did not faze the elder Mrs. Alvarez in the least as

she strutted along, gesturing and talking loud and slow, as if she had forgotten to turn up her hearing aid this morning. "Not when she did what she just did."

Bug-eyed exasperation turned to bug-eyed apprehension at that single sentence. I no longer had the luxury of quieting things down. If I wanted my plan to stay on track, I needed details—and I needed them now.

I caught the older of the two women by the arm and demanded, "What did she, uh, do?"

The grandmotherly old chin quivered. Her dark eyes shimmered. The deep wrinkles around her mouth gave her an even more dour and hopeless countenance as she said, with the kind of high drama worthy of the highest and mightiest of Texas belles, "She *told*."

Okay, I had no idea what that meant, but still, it chilled me to the marrow. I stepped back and moved my gaze from the lined and weathered features before me to Gloria's glamorous and fully made-up face. *"Told?"*

"Everyone…in…the…church," Gloria whispered.

By this time, Maxine and Jake had taken note of the three of us huddled with our heads together. I could tell this because they formed their own sort of tête-à-tête and started whispering themselves. Of course, I knew Maxine was doing that out of pure mischief. The fact that Jake had become her cohort in it so quickly could only mean…

Well, it could only mean that he was every bit as charming as anyone might hope for in a minister who hadn't yet got snapped up by…

"Oh!" It came upon me like…not like a lightning bolt, but like something lesser and yet just as out-of-the-blue and full of crackle and pop and maybe even a spark.

That's it. A *spark*. It hit me like one of those arcing sparks from an old mad-scientist movie. And all at once, I got the full effect of what Bernadette had gone and done, and why her match-minded elders were none too happy. "She told everyone in the church that we were meeting here today."

Gloria slapped her hands against her skirt in resigned exasperation. "And that she was supposed to bring lunch for the new minister."

"She couldn't have left that part out," I muttered. The meeting, most church members would have gladly missed. But a *meal?*

Gloria nodded. "We are facing a full-on church-lady throw-down potluck, with every unmarried girl around as a side dish."

"You'd better get out more chairs and flatwares, Mrs. Odessa." Gallina Roja shook her head, and when that action put the Reverend in her line of vision, she stopped cold and smiled. "It's just like her, you know. Never thinking of herself. That's a nice trait in a girl, don't you think, Reverend?"

"I agree, it's a virtue, Señora Alvarez, to have a servant's heart." He smiled, but it wasn't that wonderful smile that had won me over the first time I saw it. *This* smile held something back.

It's a virtue to have a servant's heart. But…

He didn't actually say it—and I suspect the old gal wouldn't have heard it, even if she had been wearing her hearing aid and had it cranked up to the max. But the feeling of what he *hadn't* said lingered. It hung in the air, right alongside my proverbial elephant. He could admire Bernadette for her servant's heart, *but…*

I couldn't surmise the reason behind his unspoken hesitation from the little bit I had seen of the man. I did know that he had, at times, responded quite positively to the woman I saw as his future wife and the mother of his tall, dark-haired, inappropriately shod children. When she jumped into the hot-air balloon with him, I'd really thought I saw his eyes light up. But now there was this *but*...

And not even a first-class Buttinski like me could make this match happen without knowing the rest of that sentence.

Well, maybe *I* couldn't. But Bernadette *could*. If she ever got the chance to be alone with the man.

"So, looks like Bernadette invited the whole church to participate in our council meeting." I clapped my hands together and began to hustle around the fellowship hall with all the enthusiasm and misdirected charm of that Sammy selling balloon rides on market day. "Which calls for a little bit of last-minute—" *sabotage* "—creativity on our part."

"Creativity? Is that just your polite way of saying hard work, Odessa?" I could see it in Maxine's eyes. My footloose and fabulous sandwich plan would have suited her just fine about now.

"We'll need more agendas." I waved one of the pages from the file I had stashed by my purse. For once, I had actually intended to get some things done at one of these meetings, and I didn't see any reason not to take advantage of the situation to double my efforts. "Many hands make light work. If we have a large enough gathering today, we can knock out all these concerns and have the whole flea market issue addressed in no time. Jan should really be here for this, since she instigated it. I hate the thought of doing it without her."

"You'll have to do it without me, too." Gloria stood there in her elegant outfit with her head cocked and her arms crossed. She knew I was up to something, and this was her way of letting me know she would support my folly in theory but didn't want her name attached to it. "I have another engagement."

"Well, Gloria, you know us. We're all for engagements. Aren't we, Reverend?"

"You are a dangerous woman, Mrs. Pepperdine," he muttered with a gleam in his eyes.

"All women are dangerous in some way, Reverend. You've just got to learn to separate the sinfully dangerous ones from those of us who are dangerous in a good way. Because those ones are worth getting to know."

"Can I get a big *Amen* on that?" Maxine said as she pulled fistfuls of flatware from a wide kitchen drawer.

"Amen!" I chimed in, only to have the elder Mrs. Alvarez outdo me in both volume and gusto. Still chuckling, I leaned close to whisper to Gloria. "Speaking of dangerous, what about Bernadette?"

Gloria sighed. "Dangerous to herself, I suspect. Dangerous to her own chances of finding a man who could value her, servant's heart and all."

"No, I mean, *where* is she?"

"She's pulling her van around to the back door so she can unload all the food she brought," Gloria said.

"Good. Maxine, you go help Gloria and her mother-in-law." Maxine, no stranger to church politics or to my tone when I've stopped fooling around and gotten down to business, did not argue. Next, I focused my attention on the *real* main dish at today's event. "Reverend Cordell?"

"Yes, ma'am." Not a question. Not a snappy, military-style reply meant to belittle me by making me out to be a dictator. Just simple and plain, self-assured but not self-important. Willing, but wily in his own way.

I liked the man more and more every time I crossed paths with him. Good minister material, I thought. Not to mention good husband material.

If only he could meet up with the right girl…and drive off with her before all the other potential right girls showed up.

I smiled big, and crooked my finger to bring him closer. "I have an assignment for you."

Twenty minutes later, I was gazing out at eighteen female faces. Eighteen pretty and powdered faces, and every last one of them, save Maxine's, pouting over having to sit there and listen to me talk about the flea market instead of making small talk with a certain single minister.

"First, I can't say enough how pleased I am with this tremendous turnout. It's inspiring, is all it is. Wouldn't you say so, Maxine?"

"Inspiring," she deadpanned. For a second, I thought she might even throw in a yawn.

"Now, the complaints about the flea market can be broken down into three categories. Those of aesthetics and health." I pointed to a pile of papers filled with tirades calling the drive-in-turned-weekend-marketplace a pigsty and all sorts of other names that basically meant pigsty. Most of those them bore Jan's signature, and the ones that didn't bore her signature attitude. But to be fair, there was also plenty of uneasiness about the general upkeep of the old movie screen. And serious questions regarding the condition of the portable toilets that lined the lot. And issues with the mess left behind when old newspapers, advertising flyers and food wrappers that hadn't made it to the Dumpster littered the streets and were picked up by the Texas wind and scattered around town.

"A second valid concern people have regarding the flea market involves commerce and our community. How can we make sure the sellers follow through by paying their taxes, for example? And wondering about the impact these transient merchants have on local business."

No one was listening to me. I knew it. They knew it. But the thing I knew that they didn't know was that I had lived most of my life not being listened to. It had come with the job of being married to a man who was wedded to his calling. I was used to it. I could stand here all day and blah-blah-blah and they could yawn and fidget and play with their food, and for me it would be like just another afternoon at home with my sweet but preoccupied hubby.

"And last, and probably the most troubling—" this time I gathered the last few pieces of paper and smacked them against my open palm "—we do have some reports of criminal activity."

That got their attention.

A buzz went through the room.

Then everyone clasped their eyes on me.

"Bring it on home, Sister Pepperdine," Maxine muttered under her breath.

And suddenly I wished I had prepared a big finish for this whole speech. That I had scrounged around and gotten together a few choir members with a set of drums and some tambourines to stand behind me and deliver the straight but simple message I had arrived at after looking over the material in my hands today.

Instead, I just smiled weakly and offered a one-shouldered shrug. "And it is my recommendation that this action council should compel the city council to work with existing statutes and resources to improve the overall appearance and community goodwill and public safety at the Five Acres of Fabulous Finds Flea Market.

"Oh, no. Not good enough, not nearly good enough!" Jan Belmont, wearing a white jogging suit and the red heat of anger in her cheeks, stormed into the room and up to my makeshift podium. "I did not drop everything and come over here for this meeting to hear that *that* is your plan."

Maxine turned to me and frowned. "Drop everything? What did she drop?"

"The bomb, I think." And just that fast, Bernadette was standing at my elbow, whispering, "And she dropped it on her husband. When we got there, she was packing her bags."

"No!" Maxine followed Jan as the prim woman snatched up one of the stacks of paper I had used in my talk and began waving it about.

While Jan launched into a full-blown diatribe about the low-down dirty drive-in and all the questionable goings-on going on right under our noses, I looked around. Something had gone on right under my nose, it seemed. The kind of thing that could totally play havoc with my plan—my *real* plan, not the one about the flea market.

"Where is the Reverend Cordell?" I asked the tall, flush-faced girl at my side.

"I didn't think it was right that we have Jan here and not go get Chloe, too, so we ran by the tattoo parlor."

"Is that an answer?" I kept one eye on Jan. "I don't think that's an answer, Bernadette."

"Chloe wasn't there," she said.

"*Where* is the Reverend Cordell?" I asked again.

"He…" Bernadette turned to me and bent down to whisper in my ear, as if anyone could hear a word she said over Jan ranting about mud holes and people who frequented them being no better than pigs. Pigs were a recurring theme with Jan, it seemed, and a very big deal. "Chloe wasn't at the tattoo parlor," Bernadette murmured so only I could hear, "because Sammy stole her car!"

"With her in it?" I was trying to make sense of it all.

"No. Sammy hot-wired her car while she was working."

"And the Reverend? Is he in his office, or…"

Bernadette ignored my obsession with Jake, which I took as a very bad sign. "So she took off in the tattoo parlor guy's car to try to find Sammy before he did something crazy."

"Abner?" I tried to visualize the man with the braid and the heart after God and his role in all this.

"Who?" Bernadette blinked.

Jan's voice rose, and she waved the pages in her clenched fist for emphasis.

"Abner, the tattoo parlor guy," I said. "He wasn't the one you thought would do something crazy, was he?"

"Him? Oh, no. I thought he was sort of sweet." Bernadette smiled. "And so Jake…"

I stopped her there. "He told you to call him Jake?"

"He, uh, yes, he said I could. Actually, he said I *should,* because it would break your heart if we got back and weren't on a first-name basis."

"He's on to you, Odessa." Maxine had gotten to her feet

and was huddled behind us, probably as much to prepare for a speedy exit when Jan finished as to hear what we were talking about. "He hasn't stayed single this long without learning a few tricks."

"He dropped me off at Jan's and took off to try to find Chloe before anyone—except the tattoo-parlor guy—does anything crazy."

"And that's why we cannot just let this be and hope for the best," Jan was saying. She slapped the papers down on the table one last time, faced the crowd and folded her arms. "We must get involved. We must do the right thing."

And that was that.

Meeting adjourned.

I did not announce that it was adjourned. It just happened.

Like everything else I had so carefully planned for, it had just slipped through my fingers and out of my control. My lamb was lost, the lovers were parted. The single minister was on the loose, and Bernadette was once more stuck cleaning up after everyone else at the church.

I could take that only one way.

"Maxine, I think the Lord is telling me something."

"Go home with your best friend and consume mass quantities of chocolate?" she asked, hope sparkling in the depths of her sweet brown eyes.

"I'm afraid not," I said, tugging at her sleeve and heading for the door.

Yes the matchmakers and yentas and moms who push and prod—they've always been around. Can you blame them? The job of keeping romance alive is a full-time thing, and the way some people behave, there will never be a shortage of work for those who hope to ease the way.

Chapter Twelve

How do you know when enough is enough? When it is time to let go of a hand stretched out to you in need? It's a delicate thing, not giving too much. Especially when you *want* to give so much.

There is that story about the person who frees the butterfly from the cocoon, only to find that the poor thing will never be able to fly. It needed the struggle of breaking free to strengthen its wings enough to support it in flight. If there were ever three people who deserved wings, who deserved to be able to soar, those three people were Chloe, Bernadette and Jan.

But how do you know when you've done enough? And what do you do if you're afraid that nothing you do is going to make any difference?

"Maybe it's time we faced the truth, Maxine."

We were *not* running away. The meeting was over and

our part in it was done. It is not my fault that all those silly women showed up hoping to impress the new minister with their upright, unselfish civic-mindedness and their scalloped potatoes with corn flake topping. So I saw no reason to stick around to do their dishes or listen to them… I believe the term I've seen used in the Bible is *murmur.* But in Texas we call it bellyachin', at least if we were raised right and have both the good manners and the religious grounding not to use swearwords.

Whatever term one might use to describe the grumblings going on in the fellowship hall, I wanted no part of them.

I didn't have to ask Maxine twice if she was ready to hit the road, either. We tried to get Bernadette to come along, but…well, by now you can guess how that turned out.

That's how me and Maxine ended up in my truck, aimed in the general direction of the Alvarezes' mailbox. Not that I intended to run over those nice people's mailbox, but I was going to hand over all the complaints on file, my suggestions, and the short and not-too-helpful notes from the meeting.

Jan was starting her own action council, dedicated solely to the action of closing down the flea market. Our recommendation would be to work within the system to better the place and integrate it into the community. We could not both win. Like they used to say in those old westerns, this town wasn't big enough for the both of us.

Things had gone past folks working together, and now it was going to take nothing short of a crisis to get everybody to put their personal feelings aside and deal with things reasonably. A crisis. Really. That's the kind of world we live in these days, isn't it? A world that thrives on sensationalism and loves a good scandal. The Five Acres of Fabulous Finds scandal would either come when something bad did happen on the grounds, or when Jan got a serious campaign to close the place going and something bad happened to *her*. Death threats, maybe, or a good pelting with rotten eggs.

And before you decide that egg thing wouldn't be so awful, consider this—this is Texas, where people have been known to make death threats over cheerleading spots. But rotten eggs, on a woman like Jan? Especially if they ran a photo of it in the local paper? If Jan followed through on this, things would get ugly, and one of those things might be Jan herself.

"Face the truth?" Maxine snapped me back from the image of Jan picking shells out of her freshly frosted hair, dark yellow yoke dripping from her chin onto her pristine cotton top from Talbots. "Odessa, girl, I don't recall a time when *I* ever turned my back on the truth."

"All right, then, admit defeat." I slowed my truck down while I tried to think of the quickest way to get from the church to the neighborhood outside town where the Alvarezes lived.

"Defeat? You've got me there again, girl. I didn't realize you and I had actually gone into battle."

"There's a lesson in there about putting on the full armor of God, but I tell you, Maxine, I am just too downtrodden this afternoon to try to piece it together."

"*Downtrodden?* You? A little of the air has maybe been taken out of your hair, but *downtrodden?* Not Odessa Pepperdine."

I hit the brakes. Stop sign. Which I took as an invitation

not just to stop, but to stay a while. One hand on the wheel, I shifted around enough to face my friend and ask, "You really think so?"

"I know so."

"Has my hair really gone flat? Because I took three full passes over it with Deluxe Extra Hold on my way out the door heading for the meeting." I took advantage of our sitting there to grab the rearview mirror and check it out. I pushed down on the platinum blond bubble. I know I told Chloe never to push, but this was different. This was a test push, not a trying-to-alter-the-shape-of-the-style push. After *this* kind of push, the hair springs back. Sort of. "I knew I should have stopped in the church bathroom to refluff."

"Oh, honey, with that crowd, if you had stopped long enough to tease so much as your bangs…"

"My bangs? Not them, too!" Panicked, I glanced in the side mirror to get a fresh angle.

"I was saying that if you had stopped in that bathroom for anything, those ladies would have locked you in the stall and not let you out until you told them who Chloe was and why *their* single minister was chasing after her instead of being at the church, ooohing and ahhing over their wife-to-be candidate's lemon bars or fiesta casserole." Maxine rubbed her temple. "Believe me, the fact that we got out of there with any hair at all is a testament to our flea market shopping skills."

"Flea market shopping skills? How so?"

"Stealth, Odessa, stealth." She sent her hand gliding through the air in a smooth, enigmatic gesture. "We've learned to get in, get what we're after and get out again, without alerting anyone to the fabulousness of our finds."

"Except we didn't find anything today but disappointment." I slumped in the driver's seat, both hands on the wheel. "Maybe we should just stick to treasure hunting. Finding eggbeaters and aprons. That's all I seem to be good for, anyway."

"Oh, now, I won't hear that kind of talk, Odessa."

I gave her a weak but appreciative smile.

She squared her shoulders and looked straight ahead. "You have *never* been any good at finding aprons."

I whipped my head around. She wasn't grinning, at least not with her lips, but oh, her eyes did have that special Maxine twinkle.

"All right. I get it. I don't have any call to go around feeling sorry for myself." I drove on, turning onto the curving country road that led out of town, to the Alvarez home and then…then…then what?

I had no idea where to go. It was early afternoon in the middle of the week. The flea market wasn't open. We'd already had lunch, and both of our husbands were probably sacked out on their respective couches, content as all get-out to be left alone to "watch" TV with their eyes shut.

That right there pretty much summed up my prospects these days. Shop. Eat. Try to get my husband off the couch.

I sighed. "It's just that…chairing this committee, lending support to Jan, cleaning Chloe up, playing cupid, it all gave me a sense of accomplishment. It made me feel that I hadn't used up all my usefulness quite yet. That I wasn't the big-haired-granny-lady equivalent of an eggbeater or apron."

Maxine touched my arm. "But we love eggbeaters and aprons."

I exhaled and took one hand from the wheel just long

enough to give her fingers a pat. "We do, but nobody else even knows what they are for, Maxine. They see them as just worthless junk."

The gentle touch on the arm turned into a smack on the flab—you know, that flabby upper part that goes south after a certain age. Bring the back of a bare hand down on that lovely body part and the sound it makes is part *pop,* part *flap. Plap.* I have to mention that because it gives the flavor of Maxine's outrage. She wasn't being abusive, but she did get my attention. And she didn't leave it at a *plap* on the flab, either.

"Odessa Pepperdine you are *not* worthless!" She said, it coming out all rushed and indignant. "You are *not* junk!"

"Thank you for the vote of confidence, Maxine, but I can't help but look at what I set out to do here, to get Bernadette a date, to show Jan another point of view, to break beneath Chloe's hard exterior…"

"I don't know about her hard exterior, but you did get her to fix up her hair. That should count for something."

"One out of three." I held up my index finger and pushed out my lower lip in a good old-fashioned sulk and said, "Not a very good record. I just thought I would have done better, that I'd have made more headway towards my goals by now."

"And it *is* all about your goals, isn't it?" Maxine pointed to a car pulling out from a side road as her way of warning me to stay sharp. Maxine likes to think of herself as my eyes and ears on the road, and I guess my ego-detector everywhere else. "Never mind what they want for themselves, or even what the Lord might really have planned, as opposed to what you wish He had in store."

"I only want the best for them." The truck bumped along. The Alvarez family lived in a subdivision just off a dusty old road that formed a semicircle on the south side of Castlerock. One day this would all be nice big houses, a new grocery store, maybe a country club or golf course. But now, not many people took this particular road unless they lived out this way or were up to something they didn't want anyone else to see. Not that we *could* see all that much, what with all the dust the wheels had kicked up.

Maxine waved her hand in front of her face, as if that would do any good. She coughed, even though the reddish-brown cloud remained completely outside the cab.

"I only want the best for everyone," I said, trying not to sound too pouty.

"You *only* want to rule the world, Odessa."

"You're the one wants that tiara so bad, Maxine."

She raised her hands, fingers splayed like crystal-encrusted spikes on a glittering band. "I only want to embrace my inner princess."

"And I only want…"

"To be *the* Queen Mama of Castlerock, Texas."

Now how could I argue with *that?* "It beats being an eggbeater."

"Maybe you should be an eggbeater, girl. Because you sure take the cake." Maxine laughed at her own cornball joke.

And because she laughed, I laughed, too. When Maxine laughs, everyone around her has to follow. It's infectious. But then, so are rashes and twenty-four-hour bugs and like both of those things, it can…it causes you to…it tends to… Oh, never mind about the analogy. I got to laughing with Max-

ine, and went sailing right by the turn to go into the Alvarezes' subdivision.

"About this cake…" I said, straining my eyes to see beyond the dust so I didn't miss the next driveway or entrance
to a cow pasture where I could pull in and turn us around.

"Yes?"

"Angel food or devil's food?"

"Coconut!"

"Careful what you wish for," I warned, already wondering could I get a store-bought version or would I have to
make one myself.

"I could say the same to you, Miss Queen Mama Wannabe. Careful what you wish for for other people, as well."
Her voice went quiet, and she twisted in the seat so that her
shoulders faced in my direction. "More careful still when
you take it upon yourself to try to make those wishes come
true. When you mix into people's love lives…"

"I didn't. I didn't mix into anyone's love life but
Bernadette's."

"And Reverend Cordell's."

"And Reverend Cordell's."

"And, by default, Chloe and Sammy's."

"Chloe and Sammy? I refuse to call that a love life, Maxine. That boy mistreats her."

"Okay, then, Jan and Morty."

"Again, I did not set out to meddle there, and so far I
haven't really. Other than to send David over to talk to Morty
and to try to be a friend to Jan and offer her support and advice."

"Sticking your nose in other people's marriages, even if
you use your husband's nose to do it, and lending unasked-

for advice even in the name of friendship. I don't know what you call that in the part of Castlerock where you grew up, but where I was raised, we call that mixing in."

"Fools rush in where wise men fear to tread, eh?"

"If there is one thing I know, Odessa, it is that you are no fool." She reached over and took my hand and gave it a squeeze.

Warmth and love—if you can feel love in a touch, and I believe you can—flowed from my dear sister in Christ to me. It filled my heart, even the hollow part where doubt and fear had burrowed deep. When she let go, I still felt her raising me up. When she spoke again, I knew her words would do the same.

"And if there is one thing I *don't* know, it's... What *is* that man doing?"

Pop. Talk about a way to burst a bubble of goodwill and joy between friends. Seeing a twenty-year-old van emblazoned with red-and-yellow flames on a mostly rust-colored—wait, make that mostly rusted-through-and- through—body broken down a few hundred yards ahead, with a man standing in the road waving his arms, will definitely do it.

I slowed the truck and inched in close to the steering wheel, squinting as hard as I dared without tempting the onset of deep eye wrinkles. "That's not a *man,* Maxine. That's Reverend Cordell."

Maxine shot me a look.

"You know what I mean." I veered to the right, taking my truck as far off the road as I could and still keep it out of the ditch.

I'd hardly wrestled the old gearshift into Park before Jake

had popped open the passenger door. "You two are as welcome as an answered prayer."

He started to climb into the seat, which proved an interesting task, since Maxine had not yet relinquished it.

"Hold on a minute there, Reverend. What are you doing?" she asked, even as she scooted and scrambled in my direction along the bench seat.

"We've got to get moving," he said without any explanation, as if we surely had been following his activities on some kind of minister-monitoring system and knew just where he wanted to get moving to and why.

"Get moving *where? And why?*" I asked, not taking the car out of Park.

"Out of here," he said, practically bouncing on the seat, like some overgrown kid. "Because Chloe took my car."

I blinked at the van a few feet away from us. I believed I had seen the monstrosity in the alley near the tattoo parlor the other day, but I didn't know who owned it or how exactly it had come to rest in this spot in the Texas countryside. A million questions filled my mind. And given those odds, you'd think a better one would have tumbled out of my mouth than "Why didn't you catch a ride with her?"

"I tried, but found it difficult to get in with the thing roaring off down the road at sixty miles an hour."

"Your car went sixty miles an hour on *this* road?" Again, out of the scads of pertinent and constructive questions I might have asked, I had chosen one that had all the relevance of an eggbeater in a modern kitchen.

"Odessa, the girl has stolen the Reverend's car." Maxine said it slow and forceful, the way one might explain something obvious to a two-year-old.

"I know that, Maxine, I'm just trying to…" Ignore it. Pretend it's not true. "I'm just trying to make sense of it."

"It's simple, really." Jake made big, sweeping gestures as he spoke, seemingly unaware of how many times he almost poked Maxine in the eye as he did so. "I figured at some point Sammy would come joyriding down this road in the car he stole from Chloe."

"Because this is the most *joyful* road in Castlerock."

"Because this is the most popular road for kids to meet up *outside* Castlerock," Jake said, ignoring my little jab. "Chloe pointed it out to me the day we went up in the balloon. We couldn't see it from there, of course, but when I asked her if she and Sammy didn't have anything better to do that to hang around the closed flea market, she said they usually came out here and hung around with friends."

"So you figured she would end up here looking for Sammy, too."

Jake nodded and pointed toward the stalled van. "I planned to wait for them—Sammy and/or Chloe—but instead I found her broken down, and when I jumped out of my car to try to talk to her…"

"She jumped in and took off?" I shook my head.

"You're a good man, Reverend." Maxine patted his hand. "Dumb, but good."

"Sometimes good just looks dumb to people who can't see the big picture, Maxine," I reminded her.

"The only picture called for here is a mug shot." Maxine snatched up her purse and began rummaging through it. "We need to hunker down here at the scene of the crime and call the police."

"Chloe isn't a criminal," Jake protested.

"She stole your car." Maxine's hand, her wrist and all of her bracelets disappeared inside her oversize purse.

"She *borrowed* my car. I just haven't had the chance to tell her I'd be happy to lend it to her yet."

"And to be fair, have you seen his car, Maxine?" I tsked and shook my head. "Even if she did steal it, I think the worst you could call it would be petty theft."

"Petty theft is still theft. You don't help people by making excuses. It's not your place to say one way of breaking the law is not as bad as another."

"You have a point Maxine. But I don't think Chloe meant to break the law. She's…"

"It's that Sammy. He's a charmer, that one."

"Yes. And he has led her to make some bad choices."

"Criminal choices?"

"I don't know. I admit that." Jake held up his hands in surrender. "But I do presume, from what I've seen of the girl, that she can make better choices. My faith demands that I believe she *wants* to make better choices."

"Mine too," I said softly at first and then, upon reflection and the pushing aside of my own self-doubt, a bit louder. "Mine too, Reverend."

"Can I count on you, Odessa?" he asked, his eyes unsure and his mouth showing only a hint of that fabulous smile.

"She has ten fingers and ten toes. You can count on those, young man." Maxine finally pulled out the cell phone she'd been searching for and held it aloft. "Count on her to use some of those fingers to dial the authorities and some of those toes to stomp on the gas and get us where we belong."

"You can count on me, Jake. And so can Chloe. Fingers, toes, mind and body. I'll even mess up my hair for the cause!"

"Odessa!"

I looked at my friend's earnest face. She meant well, truly she did. But Maxine was a woman who saw things the way she saw them and acted upon them accordingly. Right. Wrong. Left. Right. Black. White. She did not think of things in terms of degrees or shades.

With that in mind, I looked past my friend and asked Jake, "Do you mind if we just run Maxine home first?"

"Run me home?" Maxine bristled. She bristled so good I practically felt porcupine quills sticking me all up and down my back. "Like fire you will."

"I thought you wanted no part of this."

She sat silent for a moment, with her face turned straight ahead. Her lips twitched. She stroked the sleek case of her cell phone with her thumb. Finally, she tilted her chin up and narrowed her eyes. "What I want no part of is the two of you coming out of all this with better stories to tell than me. And for those stories to all start off with 'After we dropped Maxine off safe at home.'"

"Oh, Maxine…" Sentimental old me, my voice got all craggy and hoarse. My eyes even went a bit misty. I patted my pal's leg. "You don't want to be an eggbeater, either."

It might have been a sweet, mushy moment, except Jake clapped his hands and said, way too loudly, "Let's do this, ladies."

"You got it, Reverend." I started up the engine. "We're not done being of use yet."

"What about the van?" Maxine was still holding the phone in the palm of her hand.

"Oh, I already called Abner and told him where I'd found it. He said no problem. He knows how to start it and will come get it."

"That Abner, he is a genuinely nice guy, you know it?" I had to back up the truck to stay clear of the ditch, and in doing so had a chance to catch a glimpse of the Reverend's face as I added, "Even Bernadette thinks so."

"Bernadette? And Abner?" Jake leaned forward to peer at me around Maxine. "Really?"

"Life is full of surprises." I mashed down on the brake and muscled the gearshift into Drive. "You know he's a Christian, don't you?"

"So he said." Jake's eyebrows crimped down. He touched the rim of his glasses. "And he was really concerned about Chloe."

"Just goes to show you that God uses all sorts," I said, feeling a bit too pleased with myself for having planted that seed of a thought about Bernadette and Abner in Jake's mind.

"Even us out-of-sorts." Maxine swung her hand around in a circle like a lasso before pointing down the road and ordering, "Drive, Odessa! Drive!"

How do you know when enough is enough? Some people might think two sixty-something wives of retired ministers would have had enough adventure, would have had enough of taking risks on behalf of people who might not appreciate the effort. But as far as I can tell, there is no retirement age for do-gooders. There is no junk heap where we toss human beings and say, *That's it! She's too broken. She's too battered. She's too old.*

We are all redeemable.

We are all useful.
We all have potential.
We may just have to get creative to find it.

Chapter Thirteen

Ecclesiastes reminds us there is a time to be silent and a time to speak. The right place, the right occasion, for everything. All things in the right season.

We all have our seasons, too. The stages of a life, the ever-changing landscape of a relationship. God gave us this world of absolute wonder to help us see that even after the hope of spring has faded into the hardened cold of winter, as long as there is still life, rebirth will come.

I am not all used up just because I have seen too many summers. I will only be used up when God has gotten all the good He can out of me and calls me home, saying, "Well done, good and faithful servant."

Until then, it is my job to make myself a blessing to everyone I can. Silent? I can't be silent about the goodness of my God.

Make a joyful noise! Shout and clap and stomp your feet! some people say. When the Lord is working inside you, you just can't stay quiet.

"Yeee-haw!" The tires hit the jagged edge of the pavement, the truck bucked and bounced. We were on our way to find our Chloe, and I just had to cut loose!

"Why, Mrs. Pepperdine!" Jake pushed his glasses back into place after my driving jounced them down the bridge of his nose. "I had no idea you had so much genuine cowgirl in you."

"Cowgirl? Me?" I thought that over for a second. "Why not? I was Texas born and Texas bred, and you know what else…?"

"If she says when she dies she'll be Texas dead, do you think it would be unchristian of me to smack her one, Reverend?" Maxine spoke low and out of the corner of her mouth.

"If you have something to say to me, say it outright, Maxine." I led by example, my voice clear and my words plain. "Don't go whispering as if there were some way I couldn't hear you in this small truck cab with the three of us squashed in here like…like…"

"Sardines?" the Reverend suggested.

"Oh, don't be silly, young man." Maxine gave his arm a motherly squeeze.

"Really!" I laughed and gave him my best bless-your-heart-you-poor-simpleminded-child grin. "What on earth would small salty fish be doing driving around in a truck on the back roads of Castlerock, Texas?"

"Well, I…uh…it's just a…" He cleared his throat. He

glanced from one of us to the other and back again, as if he thought I really didn't understand the cliché he had used.

Maxine stifled a giggle. "Take my advice and stop this while you still can. If you let her get you talking about canned fish, before you know it, puns will begin flying about chickens of the sea, and once that can of worms—"

"Tuna, Maxine. Chicken of the sea is tuna," I reminded her, trying not to snicker. "A can of worms is a whole *other* kettle of fish."

"See?" Maxine poked Jake, then pointed to me. "Don't start these things around Odessa. It was bad enough you called her a cowgirl."

"What's so bad about being a cowgirl?" The road before us forked, and I squinted at it for only a second before I chose the road less traveled. No, not because of the poem, but because if I were a couple of kids wanting to get up to some misdeed, that's where I'd go to get up to it. "My Father owns the cattle on a thousand hills, you know. Maybe it's time I did get in touch with my inner cowgirl."

"I thought the plan was to be in charge of everything— and *everyone*—in Castlerock." Maxine rolled her eyes. A sort of smile played on her lips. Despite always saying things like that, and her reluctance to join us at first, that woman was enjoying this every bit as much as I was. Maybe more. She had suggested I was only now realizing how to become my best self, but I could see that she was doing a little of that herself, growing into more of the person she knew she could become, too. "How are we going to find time to run barrel races at the rodeo if we ever hope to get crowned the right Royal Highnesses of Busybodyness?"

"I just don't see a conflict in all that, Maxine." I played it real sober, shaking my head and speaking all solemn even when I added on, "Only I think we should go by the title the Royal Highnesses of Being Ourselves."

"Odessa, honey, you have got a way of getting away with far too much." She nudged me with her elbow. "But I have to admit, I like it."

"Me too, Maxine." I nudged her right back. "Let's do it. Let's us *be* Cowgirl Queens. We can get pink hats and put sparkly tiaras on the front of them, you know, like the flag bearers at the rodeos do?"

She chuckled, but I could tell, deep down she was considering it. "We don't have to ride ponies, do we?"

That got to Reverend Cordell. I guess the image of me and Maxine in pink cowboy hats and tiaras chasing down car thieves on the back of a couple of fat spotted ponies would tickle even the most righteous man.

"You ladies are wasted spending your free time at the flea market, I tell ya. You need to work up an act and take it on the road." He put his arm on the edge of the window.

"That's where we are now—on the road," I said.

"But the road to where?" Maxine looked around, leaning in and out and to the side to scope out our surroundings.

I slowed the truck down. Only then, when I found us in the middle of nowhere, did I think to ask, "Where do you think Chloe might have got to, Reverend?"

"I wanted to check all around here first." He, too, bobbed his head and bowed his shoulders so that he could peer through all the truck windows. "Obviously Chloe *was* out here earlier. But since we haven't seen any sign of her, we might try some of the places that Abner said Sammy likes to…do business."

"Business?" Maxine snorted. It was a very ladylike, authoritative, savvy sort of snort, to be sure. "That scruffy kid hardly seems the businessman type to me."

"What are you talking about? Drugs?" I started the truck rolling slowly forward again. The very notion that anything untoward might have been going on down this quiet country lane made the hair on the back of my neck stand on end. Of course, I am not naive. Well, I am not *totally* naive. I know that people do all manner of things all over the place. Even in places frequented by cowgirls and ministers. But still, the sheer isolation of this place, with this deserted road that dropped off into overgrown ditches, would lend itself quite nicely to clandestine exchanges. "I guess when I think of young people running afoul of the law, I just naturally think of drugs. Is that what you mean?"

"Actually no. Maybe. But…" He pushed his fingers back through his dark brown hair, which made the few silver strands there stand out all the more. "If Sammy sells 'em, he doesn't take 'em, and Abner felt almost certain that Chloe is clean, too."

"That's a relief," Maxine said.

I shored it up with a heartfelt "Amen."

"Abner didn't know too much about Sammy's dealings, only that the kid was into something shady and that it involved his interacting with the kind of people that gave Abner the creeps."

Maxine and I shared a look that said, *The kind of people who give* Abner *the creeps? And* we *are out chasing those people down?*

Jake stroked his chin. "No, I don't know what Sammy is up to, but you can bet it has some connection to the flea market."

"Our flea market?" I asked.

"No!" Maxine gave a backhanded bat of her hand.

"Yes." Jake spoke firmly, and with his face turned away from us. "It's the perfect cover for all kinds of mischief. You read the complaints and the police reports."

"Actually, I still have them, right...there." I dipped my eyes to show the man where I had stashed the file folder I had originally planned to dump on Gloria Alvarez's doorstep—her mailbox, really, but her doorstep in the sense that I had wanted to pawn my problems off on her. "Maybe you can figure out from those what he's up to and where we can find Chloe."

"I feel just like Nancy Drew." Maxine pressed her back to the seat to read the open file over the Reverend's shoulder.

"Odessa Pepperdine, girl detective. Or better yet—Odessa Pepperdine, agent for the Lord." I liked it. I liked it a lot. "Let's see, we could write all this up and call it *The Case of the Dubious Balloonist!*"

"Or how about *The Case of the Felonious Flea Market?*" Maxine suggested.

"I don't like that one nearly as much." I did a roundabout, which is a fancy way of saying I worked the truck back and forth on the narrow road until I had made a U-turn and pointed us back the way we had come. "I mean if you think about it... We know that the balloonist is dubious, but do we know that our flea market is felonious?"

"I think maybe it is," Jake muttered as he shuffled through

the papers in the file. "Look, there are three complaints here about 'unsavory' sorts—that's the word used by one of the people filing the report."

"Let me guess. Jan Belmont?" *Unsavory.* It was a Jan kind of word.

The Reverend did not answer me, and rightly so. Once again, the man went up in my estimation, and he didn't even realize it, I would guess.

He just went right on reading from the pages. "Unsavory sorts and suspicious types hanging around the east side of the flea market when it's not in operation."

"The east side?"

"Isn't Jan's house east of the drive-in?" Maxine pointed to her left, then to her right, and then raised her gaze skyward as if that might help her get her bearings.

Jake, too, raised his eyes. "That's the side where we parked when we went to do the tour, right?"

Fighting the temptation to check and see if there was a map printed on the ceiling of my truck, I glued my eyes to the road and said, "Yes, the owner didn't want to have a bunch of cars there when it was closed. Thought it might start rumors."

"About what?" Maxine crinkled up her nose.

"About anything." The truck thumped over a rut, and I hung onto the steering wheel with both hands. "It's Castlerock, midweek on a summer afternoon. Lots of people have nothing better to do than to speculate about all sort of things, and a bunch of cars parked at the drive-in is as good a fodder as anything."

"I bet the landowner realizes he's on borrowed time with all this." Jake closed the file and tapped the edge of it against his leg. "Only a matter of time before somebody gets fired up and holds him accountable for some of the things that go on there."

"Better someone does that than throws eggs at Jan," I murmured, thinking back to my own worries over what might happen if our resident unsavory-sort detector got the wrong people riled up. And, of course, as soon as the words came out of my mouth, I knew how it would sound to the others. And rather than try to explain it all, I decided to just go on talking to cover it up. Yes, it's a pride thing, and not pretty, but that is what I did. "I suppose that's why the drive-in owner had us park on the east side, too. The angle of the screen, and the trees and fences, they all hide that spot unless you're right up on it."

"Then that's where we have to go," Jake said. "Get right up on it, too, and see for ourselves."

"I am already on my way."

And I not only was—on my way, I mean—I got us there in good time, without so much as bending the speed limit, though I can't say the same for Maxine.

By the time we came bouncing into the pocked and furrowed entryway by the old Satellite Vista sign that once posted movie dates and times, Maxine looked truly and sounded totally bent out of shape. "Odessa, I liked it better when I was driving this heap."

"Shh. *I* liked it better when we were being quiet."

"When did *that* happen?" Maxine asked, in complete disbelief that we had ever known a time like that.

"We're starting it right now," I said, putting my finger to my lips. "We're doing the Nancy Drew thing, remember?"

"Only it's not Nancy Drew, is it?" Jake's open, kind features clouded. "I shouldn't have gotten you two involved in this. I should have sent you both home. We have no idea what we might find in there."

"Well, we are not going to drop down out of the trees on anyone like ninja church ladies!" I kept the truck rolling as quietly as possible toward the east side of the old structure. "We're just going make a pass by that secluded lot and see if either Chloe's car or the one she stole from you is sitting there."

"She didn't really steal—"

"Oh, give it up, Reverend. She did." I didn't mean to snap, but really, the man already had some gray hair. "You are too old for pretend games. Sure, you want to think the best of the girl. We all do. But sometimes the only real way to do the best thing for someone is to stop thinking the best and start speaking the truth."

"Yes, ma'am," he said softly.

The truck's tires rolled over the loose gravel strewn across the old pavement. In the silence of the cab, we heard every crunch like some crazy extra-amplified breakfast cereal.

Jake sat forward, placing his hand on the spot where Maxine usually braced herself against my enthusiastic way of negotiating the roads. Slowly, that wise and comforting smile that changed the nature of his normally normal face emerged. "And, Mrs. Pepperdine...?"

"What, Jake?"

"I think you'd make a real good ninja church lady."

I opened my mouth to laugh, or maybe it was to say something terribly, terribly clever, I don't know, because at that same instant Maxine let out such a violent, startled gasp that it completely cleared my mind.

"What is it? Do you see my car?" Jake asked.

"No," Maxine whispered. "I see… We should just go."

"What? What do you see?" I craned my neck, but at first I didn't see a thing except the trees and the heavily shaded spot beneath them where only stray shafts of light came through and fell upon…

"I've seen that cane before," I said softly.

"What cane?" Jake asked.

I stopped the truck.

"Morty Belmont's cane." Maxine raised her hand to the indicate the pale-colored staff propped against a large tree.

"It's just a cane." Jake frowned. "Anyone could have left it there. Maybe someone left it when they came to the flea market. How do you know it's Morty Belmont's?"

"Because there he is." Maxine dropped her hand and, with that movement, whether intentionally or not, brought my and the minister's gazes downward so that we finally saw what had made her gasp.

"Helen Davenport!" There, in Morty's still-mending arms, stood the woman who had sought to keep Bernadette from even meeting, much less finding romance with, Jake Cordell. "Morty Belmont is meeting secretly with Helen Davenport!"

Now who was playing at pretend? Anyone with eyes could see that this was more than just some covert get-together. They had not gone through all the machinations it would have taken for them to get here so they could swap recipes or work on a community service subcommittee. And though they were simply sitting in the grass at the base of the tree, they were close in each other's arms and lost in each other's eyes.

This was private.

This was intimate.

This was…heart wrenching.

"Should we tell Jan?" I whispered.

Maxine raised her head and, with a short, solemn nod, directed our attention through the tops of the trees, to a tiny shape on a rooftop. "I think she already knows."

Some people believe there is a lesson in every event and circumstance. That every decision we make has the power to enlighten and every choice the power to change us, for the good or the not-so-good. And that if we try, we can learn something from both. I had to wonder what lesson this day had delivered.

To everything there is a season. A time for every purpose under heaven. Among them are:

A time to weep and a time to laugh.

A time to search and a time to give up.

A time to be silent and a time to speak.

I guess the thing I had to ask myself was, what time was it now? The time to stop pretending and speak the truth? Or the time to shut up and mind my own business?

Chapter Fourteen

Noise or silence—whichever you choose, none of it matters if nobody will listen to you. You've heard the riddle, If a tree falls in the woods and no one is there to hear it, does it make a sound?

I don't know. I can only say that, in my own experience, lost in the wilderness of being a nonretired wife married to a fully retired minister, when I speak, my husband seems to pick up only noise and responds mostly with silence. I have run out of ideas about how to get and hold his attention, and frankly, it worries me.

Was that what had gone awry between Jan and Morty? Had we all become so blind and deaf to each other that taking Chloe's road, the piercings, the costumes, the car thievery, seemed the only way to avoid being as overlooked and undervalued as a…a…a Bernadette?

I've lived in the background of my own life for so long, and now these women that I had set out to help, that I have come to care for, are making me reassess my choices, making me long to find my voice. If only there was somebody listening!

"Nancy Drew, David." I had tried to keep it simple and use small words, not because I thought David needed small words, but because I thought they had a better chance of getting through. Compared with phrases like "surrendering my chairmanship of the community action council" and "dubious balloonist" and "ninja church ladies dropping from the trees," it seemed like "car thief," "creep," and "cheater" had a better chance of standing out enough to draw his attention. "I said that Maxine and I felt like Nancy Drew. Not Scooby-Doo!"

"But if you're involved with teenagers and chasing criminals away from an abandoned drive-in?" He rustled the paper in his hands and did not meet my eyes across the kitchen table. "That sounds straight out of Scooby-Doo to me."

I put my elbows on the table. Yes, I know it's bad manners, but I had cleared away the supper dishes already and the *thunk* my elbows made when they landed on the soft yellow checked tablecloth gave me a tiny bit of satisfaction. David didn't even look over the top of the sports page at the sound.

I sighed. "I don't know what bothers me more, that since your retirement you've come to learn the complexities, or lack thereof, of a cartoon mystery show, or that you haven't really heard anything I said."

"I've heard every word," he replied. This was an old trick of his. It was not a lie. He *had* heard me, just like he heard the hum of the refrigerator motor a few feet away or the *clunk-ka-chunk* of the old air conditioner turning off and on. My voice had become nothing more than the whine of an old appliance to him. And if I said that to him, he would lower his paper at last, lift up my hand, kiss my fingers, then remind me that he wouldn't be able to survive in Texas without his fridge or his Freon-cooled air—or me.

The man knew how to work all the angles, and I loved him so much I let him get away with it.

"Anyway, Maxine and the Reverend Cordell and I did the chasing." I picked up my iced tea glass and swirled the last slivers of ice around. "The teenagers—well, young adults, really—were nowhere to be found. The drive-in is not abandoned. It's where they hold the flea market, and…"

He flipped a page lazily and coughed.

I plunked the glass back down on the table. "And why do I even bother?"

At last he lowered the paper and smiled at me. "What?"

"More tea?" I asked, reaching for the tall glass pitcher of sweet tea on the table between us.

He held his glass out, and I filled it almost to the top. I know my husband, and if he planned to pretend to hear my musings about the day's events, he would need caffeine and sugar, and plenty of 'em.

"The drive-in is where they have the flea market, which reminds me!" All right, might as well get this out in the open now. It's probably already obvious, but I have reached an age that when something important pops into my head I feel compelled to announce it on the spot, for fear of it slipping right back out of my brain again. It's like I have a banana peel in my short-term-memory lobe or something, A thought hardly shows up before *swhoooosh,* it's gone again. I can't say how many times I've had something vital to say to someone and in the length of time it took to walk over

to them or dial their phone number I've completely forgotten it. So when talk turned to the flea market and I had
David's attention, I felt I needed to say, "Did I tell you about
the problem with Helen Davenport's credit card?"

"I hope you didn't. Strikes me as a bit too close to spreading gossip, my dear." Said it sort of superior and snottylike,
I thought. Not in an "I'm a better Christian than you" way,
but with that ever-irritating "men don't do this stuff, and if
women were half the men that men are, they wouldn't, either" sort of attitude. Patronizing. In fact, I think that's the
actual definition of patronizing. That almost haughty tone.
The hint of boredom or detachment in the expression. The
very man-ness of it all.

"Well, that's where you are wrong." I smiled. After over
thirty years of marriage to this thoughtful and compassionate human being who chooses his words carefully and tries
to always act in faith and do the right thing, it just tickled
me pink to be able to tell him he was wrong about something. Oh, I know, it's a fault, but as faults go, I think it's one
a lot of wives share. "It's not gossip. It's part of my work for
my action council."

"I thought you planned to resign from that."

Well, what do you know? He had been listening—a little. "No, I said I intended to resign and give all the information over to Gloria Alvarez, but then all this came up and
I didn't. And now I sort of think that I won't."

He took a long sip of tea before asking, "Why not?"

"Because it would be irresponsible. I know I started all
this for questionable reasons, but the fact is, I did start it, and
there are real problems on the property, and somebody has
to…" I finally paused to catch my breath and caught my

husband smiling down into his tea glass. "Did you think I wouldn't notice you trying to change the subject like that?"

He chuckled.

"But it isn't changing the subject, really because all of this is tied in together, which is why I can't walk away from chairing that action council."

"All right. Go on with your story." He gulped down some tea and shuffled through the remainder of the paper spread out before him.

"The thing about the credit card… It was declined, even though the cardholder said it should have gone through just fine." I was careful not to mention Helen by name, even though that was a part of the whole story and I'd have to bring it up eventually. But given the man on the other side of this pretty much one-sided conversation, he'd probably have stopped listening by then. "That made me and Maxine wonder if maybe something was amiss at the flea market. You know, had a vendor overcharged the account or something like that, but not so much anymore because you will never guess who that credit card belonged to."

"Helen Davenport."

"Helen Daven… Oh." It took me back a bit to realize that I actually *had* mentioned Helen's name, *and* he had heard me, *and* he had put a little thought into the particulars of the story.

He chuckled, but only slightly, because, you know, men don't take pleasure in anything that even borders on gossip.

"Yes, well, anyway," I continued, "now we know Helen has conducted this whole secret life on the flea market grounds—which is clearly why Jan wants the place closed forever. At this point, neither Maxine nor I think she knows who the 'other woman' is, but she knows where they meet and so she wants it all torn down to both take away their trysting spot and to remove it from her line of vision. Of course, it isn't actually *in* her line of vision unless she crawls out on the roof outside her spare bedroom. But neither she nor Morty can seem to resist doing that, so…" I gulped down a breath at last. Between the twin tendencies of David's attention to drift off and my own mind to wander, I had to get it all out as quickly and concisely as I could. "So suddenly it all fits."

"This is where your feeling like Nancy Drew comes in, right?"

It raised my spirits to know, once again, that he had heard *something* I said.

"Actually, we felt like our favorite girl detective before this, but now that you mention it, this realization did make us feel awfully clever, too."

He gave me a wink. "I can't imagine one minute of the day when either you or Maxine doesn't feel like the cleverest gal in the room."

After all these years, the man still made me feel all mushy and melty and… "What if we are *both* in the same room? We can't *both* feel like the cleverest one."

"Hmm. Good point. Let me mull that over and get back to you." He started to push his chair back.

"You stay right there, bucko."

"Bucko?" His silvery eyebrows shot up. I guess I should have taken a moment to describe my husband long before now, but I did say he was a retired minister, and I think most people who have met retired ministers already have an idea of what they look like. David fits that idea pretty well.

Ruddy complexion. Round in face and belly, but not obese. Hair gone gray, what there is of it. Last time he went to have his driver's license renewed, under the spot where it said hair color, he wrote the word *pink,* explaining that all they could see in the photo would be his sun-kissed shiny bald head. Oh, and his eyebrows, which have gotten a bit bushy with age and which shot up and stayed up when he asked, "Did you just call me 'bucko'?"

"Oh, didn't I tell you? The Reverend Cordell thinks I'm part cowgirl now."

"Cowgirl? Girl detective? Ninja church lady? Odessa, honey, I hardly know you anymore." And he wasn't all smiles and chuckles and winks when he said that, either.

"Ha! Well, I know *you,* David Pepperdine, and you are not getting out of hearing the whole of my story quite so easily." I waggled my finger at him. "The point I wanted to make was that Maxine read an article."

"Well, that settles it, then. *She's* the clever one."

"Oh, stop it." I nudged his knee with my toe. "She read an article that said that sometimes when people sneak around they build whole elaborate secret lives in order to cover their tracks. New bank accounts. Post office boxes to get bills, and credit cards exclusively for their rendezvous."

"And I thought people giving credit cards to kids was bad. But a credit card exclusively for your rendezvous..."

"David! I am trying to tell you that Maxine and I now wonder if maybe Morty had something to do with running her card up to the limit. I mean, Jan said they were having financial difficulties. How else could the man afford a mistress?"

"A mistress? Odessa, now you are the one who needs to

stop it. That is far too loaded a term to throw around when you don't know all the facts."

"I know what I saw. They were sitting in the grass, in each other's arms, gazing into one another's eyes."

"If that were all it took to be a mistress, then…then… Odessa, I am just not comfortable with all this."

"All what?"

"The speculation. The spying on people. The speed with which you reach conclusions…"

"None of that was intended to be unchristian, David. In fact, it was just the opposite. I was trying to be an instrument of the Lord." I sat back and searched my heart for any signs of malicious glee at the misfortunes of the people I had been talking about. None was there. In fact, the whole thing made me ache through and through, and had been the subject of many prayers since we had happened upon the inappropriate couple. "But in all this, my deepest thoughts and sympathies lie with Jan. I know what it's like to be a wife who raised her children and then wonders what use she is to anyone, most of all her husband, anymore. To have doubts and fears."

"I would never stray, Odessa. I never have."

"I believe you, David. But don't you think at some point in their marriage Morty said the exact same thing to Jan?"

A troubled look passed over his face. "Odessa, I…"

"I'm not accusing you of anything, sweetie. I'm just saying that there is a lot of temptation out there, even at our ages. A lot of widows and divorcées just like Helen…"

"So you blame Helen for this?"

"No...I... Well, we all have to accept responsibility for our actions. But what I meant by that was that Maxine thinks Helen is divorced."

"Hmm."

"Myself, I thought she was widowed." And off my brain went, sliding along down a new thoughtway. "We wanted to ask Jake, but he made it clear that he had no intention of discussing anything about what we saw, because Helen is a member of his congregation."

"Good for him."

"Yeah, I know." I refilled my tea glass. "But pardon me for being a little bit disappointed."

David gave an indulgent smile that acknowledged my all-too-human feelings. "If a flock can't trust their own shepherd to guard their privacy, who can they trust?"

"Of course. You're right. I told him it was exactly what you would do." I drew the cold pitcher to my chest and slumped back in my chair. "It's what you *are* doing right now, isn't it?"

"Right now?" He frowned, a bit too dourly. "Right now, I'm reading the paper. Or I would be, if I could just be left to concentrate on it."

"No, what you are doing now is acting evasive and changing the subject and teasing me to distract me from giving in to gossip and becoming a victim of my own poor guesswork."

"Hmm, *I* must be the clever one in the room, then."

"Not if I figured out your plan." I set the pitcher aside and flexed my suddenly icy fingers. "I should have thought of it. You served as pastor to Morty for so many years. You went to see him recently. You knew about this."

"If I did or if I didn't, it's not fodder for after-dinner conversation."

I sat up straight, opened my mouth, then shut it again. Elbow on the table again, I rested my cheek in my hand.

Why is it, I have to ask myself, that everyone around me is so good at making excellent points and I am so miserable about accepting them? The points, that is, not the people. David was right. Nothing I could say would persuade him to reveal anything more to me regarding what David knew about Morty Belmont. Nor would I try to persuade him.

But, oh, I *so* wanted to know what my husband knew!

"I just…" No. I couldn't ask it of him. I traced a bead of condensation down the side of my iced tea glass, my lips pressed shut tight. I understood, truly I did, but that did not make everything easy for me. That's part of the deal when you're a Christian, of course. It's not that temptations are easier to turn away, it's that you will find the strength through Christ to do what you know He would do.

So that's what I did. I didn't push for more information from David. But that did not change my emotional stake in it all, and I let him know that by adding, quite softly, "Jan is my friend."

"Since when?"

"Since I decided to meddle in her life and make things better for all my flea market foundlings."

"She's your friend because you decided all on your own to stick your nose in her business?"

"Yes. You've heard of bosom buddies?"

He nodded cautiously.

"Well, Jan and I are proboscis pals."

He questioned that with the slightest shift of his eyebrows. Yes, we've been married so long we can communicate through minute facial muscle movements. Sigh. No wonder he doesn't think he needs to listen to me. All the man has to do is sit across from me for a few seconds and he can read me like a book.

"Okay, forget bosom buddies and proboscis pals. When you get right down to it, we are, no matter what our conflicts, sisters in Christ." I waited a moment for that to sink in, but not long enough that he could make the argument that Helen might also be considered a sister in Christ. Not because that wasn't a valid point, but because—and I've already owned up to this—I don't take valid points that clash with my opinions all that well, and because it would definitely take the discussion in a whole other direction. "I care what happens to Jan. I still want things to work out well for her. I think about her a lot, and I pray for her."

His face softened, and lit with deep, admiring love. "That's my girl."

"I don't do it because I am your girl, David." I did not raise my voice or clip my words or frown and look cross at him. I just spoke my heart with calm and quiet conviction. "I do it because I am my own woman."

His forehead creased. His mouth set in a thin line. His eyes seemed to grow dark, more perplexed than perturbed. "I'm not sure I know this woman you claim to be now, Odessa."

"I'm not sure you do, either." I couldn't believe I'd said it. But there it was, out in the open, as plain as the pitcher of tea between us. "I'm not sure you have ever tried to know and understand me, all of me, not just me as your wife or the mother of your children or your helpmate, but me, the person most like myself."

"Wife and mother and helpmate, what more is there? Besides the cowgirl and…"

"You don't even know about the tiaras, much less the Royal Service Hostess Queen partyware, do you, David?"

"Tiaras? Partyware? Are you saying you're selling those self-burping container systems in your spare time?"

Oddly enough, I could sort of see where he got that. And I had to give the man credit for remembering that once upon a time Tiara glassware and Tupperware had both been sold by housewives in friends' homes. It all made sense—though more in a Scooby-Doo way than a Nancy Drew one.

I patted his hand, and this time it was my turn to smile with indulgence and good humor. "No, sweetie pie. In my whole life, you and the boys were the only self-burping things I ever had to explain to any of my friends."

He laughed and shook his head.

"I was referring to a set of serving pieces popular around the time we got married. They were made by a company called Royal Service, and I loved the black-and-gold Hostess Queen pattern."

"Uh-huh." I could tell he wasn't following, but bless his heart, he hadn't completely given up trying.

"I loved those pieces. To me, they symbolized a woman who cared about her home, serving her family, entertaining her friends and yet retaining her own individual style."

"You got this all from a few dishes?" I half expected him to whip out a notepad and write it all down to study later. It was that new a concept to the man.

"I know it seems shallow, but, well, back in those days, the way a woman appointed her home was an extension of her personality. It was a form of self-expression. Was she elegant or whimsical or pragmatic or..."

"Self-burping?"

It was my turn to laugh. "Yes. I suppose so."

"And you were?"

"A queen," I said softly.

He took my hand. "My queen."

I yanked my hand free. "Then why did you give away the few pieces of Hostess Queen partyware I ever owned to the church's kitchen and then berate me as childish for asking you to get it back for me?"

His eyes got real big. Husband-realizing-he's-been-a-jerk-big-time big. "I did that?"

"See? It didn't even register with you, David. And it really mattered to me."

"But you—"

"It really mattered," I whispered, choking back tears. I was not just talking about the dishes then, and he knew it. I was talking about everything in my life. All the new things I was experiencing. All the things in my life and the lives of the boys that had passed him by and could never be retrieved. All my hopes and dreams. *Me.*

I was reminding the man who had loved me and lived with me for most of my life that standing before him was a woman who mattered.

I just hope he heard me.

★ ★ ★

That's right, my marriage isn't perfect. What's more, my husband isn't perfect. And most shocking of all? I am not perfect! Though I do strive to come as close to perfection as I possibly can in my hair and grooming.

But then I think of the people I know who try so hard to achieve at least the image of perfection—Jan Belmont, Helen Davenport, Bernadette Alvarez, and even, in her own dark and strange little world, Chloe Morgan. What had it gotten them, this trying to make everyone believe the impossible about them? They didn't seem happy with themselves, or with their lives.

My life wasn't perfect, but I had a wonderful friend in Maxine—and, of course, my David.

"All things considered…" I stopped by the chair where David had settled down to do his daily Bible reading the next morning and dropped a kiss on the top of his dear old bald head. "I still sure do love you."

He kissed my hand.

I sighed.

"I love you, too, my sweet cowgirl queen," he whispered, his way of both apologizing and showing me he had listened, even if he hadn't known what to make of what he heard.

And as I headed out the door for my regular date with Maxine for Friday-morning flea marketing, I heard the love of my life call out after me, "Keep your eyes open. It's probably old man Jenkins wearing a rubber monster mask trying to scare you meddling kids off so you won't find his stash of—"

Clunk. I shut the door. Hard.

I love him, but if he compares my efforts to do right by my friends to the repetitive plot of a cartoon dog detective one more time…well, I might just have to take an eggbeater to him.

If only the rest of the people I cared about could be whipped into shape so easily.

Chapter Fifteen

Everyone is familiar with the saying "Be careful what you wish for...you just might get it."

And I hadn't just wished for something. I'd prayed about it. I'd worked toward it. I'd involved others in trying to make it happen. Maxine and David had both warned me about this drive to accomplish my goals. About thinking I knew better than the Lord what the Lord wanted me to do in order to comply with His will.

I admit it now, I was clearly too fixed on getting what I'd wished for.

I'd wished for attention. I'd wished to bring my flea market girls to the forefront and show them how much I believed in them. I'd wished...to shine like a diamond.

Maxine and David had told me to be careful, but maybe what someone should have reminded me of was this little factoid: The way to make a diamond is to take a lump of coal and apply a whole lot of pressure.

★ ★ ★

That morning, as Maxine and I approached the gate, Sammy did not call to us. He did not hurry over to thrust a flyer into my hand or try to charm me into taking a ride in his beautiful balloon. He didn't even look our way. In fact, he made such a point of not looking our way that it made it almost impossible not to stare straight at him and practically dare him to make eye contact.

"Cut that out," Maxine warned.

"I'm not doing anything," I protested.

"If your eyes got any buggier, someone around here would throw a net on you and sell you for bait." She held her pink pearlized reading glasses up to her nose, then moved them in and out, to demonstrate the way my eyes were bulging.

"Oh, Maxine, that doesn't even make sense." I knew what she meant, of course. And I could picture myself like some creature flopping around in a bait bucket, its eyes glazed and googy. That comparison, and my own guilt, put plenty of petulance in my tone when I justified my behavior to my observant-but-quaint-phrase-impaired pal. "I was just looking. Looking and doing are definitely not the same thing."

"That kind of reasoning is a slippery slope, Odessa. Wouldn't be a bit surprised if it was the kind of thinking Morty Belmont used when he first started climbing on the roof and gazing off toward his clandestine meeting place. Looking ain't doing."

"I'd rather you didn't compare me to that...that—" I could practically see David raising an eyebrow to let me know just how much I didn't actually *know* about that situation "—that *man,* Maxine."

"Fine." She snagged me by the sleeve of my billowy jersey fabric dress and tugged me along behind her toward the open gateway. "But I don't take back that it's that same kind of slippery-slope thinking. Looking isn't doing. Dating a boy who does wrong is not *doing,* but that doesn't mean we aren't going to go in there and let our Chloe know that we are not happy with some of her choices."

That day, we did not dawdle. We moved swiftly through the stalls using our keen eyes and what Maxine likes to call "Queen-o-vision" to scope out any potential pieces of Royal Service partyware, of which we found exactly zero. Within a half hour of arriving at the market, we found ourselves approaching Bernadette's booth, a place we don't usually reach until around or just after lunch.

Our timing was perfect. If we had taken even a few minutes longer, we'd have entirely missed the visit by the petite woman in the tan-and-brown uniform of the Castlerock Police Department. Redheaded and with her stick-straight hair caught back in a ponytail, the woman jotting something down in a black vinyl notepad wore no makeup to accent her fair skin and green eyes.

"Oh, no. We are *not* marching up to that nice police lady and demanding she let you slap some lipstick on her and poof her hair up like a pan of Jiffy Pop popcorn gone haywire."

"Hush, Maxine, I'm trying to paint a picture with words here."

The fact was, the plainness and the petiteness of the police officer created a striking contrast to our tall, zaftig Bernadette, with her long hair curled and flowing and her eyes and mouth enhanced by subtle color.

"Jake Cordell is nowhere in sight. You don't have to sell anyone on how lovely Bernadette is, Odessa."

"Get out of my head, Maxine."

But inside my head or not, Maxine was right. She had summed it all up right there. The whole thought process of the night before was still fresh in my mind. How far should you go to get someone's attention, and how long would it last? Not long, if there wasn't something more beneath the pretty surface that first attracted the eye.

That's not just my thought process, skipping like a flat stone across water. That was me actually working out how much I had undersold Bernadette in the past. How much I had assumed that nobody else would see what I saw in that strong, capable, kind young woman. But now, seeing her standing there, right beside what most folks would agree represented the very icon of the strong, capable woman, I could clearly see that Bernadette would draw anyone's eye. She commanded attention. She had not needed me, or her mother, or her grandmother, to do that for her.

If Jake missed it, then that was *his* problem, not hers.

Of course, if Jake missed it, his problem might be that he was blinded by his interest in somebody else. At that thought, I turned away from Bernadette and the officer and looked toward the health-food booth across the aisle.

"Something different about Chloe today, don't you think?" I whispered to Maxine.

She summed it up succinctly. "Pink."

I watched the young lady hand a tiny paper cup of orange liquid to a woman pushing a baby carriage. "What?"

"She's wearing pink." Maxine gave the girl a discreet wave and kept talking to me through the side of her mouth. "Took your advice and went a bit more feminine with her look, is all."

I sized up the pale green gauzy skirt with what looked like watercolor roses splashed along the ankle-length hem and the small pink denim jacket she wore over a white tank top. She hadn't done that for *me*. She had done it for Sammy, and my gut told me it wasn't to please him, but to protect him.

"Her face," I whispered again. "Something is off."

Maxine's hand froze, her fingers still curved in mid-wave. She dropped her arm to her side and narrowed her eyes. "She has a split lip, Odessa. The girl has a split lip."

"And she's not wearing her piercings," I added, in my best objective-girl-detective manner.

"Is that important?" Maxine wrinkled up her nose and squinted all the harder, just tempting me to scold her about looking too hard, the way she had me. "You did ask her to take all but her earrings out when you did her makeover."

"Yeah, but you know she put every last stud and ring right back in the second she flew out that door."

"I don't think she did. Did you see the look on her face when she caught her reflection in the mirror that day? And the way she sparkled when we all fussed over her?"

"What are my Tiara Madres buzzing about over here at the edge of my booth today?" Bernadette leaned gingerly across the glass display case as the officer moved back into the aisle and, still looking at the pad in her hand, began walking in the direction of the health-food booth.

Maxine only had to lift her eyes to indicate Chloe.

"Ahh." Bernadette stood straight and folded her arms. "You noticed it, too?"

"The new wardrobe?" Maxine asked.

Bernadette shook her head. "Her face."

"See, I told you there was something about it." I had moved around to put my back to Chloe, so it wouldn't be so obvious we were standing there scrutinizing her and talking about her behind her...behind *my* back. "And not just the cut lip, either. She's not wearing her piercings."

Bernadette nodded to a passerby, then met my gaze. "She can't."

"Why not?" Maxine, who had admonished me about making bug eyes at Sammy when he wasn't even looking at me, planted both feet firmly in the aisle, put her fists on her hips and stared right at the girl.

"That one side of her face is all puffy." Bernadette swept her fingertips over the top of the display case, as if she'd suddenly discovered a film of dust on the thing. "She couldn't get her eyebrow piercings in if she wanted to."

Maxine scowled and clenched her hands, and even her voice grew tight as she said, "Oh, I wish there was a sinner handy right now."

"What for?" I asked.

"So they could spew all the cusswords I can't permit myself to at that no-good girl-beater Sammy."

Bernadette raised her head to say something, but then her eyes shifted in Chloe's direction, and suddenly she gasped.

At that point, I had to turn to look.

Redheaded Officer Ponytail—of course, she had a real name, but I didn't know it and I did know about her hairstyle, so that was my name for her—the officer stopped dead center in front of Chloe. She flipped back a couple pages in her notepad, then one forward, not speaking.

Chloe retreated one step, then another. She set the tray of paper cups down behind her. If she could have, I think for sure she would have crawled backward, up over the table with all the health-food packages and samples on it, and hidden like a spider in a small, dark corner of the booth itself.

Maxine reached across the display case and grabbed Bernadette by the wrist. "Did you tell that lady officer about Sammy?"

"No, the officer is following up on a routine report by Mrs. Davenport. There's a reporter from the newspaper around, too, trying to figure out if there's a story here."

The officer closed her notebook and pointed to a paper cup.

Chloe reacted, and I think—though I am probably making this up because, like imagining Morty and Helen having a torrid affair as opposed to an inappropriate friendship, it made for a better story later—her hand shook as she handed the police officer the mysterious brew.

The officer lifted the cup, the way they do in the movies when offering a casual toast, then tossed back the drink.

I winced.

Maxine grimaced.

Bernadette muttered, "Yuck" and stuck out her tongue.

The officer, upon tasting the cup's contents, did the same. Wince. Grimace. Yuck.

"If we ever get a second chance with that girl, let's make over those concoctions she peddles," I suggested.

"It's prepackaged," Bernadette said. "The person who actually owns the booth has a franchise or distributorship or whatever they call it. They get the stuff in by the boxload, and Chloe, or whoever is hired to run the booth, just mixes the stuff up with hot water."

"You're kidding." Maxine clucked her tongue in classic for-shame-for-shame fashion. "And they sell that as health food?"

"I think they call it a dietary supplement. That covers a multitude of sins."

"I think there are much better ways to have your sins covered." My focus went from the officer's sour expression to the gritty residue in the cup she threw into the trash bag by Chloe's side. "And speaking of which, if we really ever do get a second chance with that girl, we need to talk to her about the Lord."

"She's hearing it," Bernadette murmured.

"From…?" I shut my eyes. *Please don't say Jake. Please don't say Jake.*

"Abner, for one."

"Oh, yeah. Abner." My eyes popped open again. "I kind of like him."

Bernadette smiled. "Actually, so do I."

I turned to look at Chloe again and tried one of David's tricks—redirection. "Does Chloe like him?"

"She listens to him," Bernadette said.

I smiled. You don't have to be older than dirt like me and Maxine—

"Hey!"

—like me and people who graduated high school the same year I did, got married as many years ago as I did, had kids the same general age as my kids, served as a minister's wife for the same number of years as I did and basically lived a parallel life to mine—

"That's better."

—to know that finding someone who listens to you is a blessing in its own right.

"Is Abner also talking to her about Sammy?" I brushed my fingertips over the side of my face.

"When it comes to Sammy, Chloe shuts down." Bernadette paused long enough to ask a browsing couple if they needed any help, which seemed to scare them clean away.

"Maybe if the three of us talked to her…"

"We've done that." Maxine put her hand on my arm. The thing about Maxine—well, one of many "things" about Maxine—is that she has this amazing sense of timing where people are concerned. *And* where making smart remarks to her best pal is concerned, but that's another "thing." Anyway, Maxine would never suggest we ignore a problem like Chloe's, but unlike me, she is very astute about how to approach individuals. She wins people over through consistency and love, not by my preferred methods—pushing and pulling and the less popular but sometimes effective hairpoofing. Chloe had balked when we tried to talk to her about Sammy, but had at least feigned interest when we spoke about what women should expect from the men who love them and about our own experiences with love. If that opportunity ever presented itself again, I knew, Maxine would jump right in the middle of it with both feet.

"I don't like seeing her hurt any more than you do. But the fact that she has gone to great lengths to hide it tells me she's not ready for us to march up and start in with our advice. It might just drive her away from us and closer to that…that…"

"Snake," I said.

"I wish he were a snake. Then I could go after him with a shovel."

"Maybe that's not such a bad idea."

"Odessa, you *can't* be advocating violence."

"No. I'm just saying maybe if Chloe won't listen to us, we should be going after Sammy."

"With a shovel?"

Another thing about Maxine is, she can have a one-track mind. I cocked my hip and exhaled all in a huff. "With our advice and Christian love."

"I bet the boy would rather we use a shovel." Maxine grinned.

If we had had coffee cups handy, we'd have clinked on it and sealed the deal for poor old Sammy.

Meanwhile, Bernadette was strumming her fingers along a metal pole that supported the canopy over her booth and sighing. "I wish I knew what kind of hold Sammy has over her."

"You don't think it's love?" I asked, then suddenly realized that the very question virtually rang with the kind of naïveté I am always professing that I don't possess. Well, okay, so when it comes to love and the bonds between men and women, I am a regular doe-eyed dope. It's not that I want Chloe to love Sammy. It was just the only explanation I could come up with for a young girl who could do anything, hanging around with a loser like that. And one who *hit* her.

"Go back over the properties of love listed in Corinthians, Odessa. Any mention of stealing or hitting in that passage?"

"I don't mean that it's real love, Maxine. I mean, don't you think she's doing all this because she's convinced herself she is madly in love with the boy?"

"No, I don't." Bernadette stopped drumming her fingers on the pole and grasped it with her hand until her knuckles went white. "I think if it was just emotional, we would all know it. Have you ever heard her talk about Sammy? About having feelings for him, or him for her?"

Once again, Bernadette, my little red-flag finder, had picked up on something the rest of us hadn't.

"There is something else there, below the surface." Bernadette pushed back her shoulders and narrowed her eyes. "And I don't think we are going to reach her for the Lord, *really* reach her, until we know the truth. It's going to take time and patience, but to help a friend, I really don't mind."

I studied her a moment, and realized that maybe I had looked at her all wrong in this respect, as well. Sensing the needs of others in order to serve them, to do whatever she could to help them, might not be her greatest weakness. Maybe, just maybe, serving others was Bernadette's greatest *strength*.

"Until then…" Maxine slapped her palm lightly on the glass, above the tiaras we had sported during our day manning—womanning?—the booth. "Is everything all right here? Did the lady officer have any insights into anything going on at the flea market?"

"Oh! Should I catch up with her and ask her for some input for the action council?" I craned my neck to try to catch a glimpse of her uniform in the crowd, moving away from us down the aisle.

"No, she only focused on the one complaint. Which the officer says they aren't really taking seriously, because Helen

can't say that no one else had access to her card, or something like that."

"Hmm…" I didn't say a thing. I didn't sneak a sidelong
glance at Maxine. I wanted to. But I didn't. However, Helen
Davenport herself had stood on this very spot and accused
me of not doing my job as the chair of my action council
by not keeping abreast of what all went on out here, so I
had to ask, "So the officer was just asking about Helen's
credit card complaint? Nothing else?"

"Yes, what else would Mrs. Davenport have to complain
about?" Bernadette scowled and shook her hair back.

I opened my mouth.

But before I could jump in and explain that I meant other
complaints *like* Helen's, not other complaints *by* Helen, Bernadette rolled her eyes and said, "Of course, given who we
are talking about here, the list of things she could complain
about are endless. Starting with me."

"Why you?" My mouth was already open, and the question came out before I could stop myself.

"According to Mrs. Davenport, I am monopolizing the
minister's time with the 'action council nonsense.'"

"Monopolizing his time, eh?" Maxine leaned in. "Is there
something you haven't told us about?"

"Nope. You were right there, actually. Somehow she
knew about us coming out here on the day of the planned
tour of the grounds. She even knew we'd been up in the
balloon together."

"Oh, really?" She could have learned about that from
Morty, what with all of us showing up in his driveway and
all. Or she might have been watching the rendezvous spot,
waiting for a certain married man to show up, but he

couldn't because, again, we were in his driveway. Or maybe the Reverend just told her about it.

"She thought when Jake got here she would pretty much be his social director and love-connection advisor, but it hasn't worked out that way, and for some reason she blames me."

"She's a poker," I said softly.

"A *what?*" Maxine's whole face scrunched up. "Odessa, have you lost your mind?"

"Why do you always ask me that?" And before she could answer, I put up my hand. "Never mind. I mean she's the kind who pokes you just before you are about to go on-stage to make a speech or have your photo taken in a large group and tells you something that's wrong with your hair or outfit or what have you."

"She does do that, doesn't she? Sort of finds somebody's soft underbelly, their most vulnerable spot, then…"

"Pokes it," I murmured.

Bernadette cocked her head. "I wonder why anyone would do that?"

A few weeks ago, I'd probably have said that she probably honestly thought she was being helpful. But now…

"She doesn't like herself." Maxine stood across the booth from Bernadette, with her own head tilted at the exact same angle as the black-haired young woman.

"What?" I asked.

"She doesn't like herself, and the only way she knows to feel better about herself is to bring other people down."

And bringing down a woman like Jan, the very picture of small-town perfection, would have been her ultimate triumph. It didn't explain everything, but it sort of made a sad kind of sense as to how she could carry on with another woman's husband and still show her face in church. She had to have convinced herself somehow that she deserved Morty and Jan didn't. Well, I know that God hates divorce, and my prayers have been for Jan and Morty to reconcile, but if ever there were two people who did deserve each other…

And even as I thought that, the still, small voice plucked at the hardheartedness of the very thought. I folded my hands together and shut my eyes. "You know, when you put it that way, I kind of feel sorry for Helen Davenport."

"No!" Maxine grabbed me by the upper arm.

"What?" I directed my attention to the place where her dark fingers were sinking into my flesh like a baker's hands in fresh dough. Mental note here—get to a gym and start lifting weights as soon as possible. Not only will it improve my muscle tone and the appearance of my body, it might even keep Maxine from manhandling me.

"Odessa, we are not going down that road again."

"What road? The one to the gym?"

"The—? No, the one that leads to you deciding for both of us that we need to try to *help* somebody that you feel sorry for."

"Oh!" I pursed my lips for just a moment. Honestly, all things considered, we really couldn't take on another foundling at this point. Besides, I did happen to know that David and Jake had Morty and Helen covered for the time being, so Maxine and I would only be interlopers there. There are lots of things I would do if led by faith, but I think I can safely say no one wants me to be an interloper for the Lord. Not *yet,* anyway.

"So, speaking of people I feel that I should be… uh…checking up on…" I began.

"Nice save," Maxine muttered.

"…how is Jan working out?"

"Fine." Bernadette smiled. Actually, she offered a fleeting facial twitch that she clearly wanted to be taken for a smile. "She really is quite thorough."

"But?" Never let it be said that Maxine let a facial twitch keep her from getting to the bottom of things.

"*But,* I have a hard time writing out a paycheck to someone who has made it her goal in life to shut down a vital part of my business. If she succeeds in closing this place…" Bernadette ran her hand over the case with the tiaras in it. "If she succeeds in closing this place, it will probably save me a couple grand this quarter alone."

Maxine went directly for the clarification. "Did you say *save* you a couple grand?"

"You two took over for a day. You know the kind of business I do here. If you add up rental fees, gas, meals, and my time away from my office, and the fact that I rarely actually make any sales or viable contacts out here, I'm losing money almost every weekend."

I looked at Maxine, gave an exaggerated shrug, then turned to Bernadette again. "We did okay."

"Oh, that's right." She touched the spot just between her eyes, as if she were pressing a button to retrieve some information. "Y'all did pretty good. I meant to ask you—what is your secret?"

Well, *that* was just the question Maxine and I had been waiting all of our lives to hear!

"You have to sell to the people who are here to buy. People don't show up at a big old flea market to plan their weddings and formal celebrations. They come for fun."

I chimed in with "And Royal Service Hostess Queen partyware." I chimed in.

"Bernadette, you have to sell more fun."

"Luckily, that happens to be Maxine's and my specialty." I gave the girl a wink.

Maxine headed straight for the display case.

"The secret to getting away with wearing a tiara is not just sticking it up on your head and plastering on a big, phony smile. No, ma'am." Minutes later, I was practically standing in the middle of the aisle, doing a pitch that would have made a carnival barker proud. "To really pull off the look, you have to have the attitude to match. It's about sparkle. It's about elegance. It's about knowing you deserve queenly headgear and all the attention that goes with it."

"And you know how we know all that, ladies and gentlemen?"

"Tell them, Maxine."

"Because we were not born yesterday!" she shouted to everyone's delight.

"And we are not quite ready for the junk heap yet," I called out in response.

"Because, friends, sisters and troublemakers…" Maxine held out her open hand to me.

I happily added, "And you know who you are!"

"…we are all wonderfully and fearfully made." Maxine raised her hands and cocked her head to make her tiara glint and glimmer in the summer sun.

"And God don't make junk!" we both said, laughing.

"Well, His children sure do!" No, it wasn't me or Maxine that shouted that above the laugher of the onlookers gathered around Bernadette's bridal-supply booth. It was Jan Belmont, malcontent. "And that might not be so bad if they didn't drag their junk out here and create a giant eyesore, health risk and breeding ground for criminal activity when they do."

The crowd mostly stood there stunned until Chloe broke through and began to applaud. Then, here and there, a few people joined in.

"I don't think there would be even that much support for her if they knew she aimed to close this place rather than just clean it up," Maxine muttered.

"That's it, Jan," Bernadette called out. "You are *fired*."

Jan set down her sign made of yellow poster board stapled to a picket. A picket she had probably bought right here at the flea market, because where else do you get protest sign pickets in Castlerock, Texas? She turned to Bernadette. "If you thought about this for one second, you would know I was doing you a favor."

Of course, Jan was doing *herself* a favor. Maxine and I knew that. But everyone else—and people had now begun to converge from all corners of our five fabulous acres— only knew what they saw. They hadn't heard the whole story, and given the situation, they weren't likely to pay attention to anything but the big showdown it seemed was coming.

And it was.

If only Jan hadn't been carrying that big ol' sign that, when she lowered it to yell at us, obscured her face and upper body, then Morty and Helen would have seen her kicking up a ruckus in the last place on earth they ever ex-

pected her to be—which I'm sure is why they chose it as
their meeting spot—as they came strolling arm in arm down
the aisle. If only Helen hadn't filed a police report about
her credit card and followed up by calling the local paper
to complain about the oversight committee not doing our
job, the lone photographer for said paper would have been
off shooting pictures of prizewinning goats. If only Maxine and I hadn't stuck those tiaras on her heads and then
acted as if we had a reason for them to be there by putting
ourselves in the middle of the fray, we would have been else-
where when the camera flashed.

If only...

Yes, be careful what you wish for. You just might get it.
And if you happen to have on a tiara or be carrying on a
tryst or trying to tear down something many people love
because you are desperate to fix your own failings, there may
be a photographer from the local paper there to record it
all on film. And, along with everyone else in town, you may
come away with a not-so-pretty picture of yourself.

Chapter Sixteen

They say there is no such thing as bad publicity. Do me a favor, will you? Next time you see the "they" who said that, kick them in the shins for me, will you?

Now y'all know I am not really advocating violence here. But I want to make myself perfectly clear, because it seems that—much to my dismay—in the town of Castlerock and most especially in the vicinity of the Five Acres of Fabulous Finds Flea Market, I have become something of a role model.

Yes, I meant to say *role*, as in a part that one might play in the greater whole. Not *roll*, as in jelly or "Pass me those homemade dinner…" or "Shake, rattle and…." *Me.* Odessa started-out-all-of-this-with-good-intentions-just-trying-to-get-a-nice-girl-a-shot-at-a-date-with-a-single-minister Pepperdine. A role model.

And apparently not a very good one.

That's the way my David tells it.

And a handful of our former parishioners agreed. At least half a dozen of them took the trouble, after that photo ran in the paper, to contact David and ask him what was going on in our home that I would pull such a stunt. He assured them the problem was not in our *home,* it was in his *wife,* or rather the woman who looked like his wife but had begun to act, to his way of thinking, like a perfect stranger. It was the first time in our married life that David had ever told another person he thought I was perfect.

I've tried saying that a couple different ways, but it always comes out just a little bit sad.

The phone rang some over at Maxine's house, too. Reverend Nash told the callers that he thought it was quite a nice likeness of his wife and thanked them for taking the time to call. He found the whole deal pretty funny and told Maxine she ought to not just buy that tiara but wear it around town so people would stop her and ask for her autograph.

He said—and the letters to the editor tended to support his line of thinking—that we had shown the world we still had a lot of fire in us. Yes, Maxine gave him the lecture about not using the word *still.* He said it was the world's word, not his. When folks saw us, they needed to be reminded that we *still* were a force to be reckoned with, and lots of them could learn from our example.

He even suggested we open our own booth at the flea market, dispensing advice and breaking up the occasional catfight.

I would have liked the idea, if I had thought I would have anything worth saying to anyone ever again.

★ ★ ★

"Hey, Mrs. Pepperdine! Mrs. Cooke-Nash! Come to take on all challengers for the title of Queen of the Lady Flea Market Wrestlers?" I suppose that Sammy thought he was being his usual charming self, but his appeal was lost on me now.

I shied away from looking at him, and at everyone else Sammy's teasing had alerted to our presence.

"Now, that ain't one bit funny, young man," Maxine called out, putting her hand protectively on my shoulder. She laughed under her breath. "We are trying to keep things low-key here. We certainly do not want to draw attention to ourselves as the ladies y'all saw in the newspaper kicking behinds and taking names the other day."

With every word, her voice grew louder, her shoulders went back a little further and her head rose higher.

"Are you kidding?" Sammy sort of loped along sideways to keep abreast of us. His flyers flapped with his every move, and he wore a big ol' grin. "C'mon. That was wicked awesome, the two of you right in the middle of things! I was right about you, Ms. Pepperdine, you've still…you've got fire in you!"

I managed a weak smile at that, but kept my gaze fixed on the gate ahead.

"My boss said to tell you, if I ever saw you back at the flea market again, I should tell you that you've earned yourselves a complimentary tethered balloon ride."

"Said it before and I'll say it again. Not enough hot air in all of Texas—including what's spouting out of you right now, young man—to lift me off the ground." Maxine held her hand up, and her bracelets went bouncing all the way down to her elbow. "But Odessa here, today just might be her day."

I glared at my friend. A one-eyed glare, with a mean set to my mouth.

She laughed.

"Y'all think it over. We can send you up any time you ask." Sammy went back to handing out his flyers.

It was hard to stay mad at the boy—particularly with Maxine chuckling about it all like that and him saying I had fire in me. Hmm. Having fire in you, at my age, is usually a problem. In fact, whole aisles in the drugstore are dedicated to fixing that problem. So I had a hard time now thinking anyone on these premises or anywhere in the town would think that was a good thing. But Sammy certainly did.

He was wrong. But it was sure sweet of him to say it.

Maybe there was hope for him still.

I lifted my eyes to the balloon billowing overhead. There was always hope, right?

I needed to believe that.

It had been two weeks now since we'd dared to show our faces at the flea market. No, that's not really the case. It had taken two weeks for *me* to get up the nerve to return to the scene of the crime—or the scene of the *crown,* as Maxine now likes to call it.

By then I had to do it, because it was the last weekend Bernadette planned to have her booth out here.

"I can't believe she's closing up shop," I said a short time later as I pointed to the sign in front of the At Your Service booth that read Everything Must Go.

"She's not closing up shop, Odessa. Just the opposite. She's expanding her hours and getting a real store downtown, not trying to run it out of her house any longer. And you know who she has to thank for that?"

"Abner the tattoo artist?" I glanced over my shoulder, trying to catch Chloe's eye.

That girl stood handing out samples at the health-food booth, in her usual place. But not in her usual attire. Today she wore a fresh green T-shirt, a denim skirt and a wide embroidered belt. The only color in her hair was the color *of* her hair and—I promise you, this is not just wishful thinking on my part—it had a little height to it in the back. She looked just darling.

I gave her a quick wave.

She smiled. Her whole face lit up, just a smidge.

Maybe I hadn't messed up everyone's life entirely. I sighed.

"What about Abner?" Bernadette's face didn't light up, but she did lift her eyes at the mention of the name.

Feeling a tad better about things, I ran my fingers along the top of the sign and said, in as upbeat a voice as I could, "Oh, I was just commenting on how nice it was of him to let you know about the space opening up in that building downtown."

"Wasn't it, though?" Bernadette pulled out a roll of small round neon-orange stickers and slipped it onto her wrist like a piece of costume jewelry. "He even offered to give me a discount on tattoos!"

I gripped the corner of the sign I had been touching. "Bernadette, you're not thinking of—"

"Not for me!" She peeled a sticker off of the roll and stuck it onto a small white photo album. "The discounts are for my customers. You know, to commemorate their wedding, or whatever."

"Sure." Maxine nodded. "Nothing says forever like a flaming skull on your shoulder blade."

"For *me,* I think I could convince Abner to do a tattoo for free."

"Bernadette!"

"I just said that to see the look on your face, Odessa." Her eyes sparkled. I didn't know when I'd last seen Bernadette Alvarez's eyes sparkle. Usually they darted back and forth and had a dark quality about them, sheltered, anxious, cautious. This was not the same girl I had spoken to weeks ago about the arrival of the single minister. This was not the woman who'd thought Chloe Morgan was too hard-boiled for us to reach. "And it was worth it, too."

I rolled my eyes. "Nice to know I'm worth something to somebody."

"You're worth the world to me," a soft voice said over my shoulder.

I knew the voice immediately, even if the volume and the message seemed exceptionally out of place. "Jan!"

"I can't believe you're out here, after—" Maxine just blurted it out, and she couldn't seem to stop herself until she literally slapped her hand over her own mouth.

Jan didn't flinch. "Well, what could I do? Hide in a cave? Act as if everything was just hunky-dory? I tried doing *that,* without much success, from the first day I realized my husband was climbing onto our roof to talk on the phone to another woman."

"That's what he was doing when he fell?"

She lowered her head and fidgeted with the large plastic container in her hands. "That's what he was doing when I popped my head out the window that day and asked him what he was doing."

Maxine and I closed in around her. I wanted to...*do* something. Pat her back. Lay my arm around her shoulders. I just...I just didn't know if she would accept that from me. I didn't know if that would be the thing that pushed her over the brink and caused her to break down here, where she had already borne so much indignity.

"In the hospital that evening, he confessed everything. The phone calls. The meetings at the flea market, where they thought I'd never see them and where they would remain in public so they wouldn't be tempted to..." She drew a shuddering breath and did not look at any of us.

I bowed my head, too, only not from shame or pain, but to say a prayer for her and her marriage. I just didn't know what else to do. I didn't know of any other way to be of any help.

"An emotional affair, he called it," she whispered. "As if that somehow would make it all hurt less."

"Oh, Jan." Bernadette chewed her lower lip. "You didn't have to come out here today if you..."

"Yes. I did. Every person has to face the truth about their lives at some point. Either I'm a woman of faith and conviction, who relies on the Lord for her hope and strength, or I'm a big fat phony. And y'all know how much I would hate being a big *fat* anything." She set the plastic container down on Jan's counter and mustered up a smile. "And I brought brownies!"

"Aren't those for the church booth?" I asked.

"I already made my contribution there." She waved toward the booth across the way. "These are for us."

"Us?" Maxine had that look about her. That "you mean there is a chance I will get chocolate out of this deal?" look.

"I asked Jan to pitch in out here today." Bernadette pried the lid from the brownie container, and the moist aroma filled the air. "I'm anticipating business will be brisk."

"It's picked up?" I asked, raising my voice above the din of the shoppers pushing past.

"It always does when you slash prices to the bone. All those people who could have kept your store afloat with a few small sales along the way just love to stop by and tell you how much they hate to see you go. Then they finally buy something—only it's seventy-five-percent off."

Maxine, who already had a brownie halfway to her lips, lowered it and crinkled her freckled nose. "I feel a twinge of guilt comin' on, Odessa. How about you?"

"Eat your brownie. The guilt will pass."

"Oh, I didn't mean you two." Bernadette spread her hands out. "In fact, I would like to make a gift of those tiaras you both admired and modeled so, um…*distinctively*. It's my way of saying thank-you for all you've done."

"All we've done? Like what?" I covered my eyes with my hand, my head down. "Closing down your business? Embarrassing Jan in front of everyone?"

"You didn't embarrass me, I embarrassed myself." Jan spoke in a voice that was hushed and hoarse with emotion. "Big time. And I deserved everything I got, too."

"No, I don't believe that," I murmured.

"I deserved everything I brought on myself," she corrected. "As for the rest of it…"

She didn't have to say the rest of what. We all knew she meant Morty and Helen and the problems in her marriage.

"As for the rest of it... I won't say I'm not angry and hurt, but...I've known that man since I was a kid, really. I have loved him and lived with him and fought with him and failed with him and I am not ready to let go of him." She began to weep softly. So softly that a passerby who could not see the tears on her cheeks might not have known it at all except for the subtle shake of her shoulders and the catch in her breath. "We're seeking counseling. We are going to try to work through it."

I opened my arms to her without thinking. I just...I just wanted to draw her close and let her know how very sorry I was about everything that had happened and how much I cared for her. "I will pray for you every day, my friend."

"Thank you," she whispered. "It's been so long since I felt that anyone was on my side. You don't know what it means."

But I did. In that split second, I knew exactly what it meant. I knew then why I had so cherished my friendship with Maxine. It wasn't because we shared a love of bacon, or a common background, or even because we both wanted to collect the entire set of Royal Service partyware, the Hostess Queen pattern. It was because, after too many years of being the minister's wife, of often having to raise our children on our own, of knowing anything we said or did or got photographed and stuck in the paper wearing would be subject to scrutiny. In a life where we felt like the people we cared for the most could, in an instant, turn against us, we had found someone to be on our side. No matter what.

And that was what, in the end, we had given Jan. And... I turned and looked at my Bernadette, who was aglow with a new kind of confidence. We had been on her side, too, when the people she had done so much for not only pushed her out of the way but wanted to keep her out of the running. For anything worth running for.

And then there was Chloe. I don't think anyone had ever been on her side. Sammy, maybe. Or maybe he had charmed her into thinking so, for his own reasons. That might have been why she felt the need to protect him. He was the one she thought would stand by her, even when she did not think she deserved it.

I blinked and suddenly realized my eyes were damp.

"Take the tiara, Odessa." Bernadette slid the key into the lock and turned it with a firm *click*.

"Only if you will let us pay for them," Maxine insisted. "Full price."

"For you." Bernadette pulled free the larger of two and handed it across the glass.

"You should wear it, Odessa," Maxine took it from Bernadette's long fingers and gently placed it on my head, careful not to flatten out my hairdo. "It looks so darling on you."

"And for you." Bernadette brought out the second one and held it out to Maxine.

She slipped it on and asked me how it looked.

"Like it's finally where it belongs," I said, though I couldn't resist adjusting it a teeny bit.

"Oh, look, the tiara ladies are back again!" someone called from down the aisle.

I looked up and found Chloe laughing and giving us a thumbs-up. My little lamb, with just a hint of air in her hair. My heart swelled. Jesus said, only not in these words, it is always too soon to give up on someone.

"I have some fliers." Bernadette pulled some pink and

white papers from the briefcase she had leaning against one of the chairs in her booth. "If you two want to help out, you certainly would be perfect to walk through the place handing them out."

"Or maybe we could go and stand at the gate," I suggested.

Maxine took the papers and began to follow me. "Odessa, what do you have in mind?"

"If you can't beat them, charm them." I gave a regal wave to the curious onlookers and marched with purpose straight ahead. "We are going to go talk to Sammy Wilson."

Jan had said it: *Either I'm a woman of faith and conviction, who relies on the Lord for her hope and strength, or I'm a big fat phony.*

And a big fat phony did not deserve tiaras or to have so many good women on her side. I still didn't know if I had anything worth saying, but I knew a message that was worth sharing with a young man who had gone astray. And I didn't see why a woman who still had a little fire in her shouldn't be the one to share it with him.

Chapter Seventeen

So that was that. We had made a difference, and we had the new compassionate Jan, the new confident Bernadette and the new cleaned-up Chloe to show for it. Now, if we could just get the men in their lives sorted out, all would be well.

"Not another project for us, Odessa!"

"Maxine, do I have to point out to you that that minister is still single?"

"Oh, no. That won't do."

"And we still think that Sammy might be bullying our girl."

"And *that* won't do times two."

"Times two?"

"Me and you, Odessa."

"We'll just have to set our minds to sorting out Sammy and if we can't do that, then to getting Miss Chloe Morgan—"

"Excuse me, did you say Chloe Morgan?"

It was that redheaded lady police officer with the ponytail who interrupted Maxine interrupting me. She had a no-nonsense look to her, she was clearly asking in an official capacity, and she was armed, so I decided not to take issue with her bad manners.

"Yes." I didn't say anything else.

Maxine, whose winning smile had suddenly lost its luster, raised an eyebrow at me.

I knew what she was asking in that sly, silent way of hers. "For once in my life, I decided not to volunteer too much," I whispered.

"Somebody get me a chair." She placed the back of her hand against her forehead in one of the worst displays of acting I'd seen in quite a while, and remember, as a minister's wife I have overseen hundred of Christmas plays and youth rally skit nights. "I think I might faint."

We had reached the gate and begun eyeballing our boy Sammy when the woman intruded on our conversation.

"Yes, Officer…" I lowered my head to read the name on her tag. "Officer Phife."

"Really?" Maxine asked, and she, too, checked the name tag.

"Bet you get a lot of jokes about that," I said.

She frowned. "Why?"

I shut my eyes.

Maxine sighed.

Old enough for the state of Texas to entrust her with upholding the law, but too young to know about Deputy Barney Fife from *The Andy Griffith Show*. It made me feel positively ancient.

"I wondered, since you seemed to know Chloe Morgan,

if you could tell me if she is working at her usual booth today?" The young woman motioned toward the open gate.

"Is she in trouble?" Maxine took a step toward that gate.

"I'll just go look for her." The officer turned away.

Suddenly I felt real helpful. "We can take you right to her."

"That won't be necessary. Please." She said "Please," but she held up her hand in a way that said *No thank you*.

"She doesn't want us to tag along," Maxine muttered in my ear. Then she stuck a broad grin on her face and gave the woman a wave. "Okay then. You do that."

I waved, too, wondering what she must have thought of the pair of us standing there grinning like fools in nurses' shoes, jersey dresses, windproof puffy hairdos and tiaras. I didn't let myself linger overlong on the matter, as I had other issues to deal with. Still waving, I put my head practically on Maxine's shoulder and whispered my plan. "We'll count to ten after she gets out of sight, then make a beeline for Chloe's booth anyway."

Maxine slapped me on the back—not like fellows do, not a great big wallop, but more a warm tap to show her support. "You are in a much saucier mood then when we came through here a little bit ago."

"When we walked through here a little bit ago, I thought it was the last time."

"The last—?"

"That's what I told David when I left. That I wouldn't even have come out today, if not for Bernadette closing out and all."

"And what did he say?'

"Nothing."

"Nothing?"

"Yes. He just lowered his paper and looked at me. Sort of funny-like, too."

"What did you do?"

"What could I do?" Stand there and listen to him tell me how much I've changed? Or wait out a lecture on what happened last time I came to the flea market, what people expect of his wife and family *and* how much I've changed? Or, worst of all, have him shake his head and say something that made it perfectly clear he hadn't heard a word I'd said? "I gave him a kiss and hurried off. I was already late getting off to pick you up."

"Well, I didn't tell my husband that this might be my last time out here. But I suppose if that's what you decide, then maybe…maybe we can think of some other place to go to…"

I raised my hand. "Okay, I just lost track of that police officer, Maxine. Start counting."

"Me, count? What are you going to do?"

I glanced at the handouts Bernadette had asked us to distribute.

"One."

Then I scanned the crowd for any sign of Sammy.

"Two."

He helped a young couple into the balloon. Then, as it rose into the air, with the ruddy-faced owner in the basket and at the controls, he twisted around and caught my eye.

"Three."

He raised his hand, checked the situation overhead, then took a step our way. "Hey, Mrs. Pepperdine, Mrs. Cooke-Nash! What was up with the police lady?"

"Four."

"She was asking after Chloe." Well, I *had* come out here to discuss the girl with him, why not jump right into the matter?

"Chloe?" He stopped in his tracks.

"Five."

"What did she want to know about Chloe for?" I couldn't actually see him sweat, but he did fidget.

Now, this boy is a cool one. Most charmers are. They don't like to let anyone see them sweat...or squirm...or fidget. So right away I had a powerfully bad feeling in the pit of my stomach about what might really be going on here with our balloon ballyhooer, our local law enforcement and our Chloe.

"Six." Maxine went right on, as if she'd taken no notice of Sammy standing there asking questions, but her eyes shifted to catch my gaze and she frowned to show she didn't like the way this was going. "Seven."

"I...uh..." Eyes on the gate where the officer had disappeared, Sammy took one step backward, and then another. Then he stumbled, not over one of the many rocks or ruts or into one of the puddles that always seemed to muck up the entryway, but over a pair of shabby, scuffed shoes.

I would have known those feet anywhere. "Reverend Cordell, what brings you out to the Five Acres of Fabulous Finds?"

"I came to lend a little support to Bernadette on her last weekend here."

"Oh?" I waggled my eyebrows at Maxine.

"Eight!" she said, giving me a thumbs-up.

I opened my mouth to tell her that she didn't have to keep counting, but before I could make a noise, something slammed straight into me and knocked the breath clean out of me.

"Chloe!" Jake reached out to help the girl up where she had fallen. "Are you okay?"

He didn't ask me if I was okay. But then, I was still on both feet. The only damage I seemed to have sustained was that my tiara had gotten knocked crooked. Of course, his lack of concern did ding my pride a bit, which was why I didn't rush to straighten myself out, you know, just so everyone could see that even though I was the classic immovable object to Chloe's irresistible—meaning she was moving at an out-of-control speed, not that she was tempting beyond all ability to withstand—force, I hadn't gotten off unscathed.

"Nine."

"You can stop counting now, Maxine," I finally said.

She held up both hands, her fingers splayed.

"Yes, I get it. Ha, ha. You're not saying it. But you have to have the last word." I held up my ten fingers to mirror hers. "You can be so stubborn sometimes, you know that?"

"I know that Officer Phife is running this way and she is undoing the strap on her stun gun."

I turned, my hands still raised, and gasped.

Jake straightened up, still holding Chloe by the wrist.

Sammy hurried back to the balloon and began calling something up to his boss. I could not hear what it was over the *whoosh* of the flames that heated the air in the balloon.

Chloe tugged herself free from Jake's grasp and struggled to find a clear path away from us through the gathering crowd.

"Stay where you are, Ms. Morgan," Officer Phife called out, but she didn't unharness her nonlethal weapon.

"It's all right, Chloe." Jake only had to extend his long arm to contain the petite Chloe.

She put her hands on his sleeve, as if she might push him away, then stopped and turned around.

"Sir, if you could just step away from Ms. Morgan." The officer came up to them then, but made no threatening moves.

"I'd like to stay close, if you don't mind," he said.

The officer crossed her arms and raised her head. "It's not really your concern."

"I think it is my concern. I'm Chloe's—"

"What's going on?" Bernadette arrived on the scene breathless, her thick hair mussed and falling over her face. "Officer Phife walked up, and Chloe just cut and ran."

Maxine threw her hands up in the air, then brought them down against her thighs with a sharp smack.

"My thoughts exactly," I said softly. The girl might have a feeling for other people's feelings, but she was clueless when it came to timing. If she had waited just ten seconds longer, we would have learned the end of that sentence. *I'm Chloe's…what, exactly?*

The redheaded lady in the brown uniform opened her arms wide. "Nothing to see, folks."

"Nothing to see?" Maxine made a point of looking at all there was to see around us, starting with my whomper-jawed tiara. "Is she kidding?"

"Move along, please." Officer Phife waved her hands in the air, the way you see people do to shoo away pigeons.

All the people pretty much stayed put.

"Chloe, whatever is going on, I won't leave you to face it alone," Jake said.

Unlike Jake, Sammy had entirely retreated from the girl. Granted, he had work to do, hauling the basket down to the ground again and helping the occupants out. Even as he directed the couple exiting the balloon area to watch their steps, he kept his eyes on Chloe and the police officer.

"I just want to ask you a few questions is all, ma'am," Officer Phife nodded toward the parking lot.

Jake inched forward.

But it was Bernadette who spoke up. "Is she under arrest?"

"I didn't do it!" Chloe flung her arms out, her lips pale and trembling.

My stomach knotted. "Do *what,* sweetie?"

She spun around to face me, and all the fight seemed to drain right out of her. "One time. I did swipe some cards one time. But you saw me and I got scared and couldn't go through with it. Y'all have been so nice to me, and done so much, and when you said you saw me steal those numbers…"

"Steal?" She might as well have said it in Latin. There was just no context for the idea of our Chloe stealing anything, and I had no understanding of how or why anyone would steal numbers. *"Numbers?"*

"Credit card numbers," Bernadette murmured.

"Like Helen Davenport's," Jake said. "It's a scam. A con. And the flea market is the perfect place for it, because different people come every week. No one notices if a new seller pops up or an old one drops out."

The officer did not confirm or deny. "Please, sir, leave this for the police."

"This is Sammy's doing." I looked to Maxine, then Bernadette, then Jake, for support of my theory—and got it. Chloe would not meet my eyes, another kind of evidence of the truth of my accusation. "He's the one behind the whole thing."

"Pardon me, ma'am—you believe you know who's running the identity-theft ring?"

"It wasn't identity theft," Chloe protested. Cheeks red and voice strained, she spoke to each of us in turn. "Sammy said it was just small stuff. They did it for kicks, because it was so boring to work out here. They just get the numbers and charge a little bit here and there. It was so small that people didn't even notice it and paid it anyway. Or if they did notice, they called the card company and they took care of it. No big deal. Sammy said if they didn't care, why should we?"

I didn't know what broke my heart more, the desperate sincerity in the girl's justification or that she was still defending that rat Sammy. "It was the young man who worked at the balloon ride." I turned to where the young man had stood not thirty seconds earlier. "His name is Sammy Wilson and he…"

And he was gone.

"Not to pull out the old cliché—" a man in the crowd tapped Officer Phife on the shoulder and pointed through the gate and the sprawling marketplace beyond "—but he went thataway."

Officer Phife turned slowly. Her once-determined expression faded. Her shoulders slumped. "Five acres loaded with people and clutter and stuff."

I blinked, and suddenly it was like seeing the place

through Jan's eyes. It was a mess. Big and noisy and dirty and chaotic.

"It would be impossible to find him in there. He could duck into all sorts of places. He knows everyone and everything, inside and out." I thought of how he had appeared from nowhere on the day we had come to unload the goods for Bernadette's booth. "And he can just slip out and through the trees where you can't see anyone…"

"Not before he warns everyone in his ring to run." The officer sighed.

"And leaves Chloe to take the blame for it," Jake muttered.

"Me?" She looked over her shoulder at Jake, who nodded, his eyes somber behind his wire-rimmed glasses.

"You don't have to take the blame for it all." Bernadette said for her friend what she had never seemed to grasp for herself. "You can just tell them where to find Sammy, and they can send a squad car over."

"I don't know where to find him. He used to live out of his car, then he stole my car and lived out of it for a couple days, then he made friends in a bar who let him stay at their apartment for a few days, but they just threw him out."

Jake poked two fingers underneath the lenses of his glasses and rubbed his eyes as he said through gritted teeth, "So, you're saying you don't know how to find Sammy."

Maxine stepped forward, her hand raised skyward. "She might not. But I do."

"Of course!" Bernadette clapped her hands. "We could see the whole grounds from up there, and if we used a cell phone we could direct someone right to him."

Officer Phife grabbed her radio and called for backup.

"C'mon, let's go." Chloe grabbed Jake by the arm and tugged him toward the balloon.

"I'd rather you stayed put, young lady." Officer Phife, who was maybe three years older than Chloe, managed to give the request an air of absolute authority. "I won't be able to bear all the ribbing if I lose track of two suspects within a few minutes of each other."

"I'll stay here with her while you go after Sammy, Officer. I think I can contain her, and as for being responsible for her, I'm her minister."

Officer Phife nodded her thanks and acceptance of the deal.

"Okay, now, can you commandeer a hot-air balloon in the name of the law? Because I don't have any cash to pay for a ride on me."

Officer Phife held her hands up, in either a sign of helplessness or a gesture meant to show she had no idea what she could do in this case or how to go about doing it.

"Here." Jake reached into his back pocket.

"Never you mind, Reverend." Maxine slapped at his wrist. "We're due a free ride."

"We, Maxine?" I eyed the billowing fabric.

"By *we,* I mean *you,* Odessa. Like I said before, there's not enough hot air in all of Texas to get me up in one of those. Now scat. Sammy is getting away!"

Chapter Eighteen

Maxine here. Do not tell me you are looking for Odessa's homey little musings here.

I mean, now? I don't think so!

This is a defining moment for Odessa. And, in many ways, for Bernadette and Chloe and, if all goes well, that sneaky snake Sammy, too. Now is not the time for setting up scenes or introducing ideas or muddling through Odessa's thought process.

This is the time for action.

I have nothing more to say.

Oh, wait… Yes, I do.

Up, up and away!

Where we normally would have picked our way gingerly through the people and the gravel and the mess, Bernadette and I charged right on through, our objective ever in sight. I don't know if it was our approach or the still-odd-angled tiara on my head that did it, but as soon as we got within earshot, the ruddy-faced man perked up and hollered our way.

"Hello! I can't tell y'all how pleased I am to have one of the queens of our fair flea market joining us for a short ride above the premises today!"

Everybody looked.

I suspect that was his intention.

"Call me Junior." He thrust his hand out to me.

"Thank you...uh..." The man was older than me, which meant he was waaaaay too old for *anyone* to call him Junior. I gave his hand a hearty shake. "Thank you. My friend and I wanted to take you up on your offer of a free ride—and fast!"

"Your friend?" He motioned toward Maxine, who was stuffing everything back into her fanny pack after rooting around to get her cell phone, which she had given to Officer Phife.

"Look, I'll explain it all on the way up," I said, tugging at the man's sleeve. "Let's just get going."

Now, you may think I was so anxious because I wanted to catch that Sammy, and that was partly true. I also figured that the longer I had to think about what I was about to do, the more likely it was that I'd chicken out. So in I climbed, and Bernadette after me.

After her, in got Mr. Call-Me-Junior, his voice booming out instructions about keeping my arms and legs inside the basket like I was suddenly going to hook my foot over the edge and climb out in midair.

The flame whooshed.

The basket jostled.

My heart stopped.

Suddenly that midair exit didn't seem so far-fetched.

And then we lifted up, up, up. Gentle. Smooth. The summer sun shone down on us through the gorgeous colors of the balloon. Blue and yellow and pink and white and green all flooded over my skin. I laughed. What had I been afraid of all this time, I wondered?

And then I looked down and remembered.

Everyone was looking up, right at me. At me and Bernadette, but of the two of us, I was the one married to a minister. I was the one who had already embarrassed herself and enough other people that she should know better. And I was the one wearing the tiara.

My hand went to it. I tried to pull it free. The teeth of the comb on the glittering band dug into my scalp, and it dawned on me that I could give it a yank and return to the ground humiliated and bald or I could let it be.

"You scan the parking lot." Bernadette, who had spent the few seconds it took for us to ascend filling Junior in on our plan, directed my attention to the grassy field filled with cars. "I'll see if I can spot Sammy in the flea market proper."

I wanted to protest. Let's face it, in the small, small world of balloon-borne flea market surveillance, casing the booths is definitely the glamour job. But I knew that if I said anything, I stood a good chance of having it pointed out that at Bernadette's age she would have the better eyesight. So I dutifully turned my eyes to the rows of trucks and SUVs and minivans and junker cars and our sedan and… "Wait a minute!"

"Did you find him?" Bernadette swung around, the cell phone pressed to her ear, and the basket swayed. "Do you see Sammy?"

I grabbed the edge. "No, I see…" Something far more curious, to my way of thinking. "I see my husband, David."

"We are looking for Sammy," Bernadette said, loud and distinct, as if she thought she might be dealing with a sudden-onset case of the condition Gallina Roja had—the inability to concentrate or understand complex instructions in English. She placed her back to me and kept looking.

I tried not to keep looking at David, winding his way through the cars to the gate, but I couldn't help it. Why was he out here? What did he want? Had he seen me?

I ducked.

Yes, I know. It was a silly thing to do, but I couldn't help it.

I ducked and sent the basket jerking around like a…a…a balloon on a tether!

"Odessa, what are you doing?"

If the movement of the balloon hadn't drawn the attention of everyone around, Bernadette's shriek surely would have.

I poked my head up.

Laughter greeted me.

I found David down below. His head was tipped back and his mouth was open, but I couldn't tell if it was in laugher or a groan.

Caught, I knew I had to make up my mind then and there. Was I going to go on trying to be the Odessa who had given up her Royal Service Hostess Queen partyware? Or was I going to be the Odessa I had always been deep down inside? The one who had befriended Maxine and played mama shepherd to a flock of wayward lambs? The one who had climbed into a balloon because she knew it was the right thing to do?

I stuck my hand up, straightened my tiara and made up my mind. "Hi, David! Can't talk now! I'm helping out in a police pursuit!"

I wished I was close enough to see his face.

But, in fact, it was not my husband's face I was supposed to be looking for, it was—

"Sammy!" Bernadette and I both called out the name at the same time. Seems the ruckus I had been making had drawn even his attention. He had stopped next to a pet-supply booth, and he raised his head, shaded his eyes and stared with his mouth open.

Bernadette spoke softly into the phone.

And before she even finished talking, Officer Phife had snuck up behind Sammy and thrown him to the ground. She might be a little gal, but she is swift and strong.

I wonder if she has a boyfriend?

"Odessa!" Maxine threw her arms open wide as the basket came bumping down to the ground again.

And just that quick, the crowd closed around us, offering congratulations and asking us what had we been doing up there anyway?

"She was just being herself," came a deep, familiar voice from the back. And then David pushed his way through to wrap me in a big, tight hug.

I started to ask him why he was there, but a commotion made everyone turn and look toward the gate, where Officer Phife was making her way along with Sammy in handcuffs! A second officer, a nice man who I think might have been a good match for the redheaded young woman, came up and escorted Sammy off.

I gasped and, like the rest of our little group, pivoted around to face Chloe—just in time to catch her trying to sneak away.

Jake grabbed her by the arm. "You have to go with Officer Phife, Chloe. Answer a few questions. You may even face some charges."

"Charges?" Her eyes grew wide. "I didn't do any—" She stopped herself right there and changed tactics. "I thought that Christians liked to preach the importance of forgiveness."

"We do. We also are pretty keen on following the laws of the land." He moved his hand to her shoulder, so it looked more as if he was offering sympathy than turning her over to the police. "Forgiveness doesn't change the fact that you have to take responsibility for your actions."

"And whatever happens, Chloe—" Bernadette laid her hand on the other shoulder "—we'll be right by your side. That is, *I* will. If you need a place to stay while all this gets sorted out, my house is open to you. Likewise, I feel that Abner won't turn you away if you need a job."

I don't know if it was the name Abner on Bernadette's lips, or the firmness of her commitment, but Jake pushed his glasses up on the bridge of his nose and studied her in a most protective way. "You might want to consider that offer a minute, Bernadette. We can find a church to do all that for Chloe, but for you to get involved—"

"I *am* involved. Chloe is my friend."

"I am?" Chloe's features softened.

"You are." Bernadette hugged the girl.

So did Maxine.

I did, too. "Call us from the station when they're done with you, and someone will come by to get you."

Officer Phife said a few words to Chloe, and she nodded and followed along.

I gave David's hand a squeeze.

He responded in kind.

Jake watched the young girl leave, then turned to the woman at his side. "Bernadette, I hope you realize what taking a public stance to help Chloe could mean for you in the church. I will back you, of course, but it could get touchy, since this also involved Helen Davenport."

One, two, three heartbeats passed, where I suspect we all—well, Maxine, Bernadette and me, at least—thought about Helen Davenport's right to judge anyone else *and* about the damage she could do should she decide to take offense at to Bernadette's decision. The fact that no one said a word was a silent testament to our faith and to the fact that our ministers were standing right there and would have pulled us back in line so fast…

"Anyway, it's the kind of thing that could be divisive in the church, especially when they've just brought me in and I haven't had time to establish myself." Jake shuffled his worn-out shoes in the mud.

Bernadette's gaze met Jake's. "Are you asking me not to help Chloe?"

He did not reply.

I wet my lips, thinking maybe I should say something, but it was the man standing at my side who stepped up and said, "Forgive me for talking out of turn, but I can provide the voice of experience here."

Everyone looked at David.

I held my breath.

"I don't know what the relationship between you two is, but Jake, I do know that as a minister, it is easy to get on your church goggles and look at everything around you in terms of what would be right for your church. Not the church, not the whole body of Christ, but your little piece of it."

"Yes, I can see how that could happen." Jake exhaled, his wonderful smile completely gone from his face.

"Unfortunately, what accommodates your church, what keeps the peace, what makes the shakers and the movers happy, is not always what's right." David turned and looked at me. "It's not right to let your church overrun the people you love. To drown out their voices or take their place in your everyday life."

"David, I never thought…"

He smiled at my unfinished thought, then looked to Bernadette. "Young lady, do not let that happen. Be true to yourself, and don't wait too long to find out who that is."

I touched his face.

"I won't," Bernadette promised. "I mean, not anymore. Jake, I don't care what the Helen Davenports of our church say. It won't dissuade me from doing the right thing. It's right to stand by Chloe and be a vessel for the love of Christ."

He nodded.

"Oh! You ought to hug her!" The balled fists at Maxine's side were proof that she thought she had to say that or explode.

I burst out laughing.

David joined in.

Bernadette blushed, but only a little

And Jake complied. Not a big romantic hug, but a sweet gesture of conciliation. Then he stepped away and smiled.

What a smile!

"That's why he hasn't married yet, you know."

That made me whip my head around so fast to look at Maxine that I thought it might have wrenched something doing it. The whipping, not the looking at Maxine.

"He became a Christian in his late twenties, and tried to set his life right by proposing to the woman he had been living with." Maxine related the story in whispers, without moving her lips hardly at all! "She went to a few church functions where she was treated like…you know…and she left him. He became a minister and promised himself he wouldn't marry any woman who couldn't stand up for herself."

"Interesting," I murmured.

"What are you two going on about? On to your next case?"

We shared a smile.

"Nope. We still haven't finished up this one," I said.

Maxine put her arm around my shoulder. "I think maybe from this point on we should leave it in God's hands."

"Maxine has a point," David said.

"I know!" I shut my eyes and shook my head. "Maxine *always* has a point."

"That's why she loves me," Maxine told my dear husband, who chuckled and nodded.

"And Maxine loves me because…"

"You don't have to explain to me why anyone would love you, Odessa." He kissed my hand. "I do. I always have, even though I haven't always shown you the way I should have. That's what I came here to say, Odessa. I don't want you to stop running around with Maxine, wearing those things and calling yourselves… What do you call yourselves?"

"I'm glad you asked," I said. "Because it means you're ready to listen."

"Bernadette calls us the Tiara Madres." Maxine pushed the crystal ornament back on her head like a cowgirl resettling her hat. "But I prefer the term Queen Mama, because…well, that's who we are!"

"Queen Mamas, huh?" David narrowed his eyes at us, then cast a sly glance at Jake. "Then what does that make the men in your lives?"

Maxine and I didn't confer to come up with an answer. We didn't play it coy. We didn't miss a beat. We looked right at the man I loved, who had finally, after all these years, suddenly looked up and found out who I was, and said, "That makes the men in our lives totally blessed!"

Epilogue

(We figured we couldn't fool you twice with putting a chapter heading on something that's not technically a chapter. Oh, no, you are too smart for that, sister queens!)

"Is that *it*, Maxine? It's been six months since that all happened. I hope I remembered everything. I keep feeling I left out a million little details."

"That's okay, Odessa, nobody wants to hear a million little details, they just want the good stuff."

"The good stuff? Like that Chloe cooperated with the state in their case against Sammy and she got probation and community service as her punishment for her part in it all? Or that Sammy went to jail for the credit card scam and they also threw the book at him for hitting Chloe? Or that Reverend Nash went to visit the kid as a favor to us and now he's involved in a prison ministry that gets him out of the house once a week?"

"And I ain't complaining about that."

Clink

"But none of that happened in the story, Odessa."

"I know, but it's good stuff that we can now catch everyone up on. Like what happened with Jan and Morty."

"You mean the Christian counseling or the second honeymoon?"

"Oh, the honeymoon, definitely the honeymoon!"

"They took a second honeymoon trip to a fancy ski lodge to try to rekindle their romance, and on the first day there, Jan fell down the mountain! Broke an arm, a collarbone and an ankle!"

"No, Maxine, she broke the arm and collarbone falling, she broke the ankle later, when the ski-lodge first-aid people dropped the gurney to ground level by accident and the ambulance driver backed over her leg."

"Ouch!"

"Ouch and *ka-ching*, Maxine. They settled for a very nice sum of money that helped dig Jan and Morty out of debt from *his* fall. And best of all…"

"Oh, yeah, this is the best part! Tell it, Odessa."

"It made Morty take care of Jan for eight weeks."

"Eight weeks."

"Eight weeks of a man having to cook and clean and deal with whatever problems the kids have."

"And even though they are grown and out of the house, kids never stop having problems, y'all."

"Give me a clink on that, Maxine."

Clink.

"So Morty got eight weeks of chauffeuring, and church volunteering, and being nurse and companion. Basically, Morty got to be the *wife*."

"You said it, Odessa. Changed his whole outlook."

"His whole outlook changed, and suddenly he didn't feel so justified in running around taking away emotional support and just old-fashioned time in the marriage trenches to sneak around with another woman."

"I hope Jan and Morty make it, Odessa. Of course, Morty and Reverend Nash aren't the only husbands doing an about-face, or in my husband's case an alley-oop off the couch."

"David certainly has come around. Not only does he actually try to listen more, he finally started using the Internet for more than just e-mailing church members, getting Bible references and reading sermons. As of this minute, he has nearly completed the entire set of Royal Service Hostess Queen partyware for me!"

"He loves his eBay!"

"And I love him."

"I'm kind of fond of him myself, Odessa. And that's not just because when he finds extra pieces of partyware that you already have, he picks them up for me."

"He's a good man. As is your husband, Maxine."

"Yes."

"As is Jake Cordell."

"Who is nobody's husband."

"Yet!"

Clink.

"We're working on that."

"Yes, we are, Maxine. Of course, we had a few hiccups at first. What with that disastrous double date."

"What were they thinking? Abner and Bernadette? Chloe and Jake? How could they have gotten it so wrong?"

"I told you, sometimes young love needs a someone wiser to give things a little push."

"Isn't the expression 'older and wiser,' Odessa?"

"I believe the expression you are searching for is 'Mind your own beeswax,' Maxine."

"We may be older, Odessa, but we've still got a lot of fire."

"Still?"

"Anyway, the young folks sorted it all out, and now Jake and Bernadette are on the right track and Abner has asked Chloe to be his partner. In the tattoo parlor, that is. They've decided just to keep their relationship as good friends."

"Which means we now know two very nice people looking for dates, so if you know anyone… We're not too picky, but they have to be Christians. Oh, did we mention that last month Chloe gave her life to Christ and was baptized in Jake and Bernadette's church?"

"Jake and Bernadette's church, Odessa? Isn't that pushing things a little bit?"

"You say that like pushing is a bad thing, Maxine."

"Odessa! Haven't you learned anything in all of this?"

"Why, yes, Maxine, I have. I'm glad you asked. Here is what I learned…."

Sisters, girlfriends and troublemakers—you know who you are—you are fearfully and wonderfully made! In other words, God doesn't make junk.

Maybe you are too young to know who Khrushchev is, or too old to understand why anyone would pierce a perfectly good body part. It doesn't matter. If you open yourself up to the experience, the Lord can use you. If you open yourself up to life, you will find purpose. If you open your eyes and look around, you will see sisters everywhere waiting for you to love and cherish and help and hope with them. If you open your ears, you will hear their joy and laughter, as well as their fears and pain.

Love one another. Pray for one another. Look out for one another.

I don't care if you have wrinkles or cellulite or have made mistakes with your marriage or your hair. God loves you, and if you are still breathing, it is too soon to give up on yourself.

"And don't forget…"

Stay queenly!

QUESTIONS FOR DISCUSSION

1) The book addresses sisters, girlfriends and troublemakers (you know who you are). Do you believe that the troublemakers in your life know who they are, that those who stir up trouble for others or themselves are aware of the role they are taking? Would you take a proactive stance, as Odessa wants to, to deal with them, or would you be more like Maxine and stand by ready to give support but not to push things?

2) Maxine compares a book to a bacon, lettuce and tomato sandwich, but Odessa feels it's more like chocolate. If you were to compare books to your favorite foods, what would they be most like? Meals or dessert?

3) The women that Odessa and Maxine interact with in the story represent different faces of womanhood. Which of your family and friends are like Bernadette, Chloe and Jan? Do you identify with any of them, including Maxine and Odessa?

4) Odessa contemplates that we value junk for its age, but not women, and tend to disregard older women in our culture. Do you feel this is true in churches as well as the world? Who are the older women who have helped, supported, guided and been examples to you? How so?

5) Chloe has a makeover to tone down her outwardly rebellious look. Have you ever had a makeover? Why or why not? Would you like one? How did it (or do you think it would) make you feel? What would you like to have done?

6) Odessa and Maxine collect dinnerware because it reminds them of something they wanted as young brides. Have you ever collected or considered collecting something from your youth? What would it be?

7) Odessa concludes "If you open yourself up to the experience, the Lord can use you. If you open yourself up to life, you will find purpose. If you open your eyes and look around, you will see sisters everywhere waiting for you to love and cherish and help and hope with them." Do you believe this to be a realistic suggestion? Do you think women of faith are as supportive of one another as they should be? Why or why not? What ways do you lend help and support to other women? How would your life change without the support of special women in your life?

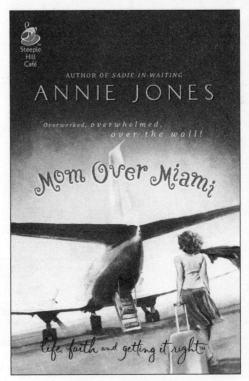

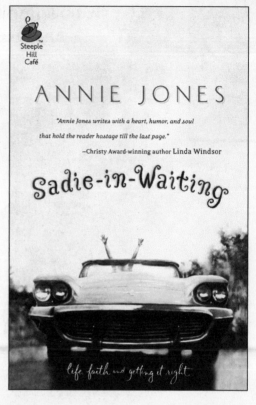

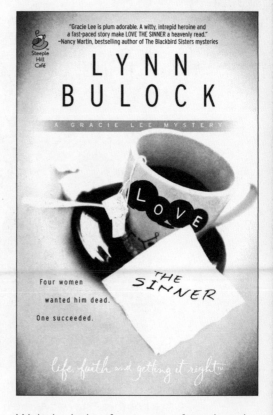

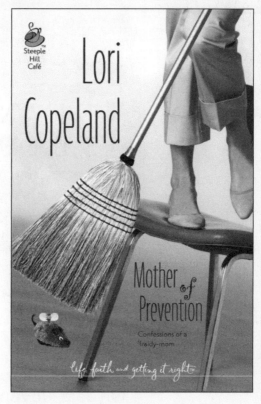

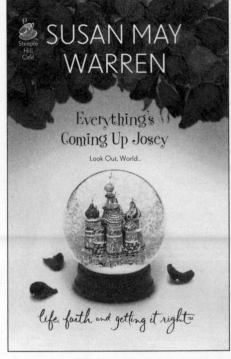